Tales of
Attluma

David C. Smith

Pulp Hero Press
The Most Dangerous Books on Earth
www.PulpHeroPress.com

Pulp Hero Press publishes its books in a variety of print and electronic formats. Some content that appears in one format may not appear in another.

Editor: Bob McLain
Layout: Artisanal Text

ISBN 978-1-68390-254-6
Printed in the United States of America

Pulp Hero Press | www.PulpHeroPress.com
Address queries to bob@pulpheropress.com

Contents

Preface

I originally wrote most of these stories in the early and mid-1970s. Those that were published appeared in the fanzines and small-press magazines of the time, most notably Gordon Linzner's important and influential *Space & Time*. Others remained unpublished when the fanzines for which they had been accepted went out of business, not at all uncommon at the time. A few others I wrote for my own practice. Some of these stories are darkly comical; most are weird or Gothic or adventurous; a few turn on matters of the human heart. I have revised all of them since their initial appearances or first drafts, some of them substantially, all of them for the better.

My initial influences in working on these fantasy and horror stories were Clark Ashton Smith and Robert E. Howard—understandable because I began writing Gothic, weird, and adventure stories with the reemergence of interest in the pulp magazine and horror story writers of the Great Depression, who were beginning to be reprinted in the late 1960s and early 1970s, when I was a young man learning my trade.

These stories were not initially conceived as being part of a particular background or imaginary world; I wrote them simply as though they were legends or stories handed down from remote times, "funny names" and all. Not until I began writing my novel *Oron*, in the summer of 1973, did it seem necessary to tie these stories into a larger framework or backdrop because the epic life of the character Oron required such a setting—an Atlantis or a Lemuria; a Hyborian Age, such as Howard had created for his stories of Conan the Cimmerian; or the Hyperborea or Averoigne of Clark Ashton Smith. The word Attluma, I hope, echoes the magical name Atlantis. The map I drew for myself of this island-continent is rather pear-shaped, a deliberate inversion of the earth's land mass, seventy percent of which is above the equator. My made-up continent is the reverse, a conceit meant to indicate that this other world is not precisely our own but perhaps mirrors elements of it.

Because the idea of a common background for the stories developed over time, the tone and mood of the earliest of them differ from those of the later ones. All, nevertheless, became episodes in a lost history with a specific beginning and end, that of the island-continent of Attluma, which existed long ago in the middle of what we now call the Atlantic Ocean. Attluma originated in some forgotten mythic time, its inhabitants believed, but the great island succumbed after thousands of years to a cataclysmic destruction brought on by the demonic forces that had been present at its creation. As their world gradually disintegrated, those inhabitants who survived traveled east and west to unknown lands—other continents—to begin new civilizations. And while Attluma sank as rubble to the ocean floor, the reality of its dark gods remained in the memory of its survivors, who brought those tales with them when they began the human story again in places strange and new to them.

—D.C.S.

Descales' Skull

1.

Dawn hung pale in the east, and the last of the stars were lost to the lifting daylight. Cocks crowed in dirty alleys. Sleepy drunkards rolled into pools of wine and urine. Women who looked better beneath the unquestioning light of evening dimness disappeared indoors.

Down the cobbled streets of Kastakuk hurried a young man not tired by the earliness of the hour. He was dressed in clothes too fine for this quarter of town; his rich cloak ballooned as he sidestepped rain puddles, and he cursed a young girl who begged him for coin. The young man turned down a littered alley, came to a door at the rear of a wine shop, and rapped on the thick wood.

The door opened inward. The young man stepped inside. He scurried down a short stairway and entered an earthen storeroom where two other men awaited him.

"Clamus, you're late," Bordogas scolded, standing infirmly from his chair. He was a thin old man. He squinted in the gloom to make certain that this was indeed Clamus.

Behind Bordogas, Sumi Dan advanced and set his great ebon fists on the one table in the room.

"I was detained," Clamus explained. He gestured as though dismissing Bordogas and his concerns.

"Never mind. Do you *have* it?"

"Right here." The young man swung aside his cloak and took from his purse a fair-sized fragment of human bone, ancient and friable.

Sumi Dan, looking upon it, sucked in a breath. At last, at last...

Bordogas the vintner hobbled to a rack of wine bottles and pulled it out from the wall, revealing a small recess in which lay other two other large fragments of bone. The old man placed them on the table and motioned Clamus to add his.

When he did so, it was clearly apparent that, by piecing the bones together, the three would have a human skull.

Bordogas whispered, "It's true."

Clamus said, "You'd better be right, you drunkard."

"I'm right. Can you feel it?" The old man reached for the bones, but Sumi Dan's gripped his wrists.

The vintner stared into the black man's eyes.

"Tell him about the curse," said Sumi Dan.

"There's no curse," the old man told him.

Clamus did not seem concerned. He smiled and said in a condescending tone, "Old bones always carry a curse, don't they?"

Sumi Dan growled at him, "Dig up a wizard's bones and he'll grant you a wish, but the bones could contain a curse."

Clamus said, "You don't believe that." He looked at Bordogas. "Do you believe it?"

"I'm not sure."

Sumi Dan told Clamus, "I've worked too hard for this. I killed men for this."

"And you didn't worry about the curse then?" Clamus asked.

"I'm saying to be careful!" the black man told him. "We need to be careful."

Bordogas told him, "We'll be careful. We're all here now. Are we ready? Sumi Dan?"

The giant said, "I killed men for this..."

"You're both cowards!" Clamus grabbed two of the fragments and fitted together the skull, then attached the jawbone as well as he could—and yelped in pain as he dropped the bones to the tabletop.

The sorcerer's skull, complete, was glowing, and it was hot. As the three men stood before it, the skull began to shiver. As it shook, a steaming fluid seeped from the jointures. The fluid sizzled and stank like burning human fat, and it turned the wood black where it slid onto the wine table.

Within a few moments, the heat lessened. The skull stopped rocking, and although no eyes had grown in the empty sockets, the thing seemed to be aware of the three, as though it were watching them from those deep hollow orbits. Watching from where? The jawbone moved, teeth grinded, and the skull spoke.

"I am—returned. You—you three men...you have done this for me?"

Bordogas and Sumi Dan bobbed their heads mutely, but Clamus bravely addressed the skull, although his voice trembled. "You are the sorcerer Descales?"

"I am."

"We have indeed restored you." Clamus wiped away the sweat on his face.

"I am returned!" exclaimed the skull. "Damn the gods! When they blasted my mortal frame, centuries ago, I swore against their names that I would return one day and regain my strength! I swore by the demons of Hell that I would walk the earth again! I promised that the one who restored my skull would have any desire fulfilled! I foresaw that someone brave would do my memory justice. And you three have done it! I congratulate you!"

Bordogas, intrigued, bent close and peered into the empty eye sockets, studied how the bones had come together perfectly. He said, "We all worked very hard for this chance, sorcerer. I found part of your bones in a sack of goods left by a mercenary. He was killed in a brawl, you see. I heard the legend from my father, so I tried to search—"

"Indeed," commented Descales' skull. "And I thank you for your effort."

Clamus told the skull, "I've known Bordogas for many years. When he told me what had befallen him by chance, I remembered a certain household that my father, a moneylender, had been forced to possess. There I found your jawbone among the debtor's curios."

"Excellent," commented Descales' skull. It swiveled so that its dark holes pointed at Sumi Dan.

"I—I was a bandit," explained the black giant. "I found your skull bone in the jewel hoard of a pyramid in the deserts. I fought other bandits to retrieve it, and then I sold it to an old witch to use in her potions. But then I told Bordogas about it when I was drunk, and he made me go back to take it from her."

"You killed her, too," said Descales' skull.

"Yes," Sumi Dan admitted.

"I saw her spirit falling into hell just days ago. She is as ugly as a toad, and very angry with you."

"Will her angry spirit stay in hell?" Sumi Dan asked the skull, very concerned.

"Forever, my friend. Forever. Demons will eat her eyeballs, which will grow back to be eaten again. And her liver, and her heart! But I owe you each a gratuity, surely, for what you have done me. I shall recompense you according to your wishes. My strength will return. I feel my shadow collecting my body even now. Go. I shall visit each of you to grant a wish. Think of the dreams I shall fulfill!"

Bordogas asked the skull, "Is there a curse?"

Something like a laugh came from between the skull's teeth. "Is not life itself a curse, full of pain and anger and sorrow? Can I change that for you? Speak carefully! Whatever you ask of me, brave men, it shall be done!"

The three backed away from the table and started up the stairs of the storeroom. Before they'd reached the door, Descales' skull had begun to glow again with warm energy. Waves of soft light surrounded it, and it slowly faded from view, staring and grinning at the men as it vanished. In a moment, there remained only a shadowy burn on the tabletop.

Bordogas, Sumi Dan, and Clamus looked at one another uncertainly.

Sumi Dan cleared his throat. "I don't care about the curse. I know what I want. And this skull had better grant my wish."

Clamus giggled and stared meanly at Bordogas. "I know what *you* want, old man! The simple pleasures are best—the finest whore from Brolio's cow pen!"

Bordogas said, "Be quiet! It's my own business!"

Clamus told Sumi Dan, "No one else will have him!"

Bordogas ordered him once more, "It's my business!"

Still chuckling, Clamus tripped up the stairs and hurried out the door to the alley.

Bordogas and Sumi Dan followed him. Sumi Dan clapped a large hand on the vintner's shoulders and told him, "Don't worry about it. We each have a second chance here."

"Yes. A second chance."

"Just speak carefully, my friend."

2.

Clamus was bathing in the warm, perfumed waters of his pool. It was late afternoon, and he was relaxing at his father's villa, humming to himself and splashing, when Descales' skull appeared. One moment Clamus was wiping water from his eyes; the next, he saw the ancient skull, yellow-white and fleshless, resting on the marble edge of the pool. Clamus waded to it.

Descales' skull said, "How refreshed you look, young Clamus, bathing in your pool."

Clamus grinned. "Why, thanks. It *is* enjoyable. I've thought things over, you sorcerer—or skull—whatever you are. I've decided what I want."

"I am at your command," said Descales' skull.

Clamus leaned against the cool marble and flicked drops in no particular direction. "Look around and you can see that I'm a young gentleman of obvious wealth. Wealth brings many things, as we know, but one can never have enough of enough. So—what I want is more. More wealth." Clamus turned a golden bracelet around on his wrist and studied the golden rings on his fingers. "Gold is what I want, old skull. Gold and more gold! Can you do that for me? I want all the gold you can give me, all the gold you can conjure!"

He slapped the water in his excitement and stared at Descales' skull as if daring it to produce such a wonder.

The skull pivoted to face a bathing towel that lay beside the pool. There was flash of light, and in the next moment, the cloth of the towel was turned into fibers of finely spun gold thread, gleaming radiantly.

Clamus gasped. He reached for the towel and felt its weight in his hands. "It's gold!" he breathed, smiling in disbelief. "It's truly gold!" He glared at Descales' skull. "Give me more! Give me all the gold in the world, as much gold as you can imagine! Gold! Gold! Gold!"

Descales's skull glowed hotly, and the benches and chairs in the bathing hall changed into solid gold. Clamus stared in awe. The columns of the chamber, the flags of the floor, the clothes Clamus had laid out on a table, the table itself—all were turned into soft, effulgent gold.

Clamus went wild. He jumped up and down in his pool and waved his wet arms, which glistened yellow because of the glow filling the room.

"More gold! More! More gold!"

The arras on the walls became golden cloth. The walls themselves, their stone and brick and mortar, changed into solid masses of heavy gold. The insects that buzzed in the air suddenly plinked into the pool. Clamus saw them sinking swiftly, like little auric brooches or trinkets.

An attendant entered the bathing hall to wait upon his master. Before he knew what had happened, the man was transformed into a solid gold statue. He toppled over and struck the golden floor—and his head cracked off. Clamus saw that the servant was gold all through.

He went mad.

"More! More!" was all he could shout, and, "Everything! Make everything gold!"

Descales' skull did as Clamus commanded. Burning with a golden radiance, the skull turned its vacant eye sockets upon Clamus, and before the young man realized what was happening, he felt the scented water begin to churn and quickly grow hot. Clamus' ecstasy vanished. He stared at the skull's malicious grin as understanding came to him.

Shouting, Clamus tried to reach the edge of the pool, but there was no time for that. Just as he began shifting his weight for a desperate lunge, Clamus felt the hot water coagulating about him, scalding his flesh. Clamus tried to push away the water around him, but when he pulled his hands up from beneath the surface, he saw his fingers covered with burning fluid gold that dripped down his arms, taking his flesh with it. Beneath the running flesh—golden bone.

Clamus tried to scream but could not. He sucked in hot, poisonous air. He lost all sensation in his legs, and when he looked down, he saw flaming liquid gold catching his waist on fire, and he smelled more of himself burning. His legs buckled beneath him, and Clamus saw the ends of his toes break the surface at the center of the pool. His feet were charred black, with golden bone showing through the ruined meat. Clamus tried one last time to shriek, to move the heavy, shining bones of his arms to swim for safety. But he fell backward into the steaming pool.

Hot liquid gold rushed into his open mouth and into his nose and eyes. As he went blind, Clamus felt his face washing away and his jaw and cheekbones turning into gold. Then his brain turned hot, and he was gone.

Descales' skull, settled on the edge of the bathing pool, felt no overpowering heat. As Clamus died, the golden glow of everything in the chamber faded. Cloth became cloth, wood became wood, stone became stone. The decapitated servant became flesh, and blood poured from his neck and ran brightly over the stones of the floor.

In the pool, what remained of Clamus floated in the hot water—burned flesh, charred bone, the water-logged husk of a torso slowly turning, then sinking to leave a dark film on the surface.

Descales' skull disappeared in a shimmer of light.

3.

Sumi Dan was by the riverbank that evening, throwing stones into the mud, when the sorcerer's skull appeared in a dry glare upon a rock behind some weeds. At first, Sumi Dan thought that the rock shimmered in the light of the dying sun, but then he spotted the yellow-white bone face and the black eye cavities and the many smiling teeth, and he became worried.

"What is it you wish," asked Descales' skull, "for returning to me my power?"

Sumi Dan didn't answer directly. He asked, "Did you give Clamus his wish, and Bordogas?"

"Clamus, yes. I will visit Bordogas after I help you."

"What did Clamus wish for?" Sumi Dan seemed uncertain about all of this.

"Wealth was his wish. As if he didn't have enough money already, he wished for more gold."

"And did you do it?"

"Certainly."

"But did he—?" Sumi Dan searched for words. "Did you curse him for it? Is there a curse to these wishes?"

"You are wise to ask," replied Descales' skull. "I merely gave him what he asked for. Speak with him when you see him about how I granted his wish. Now what would you have me do?"

Absently Sumi Dan moved his right hand to a long scar on the side of his neck, a brand marking him as a fugitive.

"What are you thinking, Sumi Dan?"

"I've been a slave most of my life," the black man answered. "I've been a slave to men in the fields, to men in the army, to men in the bandit tribes—I've never earned the respect of anyone. I've been ordered and beaten and spat on—and now I want to do all that to others!" His eyes brightened with fierce pride, and Sumi Dan clenched his fists in anger. "I want power! I want to be a leader of men!"

"So be it!" responded Descales' skull.

Sumi Dan felt a cold wind move upon him. The lambent skull glowed and gave out a brilliant radiance. The next moment, Sumi Dan found himself sitting in a large, torchlit cellar on the other side of town. He was seated on a rough chair upon a stone dais, and before him stood twenty cruel-looking men, staring at Sumi Dan as if awaiting answer to some unasked question.

"Well?" asked a man as big as Sumi Dan himself, clearly irritated. "Are you going to tell us the plan for tonight or not?"

"Plan? What plan? Plan for what?" blurted Sumi Dan. Perspiration tickled his neck as he looked upon that sea of hard faces.

"Our leader jests, Gorogi!" barked a dog-faced little man standing next to the big one. "How are we to rob the shops on Liskal Street tonight? Hurry!"

A scar-faced brute in the rear of the throng told Sumi Dan, "Our fingers itch for prize pickings!"

Thieves! Sumi Dan understood immediately. That damned sorcerer's skull had made him leader of a den of thieves!

He smiled to disguise his fear. "Well, um, I'll tell you—I, uh, I haven't yet decided—uh, decided yet, on one plan or...or the other. Tell me—Gorogi?—what do you think?"

Grumbles and whispers trembled through the crowd as the thieves looked at each other and their leader.

Gorogi snorted and hitched his belt. "I suggest what I've always suggested: Divide the men into pairs, then have one man break in while his partner keeps watch. Rotate the men. Place lookouts at each end of the street and in the alleys I told you about, and on the low roofs. And arrange signals ahead of time. Hell, I don't think my plan's any worse than some you've thought up!"

"Why, you're quite right, Gorogi, my man!" Sumi Dan enthusiastically agreed. "I like that plan! So if everyone's ready, let's all be on our way!" He rose to his feet.

"If you don't mind," suggested a hawk-faced man in the front row, "don't you think we should wait until the shops close?"

Howls of harsh laughter filled the cellar, followed by coarse mumblings among the men concerning their leader's increasingly apparent incompetence.

The dog-faced man leaned toward Gorogi and shook his head. "Don't know what's gotten into him lately," he declared. "Hope he doesn't foul us up like he almost did last week! See how he depended on you again, too, Gorogi? You ought to be leader, anyway."

The big man grinned and touched the hilt of his ugly sword.

Sumi Dan, seated before his men and recipient of their stares and smirks, cursed under his breath as he had never cursed before in his life the skull of the sorcerer Descales.

When the men finally went into the streets, Sumi Dan's nervousness and inability betrayed him soon enough, and his thieves became concerned. The giant misremembered the names of his followers and, in his haste to hurry the thieves along, gave contradictory orders. He learned that two of their number had been arrested during the last attempted series of heists in Shupath Boulevard because of blunders he himself had made. Sumi Dan was also unfamiliar with the lower haunts on this edge of town, and he continually relied on Gorogi's judgment while trying to maintain the charade of leadership. But his bumbling came to a head when a passing city guard noticed three thieves running from a jeweler's house and sounded their demise, blowing loudly on his wooden whistle.

"Damn him!" swore Gorogi. "He was supposed to've bribes the guards in this end of town!" With a lurch, he freed his sword and rushed Sumi Dan. He plunged the blade through the black man's stomach and pushed it back and forth. "We may get caught but, damn you, you'll pay for this!"

Very surprised, Sumi Dan watched as his insides drained into the street. The rest of the thieves, screaming viciously, fell upon him and exhausted their fear and anger by cutting him into pieces, even as squads of the king's guards galloped in for wholesale arrests. Swords jumped in the moonlight, and a few howls sounded out before the dogs were hauled off to jail.

The ruins of Sumi Dan stained the cobblestones, with nothing left to identify him except that long scar on one side of his broken neck.

On a low roof above the street, Descales' skull glowed brightly.

4.

Dawn was not yet gray in the east as Bordogas sat sleepless in his musty room above the wine shop, shivering as he awaited—what? The skull? The fulfillment of his daring wish? His imagination went in every direction in a perplexity of images and desires. As he stared at a corner of the room, light shimmered into being on a low bench behind him and hardened into the ancient sorcerer's skull.

"Bordogas."

The vintner turned, hand to his pumping heart, not knowing what to expect. When he saw Descales' skull, he smiled. A craggy, broken-toothed smile.

"What is your wish, o Bordogas?"

The vintner took in a deep breath, and he felt his collected fears slip away as he looked upon the living skull. "I'll tell you," he said softly, but then worry touched him. "Have—have you visited the others yet?"

"Yes."

"And granted them their wishes?"

"Yes."

"And—they got what they wished for?"

"Assuredly, good Bordogas. Are you, too, worried about a curse?"

"Yes. I didn't know if—"

"The only possible curse," Descales' skull reminded Bordogas, "is one you might bring upon yourself. Is that not what life is, after all—making choices and anticipating outcomes? Even I learned that as a young sorcerer."

Bordogas nodded quietly, as though he, too, had already given this matter grave thought. He stood, rubbing his back, and stepped to a low table in the corner of his room. With his back to the skull, he said, "I know how ugly I am. I have always been ugly. Hideous beyond the slightest mark of beauty, and so—I have never known the caresses of a beautiful woman. I have no real desire for anything else. But I am old, and I don't want to die without knowing the love of a beautiful woman."

Bordogas reached for something on the table; he turned and showed it to the skull. It was a small figurine of a woman, carved of ivory and slim, perfectly done, its hair finely painted and its lips rouged—the portrait of an exquisite beauty done by a consummate artist.

"I bought this at a bazaar," said Bordogas, "when I was a young man, and I've dreamed of knowing such a woman. Impossible—"

Suddenly he yelled and released the figurine. The ivory, glowing hotly, fell to the floor and shattered, sending up a white mist that quickly straightened into a slender pillar of smoke. Bordogas cried out and stepped away.

The white smoke congealed into the figure of his statuette, life-sized, and of real flesh, real hair—

Bordogas dropped to his knees, overcome by the beauty of the woman who stood before him.

She was more stunning that Bordogas had ever dreamed. Her face was a smooth oval with great dark eyes and full lips, framed by cascading black hair. The thrust of her full breasts complemented the sweet curves of her round hips, which tapered into legs long and sleek. She was wonderful, and posed for the old man with her body thrust forward, arms poised for embrace, lips parted in the expectation of fulfilled passion.

"Bordogas? Bordogas, I love you—"

Her voice was a melody of urgent yearning and husky demands. Bordogas found the strength to stand, although his legs were weak and his arms shivered. He reached one hand toward the woman's fingers, and at the touch of her, the old man shuddered, a withered leaf touched by the stark beauty of cold winter.

The remarkable woman now glided to Bordogas and cupped his creased face in her hands. She burned a cold kiss upon his wrinkled lips. Then she released him and whispered again, "I love you, Bordogas—"

She turned from him and circuited the room, touching everything that was his, identifying it with herself. Bordogas watched, breathless. He was a prisoner of her undulant hips, her slim legs, her curving back and flowing hair. She tilted her head to smile at him, and Bordogas' heart raced. She whispered to him, "I love you," forming the words with her tongue and perfect lips.

With shaking hands, Bordogas poured himself a cup of wine, drank it, and sat on the edge of his bed.

The woman glided to him, crossing before an open window. The first sunlight of the morning touched her flesh, making it glow. Bordogas swallowed with difficulty.

The woman crawled onto the bed and crouched beside him, pressed her hands to his chest and kissed him open-mouthed, forcing her wet tongue around and around. Bordogas had to push her away and cough for air.

The woman laughed, teasing him. Bordogas smiled weakly as she bent over him and kissed him on the chest, trailed her kisses down his belly and licked his navel, kissed lower still.

Bordogas felt his chest becoming hot. Only a small tunnel remained in his throat for air to enter or leave. He lay back and stared at the ceiling, then down at the woman, and tried to smile. His penis was as solid as it had been when he was a young man, but he was short of breath.

Like cool silk drawn over tired muscles, the woman moved upon Bordogas. She slipped herself onto his penis and began pushing with her hips.

Bordogas should have been happy. He saw her smiling down at him. He tried to return her smile because, as she had said, she loved him.

The woman moved faster. She leaned on Bordogas; her hands dug into his thin flesh; her weight crushed him as she moved.

Bordogas looked up at her wild eyes. Still she smiled. Bordogas could no longer speak. He tried to draw in a breath, but he couldn't manage it. Fear gripped him.

The woman pushed, pushed, crushed him, leaned back, leaned forward, moved faster—

Bordogas tried to rise. He waved his arms and attempted to kick his legs. Ecstasy began to build in him, very warm, but at the same time, he couldn't breathe, and his heart hurt. He was becoming numb. The beautiful face framed by dark hair was now a blur, a white oval with two deep black cavities for eyes and sharp teeth pulled into a frightening smile. Bordogas' chest burned; he had a sensation of complete panic, but he could not move. His heart was on fire. He no longer felt glad, and now he couldn't collect his breath at all. Something broke inside him. He stared as his arms went still, and his legs, and he was no longer free to move.

His body was wet with sweat. His dead fingers were curled upon the sheets, and his bony legs twisted. Above him, a white vapor dissolved in the bright morning that filled the room.

From its bench in a corner of the room, Descales' skull also vanished. A warm glow, a bright light, and it was gone.

5.

In the dawn-lit sands of a timeless desert, the citadel of the ancient sorcerer Descales rose once more. The stone blocks and winding stairs, the vaulted chambers and sunken corridors were all come to life again within this fortress of dark aura. The crawling things of the sands avoided its shelter, and even the good sunlight held back from the citadel's perimeter.

In a high room, Descales gloried to be in human form again. He walked and touched and sat and stretched. The skull that had been brittle was now hardened and eternal; over it were fashioned living muscle and flesh, tissue molded by gramarye from the dust. In the orbits sat luminous eyes; in the cranium pulsed a wet, designing brain.

Descales' tomes of wizardry and knowledge, also resurrected from the dust, sat tall again upon their shelves, and their passages the sorcerer had rememorized. His ancient incantations yet accomplished wonders; the fruits of their sorcery sat all about him—strange plants made alive again from poisonous old seeds; oddly shaped shadows that moved on their own, alive in a fashion although eyeless and voiceless, some kept within cages or caught by spells so as not to roam free; and in secret rooms and cellars, peculiar contours and angled sigils carved into the stone blocks according to the rules of mysterious geometries. These contours and sigils would serve the sorcerer as doors into other secret rooms and cellars deep within citadels far away, towers and walls built beneath very different skies. The piceous desert nights guaranteed a resurgence of magic more malignant than had been practiced since Descales had originally been slain by the young gods.

In the tall chamber where he now sat, there hung upon a wall Descales' curved silver mirror. By the power of this mirror, the sorcerer could see wherever he wished, visiting by sight lands and skies in this world as well as others. This morning, the sorcerer saw in his mirror layers of smoke, fumes from burning gases, rocks dripping with molten liquid, and a million or more flitting shapes that seemed to be insects but, in fact, were souls, damned and forgotten in this lost, low place. Here was Hell, the Hell to which the fallen of the earth came to suffer torment for excesses of greed or stupidity or even mere foolishness.

The flames and gases singed the edges of the silver mirror. In a distant corner of the lowest of pits, Descales saw three shadowy figures writhing in torment. They were being roasted on metal spits the way a hunter cooks a caught bird, and their smoking bodies were being devoured by ravenous demons of insatiable appetite. Yet even as the monsters picked the meat from the bodies, the flesh reappeared on the steaming bones and was again roasted to tasty perfection. The victims screamed endlessly, their lungs never tiring of the agony. Descales laughed and laughed, and he spoke to those men across all the barriers of time and space.

"I know you can hear me. I know my words can echo in those tunnels! Suffer as I suffered, fools! You weighed your greed and lust against my sorcerous strength—and now you have only yourselves to blame! Ha, the witch! Look out, Sumi Dan! Here comes your witch!"

Sure enough, the wicked crone whom Sumi Dan had killed to obtain his portion of Descales' skull came flying toward him. She was greasy and green, a colorful shadow, but her eyes were yellow and her mouth all black with hate. She reached one long, snake-like, green hand into Sumi Dan's screaming mouth and retrieved a length of his insides. This she ate, slobbering the blood all over the agonized black man, who watched her in horror. When she was finished, she wiped her lips and flew away.

Meanwhile, thousands of old spirits no larger than wasps swarmed around Bordogas' head and crawled into Clamus' eyes and ears. What could the suffering men do? When they tried to wave the demonic insects away, their hands became smoke, utterly useless.

Descales continued to laugh. "Here is the secret of my sorcery! Human weakness is more corrupt than any dark art! The gods sent me to Hell, but I knew that anyone who saved me would be taken into Hell to replace me! Who will save you as you saved me? No one!"

And proud Descales watched in satisfaction as a variety of demons gorged themselves on Bordogas' eyeballs, Clamus' baked thighs, and Sumi Dan's smoking liver. The greasy old witch returned to further torment Sumi Dan, and the sorcerer laughed grandly, a laugh that echoed throughout Hell and into eternity.

The Generosity of the Gods

Long ago, on high Mount Domasgotht, dwelt the gods. Remote above the clouds, they lived in the splendid ennui that is the privilege of deities. The gods were many and diverse. They played tricks on each other and on us, too. When people prayed to them and invoked their names in blessings, the gods generously ignored these worshippers, or at least regarded them with amusement. They appreciated the aroma of animals burned in their honor, and they were entertained by the music and dancing of the people below. But when anyone blasphemed the immortals, the cloud-dwellers were wrathful and merciless. The gods do as they wish, and it is best not to draw their attention at all, even with sincere worship. Even good intentions can pique the temperamental immortals, let alone deliberate provocation.

On a sunny afternoon, Obroc the Kurstikan and his companion, Cedes the Bent-nosed— two fishermen notorious for their inability to net any fish—beached their salt-rusted dinghy and retreated up the hot strand toward town. These two were the closest of friends, inseparable, and allied in their complete ineptitude. They blamed their consistent failure to tempt any spawn of the provisioning sea upon the gods who ignored their petitions for prosperity. They would do anything to assist each other through the troubles of life; why, then, would the high gods not do the same for them?

Striding the narrow streets of Semkorra and doing the best they could to ignore their empty stomachs and dry mouths, despite the temptations of food sellers and beer vendors, these two as usual railed against the immortals. Obroc, a big man confident in his swagger, said that he only half-believed in the gods, anyway. Cedes, slender as a length of bone and with no more than a bone's worth of meat on his long frame, subscribed to idea of the immortals, but he couldn't understand why the almighty deities were prone to such pettiness as, for example, forbidding their followers to use certain words or take certain actions deemed to be profane. Surely the gods can do and demand anything, but if they were all-powerful, then what harm could people do to them? And if the immortals imposed restrictions to secure the devotion of people, why would anyone who already believed in the gods need to be restricted in the first place?

"For instance," said Cedes, kicking up dust from the cobblestones, "the name of the god of my temple is unspeakable, yet I have little doubt that if I spoke it in a loose moment, he would not damn me forever but attribute the action to the ineffectuality of people, the very thing that sets us apart from the gods."

"Well, then, why don't you?" said Obroc, perspiring uncomfortably. "I'm certain the gods could forgive the trespasses of two puny men on a hot, fishless afternoon. If we blaspheme, at least it will prove our point. And if the gods should take offense at us, I'm certain their hearts are big enough to forgive us."

Cedes looked at him and rubbed the sunlight out of his eyes. "What? Do you really want to?"

"Certainly. Nothing will happen. But if something does, at least it will liven a dull day."

"I think you're approaching this a little too light heartedly."

"Didn't you mean what you said?"

"Well, of course I did. But I was only speaking generally. I didn't mean me, personally."

"You're just trying to get out of it. I think we should undertake a little blasphemy to prove to everyone that the fat old temple priests have been pulling our legs all these years. I think they play dice with their 'gods' after hours, and use that Miridian wine for more than sacrifices."

"You're awfully close to blaspheming now, Obroc."

"Relax. It's human nature to question and profane. The high ones know that. They made us this way."

Over a bottle of cheap wine paid for with the last of their coins, they determined to test themselves and the gods. Emboldened by the bad drink, they made their way down shadowy side streets and at last climbed the steps to the doors of the first temple they came to, that of Yem-yur.

A wizened priest at least as old as Yem-yur himself approached the fishermen as they entered and asked if they wanted to buy sacrifices to give up to the god or if they were only going to pronounce self-condemning prayers or debase themselves in some other fashion.

Obroc, feeling the drink, balancing himself as well as he could on sandals that kept sliding out from under his feet, said boldly, "We've shown enough patience with these gods. I think it's time they showed a little patience with us!"

"Blasphemy!" said the priest, backing away from them. "Blasphemy in the temple of Yem-yur!"

"Blasphemy and burps, too," Obroc told him, following through with a particularly dramatic belch.

He then slapped Cedes on the back, pushing him ahead as they both moved farther into the temple.

Cedes had promised to blaspheme against Omidom the unspeakable, in whose temple he had occasionally found himself, going there to petition the Nameless One for divine assistance in directing some quick-moving fins into his fishing net. Obroc, for whom one god was much the same as any other, decided to desecrate Yem-yur, whose face no one had ever looked upon, because that was the god whose house they happened to be in.

In the rear of the temple, a mighty image of the Yem-yur sat under a great shroud. This was the eidolon that legend said had been constructed by blind men overseen by the god himself. Obroc pulled free the cover, and it fell in layers at the base of the idol. The defiler kept his head bent and said in a low voice, "Yem-yur, you claim to be a god. Surely I am no more than an insect to you. Let us see what troubles you take when offended by a mere insect." And with that, he drew up his head sharply, stared into the chiseled visage of the god—and let loose a terrible scream as the light faded from his eyes.

At the same time, in the hallway just outside the sanctum where Yem-yur's image rested, Cedes said nervously, "Great Unnamable One, what I do, I do to test the truth of your heavenly power. Therefore, I speak your name, Unspeakable One, potent Omidom." And as the syllables fell from his tongue, his jaws tightened and he could speak no more. Cedes gurgled and coughed and spat and wheezed, but his throat was now an empty fountain.

Obroc, sobbing, came stumbling into the hallway, crashing against the walls as he felt his way, and finally dropped to the floor, waving his hands before him. "Cedes! Cedes! What have I done? Yem-yur has cursed me for my impudence. I am blind! Where are you, Cedes?"

In answer, his friend took Obroc in his arms and trembled like an animal, whining and puling, rubbing Obroc's hand all over his mouth.

"What?" asked the blind man. "Has the unspeakable one stolen your voice?"

To which Cedes vigorously nodded his head in Obroc's grasp.

For a moment, they both sat silent in self-pity. The house priests gathered about them, and the temple hierophant said to them in a somber tone, "You foolish defilers. Did you really think that the gods would take no notice of you? What arrogance."

"No. No. Listen to me, please," begged Obroc. "We are fools, yes. But is there no way the great gods will take pity on us? Pray to them, please, to reissue us our senses. We will become slaves to them. I will do anything for them. But I beg them to make us whole again!"

"You have proven already that you are slaves to them, poor gentlemen," whispered the learned flamen. "Yet they sometimes can be generous. You must go to them. Go to where they live upon Mount Domasgotht. Present yourselves to them, and beg with all your hearts for their mercy. If they see fit to do so, they will return to you what they have taken. This is the only prayer I can offer you."

At this both men whimpered like beaten pups, for the chance of clemency was a benevolence that brought the tears to their eyes. They arose and left the temple, speechless Cedes leading the sightless Obroc. They made their way through the crowded streets to a back alley, where they slept the night, and where they lived for some weeks as mendicants, begging and cadging, relying upon each other as never before, living leanly and saving every spare copper for provisions for their peregrination. On the anniversary of their profanation, they set out.

The gods did not treat them kindly on their long journey. The cloud dwellers tested the amerced men's mettle and fortitude, deeming in this way how greatly the trespassers valued the senses they had lost. Through blasting weather, through violent storms and withering heat, the fishermen continued, each holding up the other, the one seeing to lead, the other groaning both their excruciations. They passed through forest and fen and desert, and at last one morning awoke to find before them the stony base of the home of the gods, stark in the sunlit mists.

With renewed vigor, they took up their challenge. Ever upward they moved, cutting their hands as they proceeded, stumbling sometimes but recovering the same ground in their determination. They imagined that the immortals watched them disdainfully. With one brush of their hands, the high ones might sweep the two of them into eternity. But still they persevered. They rested in small defiles, thin delves in the sheerness, and did what they could to ward off the strangling cold. They knew that they had given up long ago were they seeking less precious things, treasure or lost magic. But they were searching for parts of themselves, and their regret and hope and shame spurred them on.

They reached the pinnacle one midmorning. Cedes stood upon the flat mountain top and hoisted his eyeless companion up after him.

"What do you see? What can you see?" asked Obroc.

In truth, nothing was to be seen for the blinding mists, great gray clouds, and vapors that held everything in timeless suspension.

Obroc's heart was wild in his breast. "They must be here!" he cried out. "Yem-yur! Mighty Omidom! Forgive us our crimes! We come to beg you for your kindness! Do not fail us as we have failed you!"

There was a roaring thunder upon the mountaintop. It might have been an echo of creation—or the sound of ultimate destruction. From the mists came a voice so large and grand that it struck Obroc and Cedes as a physical blow, like a wave smashing a man tossed in a stormy sea. It was the voice of a god.

"I am the Unspeakable One. You, Cedes, dared to say what is ever to be unsaid. I blast you with my vengeance, and you dare to multiply your impudence by intruding upon this, my home?"

Cedes unleashed a pitiful groan. Long tears sped down his face.

"And you, Obroc," came the voice of Yem-yur. "Do you likewise?"

"O Yem-yur! I come only to plead your divine leniency! Forgive my insubordination."

There was further rumbling, as of distant earth seizures growing nearer, while the two gods debated between themselves.

Then said Omidom, "You have tested our patience, but we are gods. Great is our retribution, yet great is our mercy. You two have suffered together for your sins. Nevertheless, you must remember always the crimes you have committed and the punishment you bear."

"Oh, we will, we will," promised Obroc.

"Here, then, is how merciful and generous the gods can be!" said immortal Omidom.

Immediately the two fishermen felt themselves embraced by a cold wind. They were trapped within a whirlpool that lifted them into the air and, a moment later, set them down on the seashore, next to their old dinghy.

"Where are we?" asked Obroc. He was in a gray fog, no longer in complete darkness, and he tried to take a step forward.

When he did, he felt something heavy pull at him, and he realized that Cedes was alongside him, pressing close to him.

In fact, Cedes was now attached to Obroc, leg to leg and hip to hip, so that the two were now one, truly inseparable, sharing a third leg between them but bending awkwardly above their waists in order to move their arms and hands.

"What has happened?" groaned Cedes, who suddenly became aware of his own voice. "I can speak! I can speak!" he yelled, flickering his eyelids.

"And I can see!" blurted Obroc, wagging his tongue in his hollow mouth as the gray fog lifted.

Both then they realized how generous the gods had been, for the two of them had their senses back, but at a cost. They limped along the shore, managing as best they could in their freakish union, ignoring the stares and derisive hoots of others on the beach.

"They'll never let us forget," groaned Cedes, his eyelids moving rapidly as his voice issued in currents from his eyeballs.

"They've tricked us!" complained Obroc. "I can see, but only when I keep my mouth open! I have new eyes, but if I talk, my teeth get in the way of my vision! Oh, cruel gods!"

"Oh, wise gods," corrected Cedes. For he could speak as his friend had seen. And Obroc could see as his companion had spoken.

So they remained for the duration of their lives. Obroc and Cedes, the closest of friends, returned to the temple of Yem-yur and were taken in by the kind priests there, who fed them and kept them warm and exhibited them to believers as an example to avoid. So they lived out their days, the two poor fishermen become one in their pride, ever mindful of the blasphemy they had perpetrated upon, and ever mindful of the generosity of, the gods.

Feasting Shadows

In the cavern, a thing moved in the darkness, a living creature. Its wet substance made no sound as it stretched in many directions at once, following an old habit of sensing a path, then pushing itself along it. It had no eyes but many mouths on the bottom of it, and so it ate by pulling into those mouths whatever it found on the surfaces it crawled upon. Organs to hear were somewhere in its bulk, and it was aware of even slight scents. It had memory. Throughout itself, it remembered the strong odor of incenses burned in its honor in the old days of glory, and it could yet hear on the walls of the cavern and its tunnels the vibrations of echoing screams of terror.

It stopped and waited.

Listened.

Tasted the damp rock beneath it for clues to anything nearby.

And began moving again.

The creature had lived in the cavern for longer than it could remember. Once gigantic, it had melted over many foodless years so that now it was but the size of ten human beings. It subsisted largely on whatever grew or reproduced in a pool near the mouth of the cave. Sometimes it followed the thin rivulet that coursed through the cavern to the world outside and there took in small things of the forest before returning to the safety of the deep cavern.

Stretching now, it found things to eat in the pool, minnows and frogs, and as it did, it held onto the memories of ancient days, the old days of feasts and ceremonial fires. It remembered when the first humanlike beings had seen fit to sacrifice to it thick prehuman flesh, and it remembered its first taste of subhuman meat— the hairy men and women and children given to it in fearful worship. It remembered the orgies of beginning religion, the songs and the dances and the sacrifices and the feasts.

****

"I'll start a fire," Pel said, kneeling to gather whatever twigs and leaves had blown into the front of the cave. The sky thundered, and the rain that had driven Jenta and him to seek shelter came down harder, the fat drops slapping on the ledge of the cave mouth and sending waterfalls over the edge into the forest below.

Farther in, Jenta said, "This is the one. I was right. This is the one."

"You and your father?"

"Yes."

Pel now had a small pile before him and was striking flint and steel to it. Sparks came, then smoke, then real flames. He carefully added larger twigs to the fire, then stood and looked at Jenta, barely visible in the shadows, as slender as she was. "Has anyone even been here since you and your father?"

"I doubt it. It's so hard to get to." She moved farther away from the light of the small fire, feeling her way along a wall. "But here are the marks." She turned and faced Pel. "Are the torches still wet?"

"Every one of them."

"Curse it." But Jenta wasn't terribly angry; she was too excited to be angry, thrilled at having found just this place more than ten years after she, as a girl, had been brought here by her father, who had stumbled upon it when he was himself a boy.

The marks and symbols on the cave walls had confirmed then for Jenta's father, as young as he was, that this cave was an ancient temple, perhaps the first temple in the world, reaching away to the beginning of everything, back to the time of the Ancestors and the first gods whom the first people had worshipped. The names of these deities, no more than human grunts or raw syllables then, had become as forgotten as the lost gods and goddesses themselves, yet Jenta's father had been convinced that those must be the very names cut into the walls of this cave in symbols so old they matched no existing tongue.

"This one," Jenta said.

"Come over here and dry off," Pel said.

"No, I'm all right for now."

She was in no more than a tunic and vest and short woolen breeches and boots, and soaked through. He at least had worn his leather vest and heavy trousers.

He had brought along parchment and charcoal, anticipating that he might need to draw a map so that they could make their way safely back home if they even managed to find this place.

Now Pel rolled a length of parchment into a tube, shoved twigs and dried grass and bark into one end of it, then placed that end into the fire to make a kind of torch. It would burn quickly, but for now, he carried it to where Jenta was standing, hands pressed on the rough cave wall.

He asked her, "Which one?"

"See the circle?"

They could distinguish it now by the light of the torch, a circle the width of her arm with a large symbol in the center and words or signs drawn around that symbol.

Jenta said, "My father thought it was a sign for Erith, the god of the mountains."

"It's very crude."

"These must go back to the First Families, even to the gods themselves when they lived on earth with us. Can you imagine it?"

Pel was uncertain about the gods. He had visited the Imnu Sher, the House of Thought, in Sorkendum, and spent time there among the wisest men and women in the world. Those learned souls maintained that even the gods themselves were subject to natural law, just as everything was. Human beings cannot force nature to follow their will; neither can the gods do that; nature itself has no will, no reason, only an appetite and the desire to continue as it is. Given those facts, some at the House of Thought speculated that the gods were no more than demons or animals, sufficiently frightening to cause people to worship them, but not immortal or outside nature.

Pel himself could not believe that the gods were animals or monsters; the world was far too ordered and rational for that to be true. The gods had given human beings the power of reason, so they, too, must be reasonable, just as the world itself was, in its patterns and intricacies. This is why the gods were worshipped, because they had created a wise order to everything.

The flame of his torch had come down nearly to his hand. Pel set the parchment on the ground, where it gave off light as it burned itself out.

"I want to keep looking," Jenta told him. She turned to walk deeper into the mountain.

"No, no." Pel put his hands on her shoulders and turned her around. "We know how to get here now. We can come back when it's dry. Or at least keep our torches dry next time."

"I'm not afraid of the dark."

"All you need to do is trip and fall, then how do we get back?"

Thunder came again, but farther away.

They looked at the cave opening and saw that the rain was not falling as strongly as it had been and that the sky was brightening.

"Just wait," Pel said.

The creature of shadows remembered the days of sacrifices and feasts. It had witnessed the rise and fall of the tides of humanity. From the primitive tribes had emerged others, and they too had held in reverence the god-thing of the cavern. To it they had offered, at every new moon, maidens of softer flesh than the hirsute ones. After these had come a people tall and clean-limbed, intelligent and proud. They had appointed high priests to officiate holy god-thing ceremonies. Toiling workers of these people had transformed the harsh rock of the underground into the rude walls of a temple. Here the women were kept, raised to obey the interpreted wisdoms of the undying creature of the cavern. And they were sacrificed with precise regularity, singularly or, in times of strife or celebration, with hosts of other maidens and children and people taken in raids. Then there was the Song of the Feast, and the Dance of the Feast, and the Culmination Feast.

The creature remembered conquests, the overthrow of one type of human by others. It remembered being taken to a mighty city and placed in a great brick house erected in tribute to it. It clearly recalled feasting on beautiful virgins, devouring them in the whispering light of torches and the aroma of burning incenses, under the auspices of conniving priests certain that they could control the god-thing.

They could not. It was what it was, and they were what they were—human, and that was all there was to them. Attacked as it had escaped the city, it had feasted mightily, and then it had roamed forests and swamps, crossed rivers and pulled itself over mountains. It would have continued in this way for all of its days except that men riding animals on four legs had discovered it and poured oil on it and set it afire. It had felt pain. The fire was not the worshipful fire of torchlit temples but a fury that even the thing itself could not defeat. It had pulled itself in two, leaving the fiery part to burn and die, meanwhile thrashing as the men attacked it, and their horses, the four-legged animals. It had eaten as many of them as it could, and the screams were good. In pain, the thing had continued moving, enlarging itself with what it found and gradually healing, until it had returned to this cave, its temple.

By then the old tribes were gone. Modern barbarians and soldiers and sorcerers and seekers of truth occasionally ventured into the cave, curious or delusional, to provide themselves accidentally to it. Yet they never offered songs and dances. The time of the Song of the Feast and the Dance of the Feast and the Culmination Feast was long past.

Now the creature perceived noises, sounds like the voices of humans from long ago. Its sensations increased; it scented whatever was in the cave. It stretched toward the mouth of the cave, sensing its path, sensing human beings.

Jenta let out a sound of surprise as the ground gave way beneath her, dropping steeply, and she nearly lost her balance.

Pel went to her but stepped carefully, taking care in the darkness. He put out his hands, found her, and helped her steady herself.

"Enough," he said. "We can't see anything. This is pointless."

But where Jenta had nearly slipped, there was matter on the cave floor. She knelt and felt for it and asked Pel to help her. Twigs, brush, leaves—all manner of material for him to gather into a pile and set afire with his flint and steel, which he quickly did.

As the flames and smoke lifted, Jenta held up her right hand, brightly lit in the glow of the little fire.

"Listen." She leaned toward the depths of the cave, where the path descended farther into the mountain.

"I don't hear—"

"Listen!" And then, "Animals? People?"

"Echoes," Pel told her. "Our own sounds coming back to us. Here." He scraped his boot on the cave floor.

From deep in the mountain, he and Jenta heard a similar scraping sound answer them.

Jenta stood and, by the light of the little fire, turned to the cave wall near her to see what was there. She told Pel, "We never got this far. My father would be astonished."

Pel said, "These symbols are different."

"Older, aren't they? These are even cruder than the others. See here?"

Inside a great circle was an odd shape with smaller circles within it, like eyes or mouths, and signs or perhaps words scratched beside it.

"If only we could read these. Where you going?"

Pel had stepped away, going back up the incline. "More twigs for the fire. Then we're going."

"Yes."

"The rain has stopped."

The small fire was weakening, but by its light Jenta moved a few steps farther to study the extremely crude scratches, and she heard the scraping sound return.

She scratched her boot on the floor and heard the sound come back to her, louder now, nearer.

Pel returned with a small armload of dry brush and twigs and added them to the fire. It blossomed suddenly, opening with brightness and jumping flames.

"There," he said, and stood.

Jenta stepped onto something that was not the floor. "Pel?"

He saw the darkness change behind her, as though the darkness itself were moving.

Jenta said, "It's mud." She tried to lift her leg and pull away. "Pel!"

"I see it, I see it!"

He hurried to her, nearly falling, and in the bright light of the fire behind him saw a wall of gray paste taller than himself push toward him, an appendage that folded about him.

"Pel!"

He groaned and lost his breath. The thick paste held his arms at his sides and tried to wrap around one of his legs as it lifted him toward the ceiling of the cave.

Jenta screamed as she saw it happen while the mud or paste moved around her own legs.

She *screamed*.

And the creature trembled with excitement at her scream, the sacred Song of the Feast.

Pel was upside-down. He remembered one summer as a boy when he hung that way from the limb of a tree. Then the mud or paste pushed him down to the floor of the cave and moved over him with teeth of sharp pain, and he was gone.

Jenta screamed again and tried to lift her legs, looked at the fire as if it were the only thing that could save her, and stretched toward it.

She pulled her legs free and jumped toward the fire. She looked back and saw whatever it was, gray, wet, a thing made of mud, pushing toward her. She moved to the right, to the left, tried to back away and nearly fell into the small fire.

The Dance of the Feast.

The creature stretched an appendage to seize her around the waist. It did not wish her to reach the fire. The flames of the fire were harmful, it remembered. But it appreciated these moments as she continued to scream and tried with her dancing to escape.

Finally it wrapped itself fully about her and pulled her beneath itself.

The Culmination Feast, such as the thing had not experienced in longer than it could remember.

The small fire burned out.

The creature pushed itself in the opposite direction, sensing its way, returning into the darkness of its temple.

Dark of Heart

We run heedlessly into the abyss after putting something in front of us to stop ourselves from seeing it.

—Pascal

1. A Prince Seeks Aid

Drenched with sweat beneath his leather and steel armor, the sergeant crossed the wide yard to the stockade. The two young bucklers on duty had found a bit of shade but, as the officer flashed a clay seal, they quickly rose to attention and slapped their chests in salute.

"Never mind that," the sergeant told them. "Just get it open."

The recruits pulled on iron rings stapled to the stockade doors and swung them back. Clouds of dust lifted inside, cut by shafts of burning sunlight from the yard.

The badge moved down a gloomy hall, personally offended by the stench of this pen. Only one prisoner was here, yet the place stank of the hundreds who had passed through already, all of them little more than wild animals

He stopped at the third cell on his left and looked in.

Another wild animal. In a corner, a brawny, bearded man in worn trousers and leather vest and boots sat sprawled on a pile of straw. His legs were free, but a length of heavy chain connected manacles on both wrists. Despite the chain, he was flicking pebbles across the floor at a large spider in an opposite corner of the cell. The spider had caught an insect, and the prisoner was intent on killing the spider. Preoccupied, he did not look at the badge, but he said, "I thought prisoners were beheaded at dawn."

"Prisoners *are* beheaded at dawn, Captain Dathien. This is something else."

"Well. Something else."

"On your feet."

The sergeant inserted a wedge-shaped key into the lock and opened the barred door. The hinges squealed like wounded animals. The prisoner stood and, as well as he could, stretched his heavy arms.

"Walk ahead of me, Captain. Outside. To the officers' barracks."

"I could turn and strangle you with this chain, Sergeant, and be done before you could stop me."

"It's too hot for that."

"Maybe." But he went, out of the stockade and onto the wide grounds. The brilliant sunlight was painful and immediately blinded him.

"Personally," said the sergeant from behind, "I'm glad you killed the son of a bitch. The rest of us wish we'd done it."

But it was too hot, as well, for any show of amity. Besides, Dathien was intrigued by the troop taking their rest in the shade of the officers' barracks and by their mounts, which were watering at troughs not far from the soldiers. The men were of the royal guard, and their animals were perfect, too purely bred to belong to any but gentry or nobility. No one on this frontier had horses as good as those.

The two of them went up a stretch of stone steps and across a wide wooden porch to the front door of the officers' barracks. Two stories, solidly built of stone, the mess and offices on the first floor, the barracks upstairs. Dathien knew it well; he'd lived here for two years. Given the chance, he could break out from it and make it over the walls to freedom.

If not for the chain.

Inside, two more on duty fisted their chests as the sergeant guided his prisoner toward the mess hall. He stopped him just before the entrance. The hall was open. No more doors.

"Here's where I leave you, Captain."

"What about this?" Dathien lifted his hands.

"That stays." The sergeant slapped his chest, pivoted, and walked away.

Dathien eyed the other two. They watched him without emotion. He turned and entered the mess hall.

A single figure stood at the opposite end of the long central table. Dathien knew him on sight—Eam, first in line for the throne of Kormistor if he could keep head and neck together long enough to take that seat, given his brothers' jealousies and the moods in his father's unfriendly throne hall. He was Dathien's age, of thirty years, and taller than average, as tall as Dathien but not as hardened, and with features more refined. He wore a thin moustache but no beard. His chin was strong, and his bearing authoritative, as it should have been, given the badges on his armor and the seal on his helmet, which sat in front of him on the mess table.

He apprised the prisoner frankly, then said, "Captain Dathien. You know who I am?"

"I do, my lord."

"Step ahead. There is food, as you see, if you're hungry. And wine."

Dathien told him, "Of course I'm hungry," and moved to his end of the table, where there were a plate of smoked meats and vegetables, a ceramic cup, and a flagon of wine. He poured wine, gulped it, then began moving food from plate to mouth.

"So that we are clear on matters, Captain, I didn't bring you here to discuss the murder of Captain Berrak."

"No?"

"Personally, I'm glad you killed the son of a bitch."

"I seem to be everyone's favorite cutthroat today."

"I'm here to offer you a chance to pardon yourself before the throne."

"I'm listening."

"You're not a native Kormistoran," Eam said. "You're from Midriga."

"Yes."

"That's wild country. Not what I would call civilized."

"No."

"I need your help, Midrigan. We can be of assistance to each other, if you agree to my terms."

"As I said, Prince Eam, I'm listening."

"Fifteen days ago, my sister, Amyra, left the capital in a caravan for Csithuum. She is pledged to marry Prince Terias in a month's time. But she has been abducted."

"By whom?"

"We don't know."

"But who were the men who attacked her caravan? Were they Midrigan?"

"It wasn't attacked by men. It was attacked by flying creatures. They came from the north. Took everyone—people and horses, pack animals—and flew back with them."

"Toward Midriga."

"That's correct. Into the mountains. What kind of animals are those, up in Midriga, that do such things?"

"They're not animals, Prince Eam. They're demons."

"Demons?"

"There are renegades in the mountains, and they're capable of anything. They worship devils. Do sorcery. What do they want with your sister?"

"That I do not know."

"Did they attack this caravan because of her? Or was it simply for loot?"

"I don't know that, either."

"Lord Prince—what *do* you know?"

"I have a name. One man lived, he crawled away, and he heard a name from one of the guards, if it *is* a name."

"Tell me."

"Sogrul."

Dathien grunted. He poured himself more wine.

"*Is* it a name?" Eam asked.

"I fought him once. He's a pirate. Or he was. Whatever he is now, since he's been up in the mountains, he was raiding the river settlements five years ago for whatever he could get, him and his scavengers. Gave me this." Dathien pulled back his vest to show where a long white scar cut across his hairy chest and down his midsection.

"And what did you give him?"

"A trip to Hell, I think. I nearly cut him to pieces. His band left him for dead, but I heard that he made bargain with the shadows to stay alive."

"But how could he have made it into the mountains if you'd wounded him so badly?"

Dathien shook his head. "Maybe more of your flying creatures came for him. If it's the same man, even. But I know of only one pirate named Sogrul, and he'd dare anything, even demons."

"Would you welcome the chance to confront your old enemy, if this is he?"

Dathien frowned. "I killed him once. Anywhere else, that would be sufficient. But I'd welcome the chance to be quit of your stockade and this post and scum like Berrak. Your officers here are no better than Sogrul's jackals. What else are you offering?"

"Your freedom—and that is all. In return for the guidance you give us in helping to retrieve my sister."

Dathien told him, "I could cut my way to freedom. And your sister's likely dead already."

"We don't know that, and I refuse to admit it until I have the facts."

"Which is why you're moving west."

"My company and I are joining another troop that at this moment is sailing upriver. Csithian, sent by Terias. We're to meet tomorrow evening at a village north of here. From there, we head out to sea and up the coast."

"The coast is stormy. It can be a treacherous journey."

"Do you know another route?"

"The coast is safer than going overland. I know some currents that will keep you away from the rocks, but it will add a day or two."

"I want to remain alive to find my sister."

"Remaining alive is something else altogether, Lord Prince. I'm surprised I've lived this long, myself."

"Dathien...I am bound by an oath to Terias to do all that I can to establish this marriage. He and I are brothers, now. But we'll go to war if I do nothing."

"It doesn't take much for princes to go to war," Dathien told him. "And *you* won't die in a war. Other people die in your wars."

"And what would you do if she were your family?"

"I don't have any family. I killed my family."

"You killed your family?"

"In a feud. Over a matter of gold, as I recall. We had a pact, and they turned against me, my two brothers. I've been in the mountains, Prince Eam. I killed a magician there to get his treasure. I came back with the treasure and some cuts and bruises for my trouble, and my brothers ambushed me."

"I've never heard of such a thing."

"As you said, we're not civilized up in Midriga. But the treasure was lost. It fell into the river and was swept away in the flood."

"Is that your price now to help me? Treasure?"

"Whatever we find up there, these victims—from this caravan or from anywhere else—I want their gold and their silver."

"I am offended, Captain."

"It's not doing them any good."

"You and I are different kinds of men."

"We are, indeed."

Eam, after a moment's consideration, said, "I agree to your conditions."

"I want weapons. I'm not going like this." Dathien stretched the chain to its length.

"That's understood. I trust you to keep your word, Captain. I am a man of honor. Are you a man of honor?"

"That's why I killed Berrak. He had no honor."

"Truly? Is that what happened?"

"He gave me his word and he went back on it. A matter over a horse," as I recall.

"Is that a good reason to kill another man?"

"Lord Prince, give me a good reason *not* to kill other men."

2. The Witch Woman

Under starlight, two galleys, full-sailed, pushed northward, tacking against tall waves and strong winds. Dathien's warning had been correct: the coastal route was perilous, and fighting the powerful northwest winds cost the crews great effort, as well as who knew how many days? But they kept to Dathien's directions and so avoided currents that would have sundered them on the rocks. When the winds died, the soldiers on both galleys lifted the oars, singing and grunting as they cut the dark waters. Dathien joined them. And so they made their way, despite hot suns, despite mists that followed them steadily the farther north they went.

They passed small towns that diminished into villages and then into mere settlements. And beyond, inland, great forests grew into a deeply shadowed canopy that filled the world to the clouds. Then even those endless treeland stretches fell back as the great mountains began, as silent as memories, as ancient and vast as thought. Mists crept about them, lightning danced on their heights, and sunlight retreated into their shadows.

After many days, as a warm dawn awoke, Dathien, on the forward half deck with Eam, pointed ashore. "Here," he said. "Before we do anything, we must meet with the witch woman."

"And who is that?"

"Leja. Another renegade. She uses magic, and she knows the mountains here. If Sogrul is near, she can tell us."

"Is this the best way to proceed?" Eam asked.

"Better to speak with her and get the truth than deal with anyone else we may encounter."

"You trust this woman?"

"We've bargained before. She'll demand a price."

"And what will that be?"

"She'll decide. You've bargained with men in your throne halls."

"Of course."

"Leja will be more direct."

The strong-keeled galleys were run aground on the stony beach. Eam chose ten of his guardsmen to accompany him and Dathien and further men from each ship to stand guard through the day.

"We'll return tonight," Dathien told one of these men. "Start a fire when darkness falls. You'll want the light."

"We understand, Captain."

"And use your weapons if need be. You're being watched." He indicated the forest all around.

"Let them come, sir."

"No, young man. Let them stay away."

The forest was cool and damp. Dathien led the way with a light step, but Eam and the men behind him smashed through the tangled vines and growths, hacking with their short swords and stamping with their boots, alerting the wild to their passage as surely as if they had been calling out with trumpets and drums. Dathien had anticipated it and expressed little concern. If Leja were still alive, she would have seen them coming days ago. And if Sogrul were on his mountain, likely he would be aware of them, as well. We cannot pass over the earth without the earth feeling our tread.

At midday, they stopped to eat. Dathien warned the men to use the rations they had brought with them and not to sample anything growing nearby. "The water is safe," he told them. "I've fished here. But stay away from the plants and roots."

"Poisonous?" one of the men asked him.

Dathien grunted a response.

Early in the afternoon, they came to a broad river. To the west, the waters moved dangerously in a rapids before turning north under heavy foliage.

"Down there," Dathien told Eam, "is where I killed Sogrul. Him and four of his men."

"In the rapids?"

"At the bend. And beyond that is where I fought my brothers."

"Those are fast waters. I wouldn't trust rafts."

"We'll cross down this way." He nodded to the east. "It's shallower, and the current is slower."

They did so without incident, waist-high in the bright water, continuing on the other side through the endlessly same undergrowth and foliage, roots bigger than men and trees sky-tall.

As the afternoon sun began to decline, Dathien led them into a clearing where one hut stood amid the ruins of many others.

"The village of my people," he told Eam.

Aside from the single small hut, all that remained was burned wood and crumbling stone, everything overgrown with tangled, eager forest life.

"A raid?" Eam asked him.

"Some years ago, after I left."

"Who attacked them?"

Dathien shrugged. "It could have been anyone. Feuds are common here."

"And the witch woman—she's one of your people?"

"No. She claimed it afterward. You take what you can find."

Leja's hut was decorated outside with hanging skulls of men and beasts, carved lengths of bone, and leather skins painted with symbols. Eam noticed that some of those skins, stretched wide and stained with forest dyes, were human.

You take what you can find....

He followed Dathien to the open door of the hut, through which he saw the flickering of an early fire.

Dathien told him, "You and I will enter alone," and Eam ordered his guard to stand at rest. Then he followed Dathien into the hut.

It was dim, with only that fire in the center of the earthen floor to light against the crouching gloom. Thick smoke pulled upward and out a hole in the thatched roof. The smoke was aromatic. No doubt, Eam surmised, the witch woman had placed herbs or leaves onto the coals to befog him and Dathien or attempt to manipulate their reason.

She was not, this witch, what Eam had expected. She stood opposite them, on the other side of the fire, watching them as they watched her, allowing Eam to judge her. She was attractive, quite attractive, in fact. Mature—the prince's age, and Dathien's, or maybe a few seasons older—and dressed in animal skins about her hips. Dark hair fell about her face and across her shoulders to her deep breasts, which were bare, as were her arms and legs. Her sun-colored skin glowed in the firelight so that the painted designs on her arms and breasts seemed to move or breathe on their own. Perhaps it was the color of the dyes that made them move in the waving flames.

"I know why you are here, Dathien." She lowered herself and sat now, legs crossed, on her side of the fire.

Dathien nodded, spoke her name—"Leja"—and motioned for Eam also to crouch on the earth, as he did himself.

She looked at Eam. "You must pay me for whatever I know that may be of help to you."

"I understand. What is your price?"

"A man of your guard. Just one. I will take just one."

Eam looked at Dathien.

Dathien nodded to him.

Eam asked Leja, "For how long? To be your servant?"

"To be whatever I wish him to be. Is one life so valuable to you?"

"No. He will do as I command him. Now tell me what you know about my sister and the caravan."

"Sogrul has taken the princess, certainly. Her and others from that caravan. Them and many others. They were taken to his mountain. Sogrul has not left his mountain for some time. Years."

"Near here?" Dathien asked her. "How far?"

"Not far. A day. My understanding is that he is in a cave high in the mountain of the dragon's jaw."

Eam looked from her to Dathien. "What mountain is that?"

"An ancient temple," Leja told him. "Very old. Older than people. Dathien has seen it."

"Only from a distance," he reminded her.

"A demon holds that mountain," Leja continued. "You will feel it as you approach, the strength of this demon. Your warning is this: Do not sleep."

"Why not?" Dathien asked.

"The demon comes to us in dreams. That is how it lures its victims into its mountain."

"And my sister is there? What sorcery is this?" Eam's voice began to rise with anger.

Dathien reached over and gripped his forearm, cautioning him.

Eam, resentful, pulled away. He asked the witch again, "This demon holds my sister?"

"I will send my sight." She reached down the front of her rough skirt, felt about the folds, and pulled out a small purse, the dried liver of some animal. From this she withdrew a pinch of powder, then returned the purse to her skirt. The pinch of powder she threw into the fire. Immediately the orange flames sparked and turned into tongues of sapphire.

Eam frowned, unconvinced by this trick.

Leja leaned close to the fire. Her breasts swung beneath her long hair, and the designs on her arms moved on their own across her damp blue skin.

"The mountain is guarded," she told Eam and Dathien, "by his flying creatures. His or the demon's. It is difficult to see within. The demon is strong and protects this place from my sight."

"What of my sister?" Eam asked impatiently.

The blue of the flames faded, and Leja sat back. "I may have seen her face. He guards this place strongly."

"This is ridiculous." Eam rose and looked down at Dathien. "You trust this woman?"

"I do, Lord Eam." He pushed himself to his feet, as well, and Leja rose. Dathien asked her, "What else?"

"The demon owns Sogrul. Whatever bargain he made with the shadows, they own him, now."

"Yet this was done by his command?" Dathien asked her.

Leja shrugged. "It does not matter. Sogrul and the demon are one thing, now."

"And all you saw of my sister was her face?" Eam asked her.

"Yes."

Eam's tone was cold. "A woman dressed in animal skins and a dying man hiding in a cave. This," he faced Dathien, "is why you have brought me here?"

"I trust her. And you and I have an agreement."

Leja said, "To confront the elements of this world rather than its illusions, Prince Eam, one must be dark of heart. Life itself is dark-hearted. Are you so certain of yourself?"

"Certain enough that I feel no compulsion to explain myself to such as you."

"What would you have the weak do when you give them so little power, Lord Eam? Women in animal skins and dying men— what should the broken do with their pain, and the dying?"

"They should die, witch." In his dark mood, he turned and left the hut.

Leja looked at Dathien. "He is a fool." She followed Eam through the open doorway, and Dathien came after her.

Eam and his men were in a half circle outside, watching as they approached.

"My price, Lord Prince," Leja called to him.

Eam pulled some coins from his belt and held them up so that they caught the sunlight. "I'll pay you in silver," he told her. "Even you can use real money, no doubt."

Leja shook her head. "We agreed." She smiled, showing her teeth, and walked in front of the soldiers. She looked them up and down, one after another.

Eam frowned.

These were young men, all of them, certain of themselves, some of them very vain. Leja paused before one and watched his eyes.

"Stay with me," she said to him.

The young man showed a wide grin. The two on either side of him slapped his shoulders. He told Leja, "I'll stay...if you think you can handle it."

"Let me try."

Some of the men laughed and made obscene gestures to one another.

Still grinning, the youth looked to his commander. Eam jerked his head in assent.

Leja caught a look from Dathien, nodded to him, and led the youth toward her hut.

He told her as they stepped inside, "Some of 'em like me to keep my armor on. Are you that way?"

Eam waved a gloved hand, motioning his troop to return down the trail they had taken. He and Dathien fell in behind.

"A waste of time and the waste of a man," he grumbled. "I distrust these spells and tricks."

"Then don't believe the spells and tricks. But if she says Sogrul and your sister are on that mountain, then that's where they are. She knows these forests and—"

He stopped at the sound of a scream behind them—the soldier they had left with Leja. The scream hung in the air, a single pleading, prolonged note that held—held—

"Damn it!" Eam pivoted and reached for his sword.

"No!" Dathien yelled at him.

"What's she doing to him?"

"You paid the price. Let her be."

"What is she doing to my guardsman?"

"She won't eat him all at once, Lord Prince."

"Her? Human flesh?"

"We're meat, Lord Prince," Dathien told him. "Don't forget it. You are. I am. We're meat."

3. The Dragon's Jaw

At the first light of morning, Eam told the captains of the war galleys to wait three days, a full three days, before taking to the waves again, thereby allowing sufficient time for the prince to return with his sister and anyone else who might survive the adventure in the mountains. Then he and Dathien and forty men, twenty from each ship, moved up the beach and returned to the forest.

Eam's chosen forty did not include any of the guardsmen of the previous day who had been with him at the witch's hut.

Prudently, the prince had taken Dathien's advice not to continue with those who had witnessed the barter with Leja. Doing so would only increase the chance of disaffection and bad temper among men who, although well trained, nevertheless would likely serve their master better, and themselves, the less they had of such matters on their minds. The trail ahead promised sufficient peril and uncertainty; why enlarge the concern with worries about what might be waiting behind?

By the same rationale, Dathien took them on a path that steered away from the vicinity of his former home. And as on the previous day, to Dathien's annoyance, the soldiers and guardsmen as they crashed through the forest made noise sufficient to rouse a sleeping dragon. It was the carelessness and arrogance of it that chafed. Had he himself been an enemy in this forest, he could have moved into them and one by one slit their throats on the trail, taking each man silently and by surprise, finishing them all before midday.

Yet there was no enemy around them, Dathien realized. Years ago, as a young man living in this forest and others like it, he would have heard bird calls from far off, musical whistles and chirps, the sounds men make to each other as they track their prey. He would have caught the lingering scents of strangers that had recently come through, noticed boot prints on the soft ground, or caught sight of finely broken leaves and branches that showed where others had crossed. Yet there was none of that here.

Surely, Dathien thought, it is because of the demon that holds the mountain, or perhaps because of Sogrul himself. Cautious animals and men and women had learned to stay away lest they provoke the evil that was here now, provoke it or, through some accident, fall victim to it otherwise.

At midday, the forest gave way to a wide clearing, a stony plateau that overlooked a bottomless gorge and, across from it, their first sight of their destination, the rocky height of the mountain. The troop halted to have a meal, the men unbuckling their harness and removing their helmets.

Eam walked near the edge of the precipice and strained to see the bottom of the chasm. "How do we cross?" he asked Dathien.

Dathien pointed northward to a natural bridge that spanned the width of the gorge. Eam saw where the bridge joined the mountain at a small plateau, far on the other side. Upon the plateau stood two tall columns topped by a great natural stone arch.

"That's the dragon's jaw," Dathien said, indicating the arch. "The columns are what's left of a temple. Or what could have been a temple."

"You've never crossed that bridge?"

Dathien frowned and shook his head. "I don't like it up here. There's nothing good about this place."

"I can sense it," Eam told him. "Can't you? It's...a feeling of overwhelming sadness. Profound sadness."

"It's all the death here, Lord Eam. This land is old with death." Dathien pointed behind them, to the south, where a great pile of stones stood just inside the tree line. Curious, Eam approached the stones and, as he came close, noticed an order to them. There were images still visible in the weathered stones.

"Unusual," he said.

"Look closer, Lord Eam."

Eam studied the designs, some of them almost indistinguishable now as being anything intentional, and winced. "Faces," he said. "Animals, some of them. People, perhaps?"

"I wouldn't call them people," Dathien said. "They're older than people. Maybe older than whatever was here before us. I don't care to contemplate the things that were once alive in this world."

"Is life so old?"

"I think so. Old enough that, whatever was here, we're small by comparison."

"I can see why you dislike this place," Eam told him. "We are not welcome."

"No. We're not welcome. And we don't matter."

A short distance into the forest, they noticed the remains of an animal. It was enormous, reduced now to the skeleton but with the skin dried on it and some old muscle and gristle. It had horns and spikes of great length, and its thigh bone was as tall as Dathien. Neither he nor Eam could identify the bones.

"What is it?" the lord prince wondered aloud.

Dathien shook his head.

"And what killed it? Where did it come from?"

Dathien looked behind them. "From the mountain. I never heard anyone here talk about such animals."

"From the mountain?"

"Across the bridge."

They returned to the men, sat on some rocks, and opened the rations they had brought.

Dathien asked the prince, "Don't you have people to wait on you?"

"And servants to cut my meat into pieces for me? We're not quite as decadent as that, Captain, whatever you may have heard about the royal family. I don't have others mount my horse for me, either."

"Do you have any affection for your sister?"

"Some. I've met her only a few times. She was raised in another city and prepared there for this marriage."

"You're right. We are not the same kind of man. I wouldn't risk so much for someone I barely knew."

"It's a matter of blood. She's the throne. I am the throne. I wouldn't expect you to understand. You spilled *your* family's blood in feuds."

"You do the same, Lord Prince, but on a grander scale, that's all."

Eam smirked. "I take your point, Captain."

"The best thing is to stay alive for as long as possible," Dathien told him. "Whatever kills me finally or eats me will pay for it."

The prince chewed thoughtfully on some of the jerky he had brought before asking, "Do you believe that Sogrul truly made bargain with demons for his own life?"

"I've seen things just as strange as men making bargain with demons."

"Such as the witch woman?"

"Yes."

"Why do they do it, your renegades and witches and pirates? Bargaining with demons and skinning dead men?"

"This is the last chance they have of staying alive, Lord Eam. They're at home here. They don't belong anywhere else."

"Is that sufficient reason to dare such sorcery?"

"They want to stay alive. Everything living wants to stay alive."

"True enough. I certainly intend to. But your pirate friend may not do as well. If Sogrul has harmed my sister, he will bring out my rage, be sure of it. I have a hot heart. He, too, will pay for what he has done. Captain, you are not trying to run away, I notice."

"No."

"Why not? You could disappear here, and my men and I could not stop you. Become a renegade yourself. Are you so honorable?"

"Not at all. I want that treasure."

"There are other treasures to be had, and they'd be gained with less danger and far less difficulty. What holds you here?"

Dathien considered the question and at last replied, "It is a harsh land, Lord Prince, and I left it because I'm restless, but it is my home. I am a son of this land."

"As I am of mine. We cannot—"

Eam was interrupted by a scream from one of his men. Immediately, Dathien was up and running. Sword drawn, he shoved men away in every direction until he reached one of them writhing on the grass. His face was blackening, and he kicked his legs frantically as he dug at his throat. Beside him lay a piece of blue fruit, half-eaten.

Ringing soldiers watched as he died at last. And every one of them gasped as the corpse's throat bulged, moved on its own, and broke open. Thin black feelers reached through the flesh, and a barbed worm squirmed out, larva white and trailing red mucous.

"You damned fool," Dathien said, kicking the body so that the worm tumbled to the ground. He stepped on it, crushing it. "That's what your rations are for!" he announced in disgust. He reached for another fruit from a bush and halved it with his knife. At the core was a tiny, curled worm; Dathien showed it around, then threw it to the ground. "Bury him," he commanded irritably. "And unless you want him mutilated, pile his armor and some stones over the grave."

They did it, several of the guardsmen, turning over the soft earth within the forest. When they were done, they moved double time to catch the rest of their troop moving north.

By late in the afternoon, Dathien judged that reaching the bridge before sunset was unlikely and crossing it in darkness, foolhardy. He asked Eam, "Can your men stay awake until dawn?"

"And cross it then? I'd prefer to do it now."

"I'd rather have daylight. And we could all use the rest."

"So long as we don't sleep? What sort of warning is that? You still trust your witch?"

"I trust her. Tell your men to bivouac, but everyone keeps alert and no one sleeps."

Eam, tired himself although loath to admit it, ordered the men to make camp, have their rations, and take their rest. "But we all keep watch tonight. No sleeping."

Night fell quickly once the sun dropped beyond the mountains. Campfires were lit. Swords were sharpened, garments repaired, and the dice and cards brought out. Talk continued into the night, the tall tales and ribald jokes. Speculation as to what waited on the other side of the bridge was met with boastfulness, the certainty that weapons and quick wits typically prevail, whatever the situation.

At a fire, one of the guardsmen said, "I seen some bad things, but my brother told me he was someplace once where the ground itself ate you up. One of the islands. Man'd be walking and then go straight down. Eat him alive."

"There's no such places," an older man told him.

"My brother says there is, and he don't lie."

The older man grunted and got to his feet. "Maybe he don't lie, but there's no such places." He walked into the darkness just beyond the firelight. In a moment, the others heard him urinating in the woods. Then he grunted again, and the leaves rustled.

The men at the fire looked at one another, and one of them called out, "Hie!"

Silence.

"*Hie!*"

No reply.

The guardsman with the brother who'd been to the islands stood and drew his sword. "Who else?"

One of the others got up, as well.

They walked to where the older man had been, called out for him, then slapped the shrubbery with their swords.

"There's blood," the second of them said, "but no sign of him."

They returned to the others, the one showing where he had fresh blood on his fingers.

A youth at the fire said, "Maybe the ground ate him up."

They regarded one another uneasily.

"That's not what it was."

They turned toward Dathien as he stepped toward them.

"Stay by the fire."

"What's out there, Captain?"

"Anything. Wolves. Renegades. Ghosts."

"Demons?"

"Whatever lives at night and looks for meat."

"Can we help him?" a guardsman asked.

"The man they just took?"

"Yes."

"He's inside something's belly. You keep by the fire."

"Yes, sir."

"And stay awake."

Dathien built no fire of his own but settled himself against the bole of a tree, positioned comfortably within the great roots of it, and variously watched the wide black wall of the mountain across the gorge or turned his sight to the tall sky with all of its stars. Twice he saw stars lose their hold and fall to earth, trailing streaks of white fire.

Eam was restless and could not remain still. He paced, occasionally asked Dathien questions that had no answers or that answered themselves, or he sat apart and brooded. Only once did his attitude change, and that was in the deep of the night, when the breezes fell still, nothing moved, no sounds came from any direction, and the darkness itself seemed to have stopped where it was, so that morning would never come.

From somewhere in that wide silence there rose a scream, and then a man's voice calling, "They need me! They need me!" There was the sound of running, and then the cry of a man going over the edge into the gorge, his voice diminishing as he fell.

"Stand back!" Eam yelled to everyone. "No one move! What happened to that man?"

For a moment there was confusion, until a guardsman stepped forward to tell Prince Eam, "He fell asleep, my lord. Only for a moment."

Eam looked at Dathien, who shrugged and returned to his tree.

"No one sleeps!" Eam commanded.

"No, sir. We won't, my lord."

"I'm not losing any more men up here."

"No, sir. No, my lord."

"No more," Eam repeated, and walked away to sit in the shadows, muttering to himself, "Witch!"

With the first light of dawn, the troop continued northward, Dathien and Eam leading them. By midmorning, they came to where the great rocky span lifted out from the wall on their side of the gorge and reached all the way across, turning slightly before it met the plateau beneath the columns and arch opposite.

Dathien and Eam were looking at a small forest of white and purple growths that had sprouted from the south side of the mountain.

"I've never seen plants like those," Eam declared. "They're huge. Are they flowers?"

"Flowers of some kind," Dathien said. "But they're bigger than that animal skeleton."

"How are they able to grow there?"

"Sorcery. Now what about the bridge?"

Eam had to decide whether to leave some of his men here or take them all across. Dathien retrieved a heavy length of tree limb from the forest litter at their feet and, as strongly as he could, heaved it out over the span.

The tree limb flew straight until, caught by a rising wind, it was snatched from its path and pulled far out to drop to the unseen bottom of the gorge.

"We stay low," was Dathien's warning. "And your men should tie themselves together to weigh themselves down."

Eam agreed and ordered his company to do it with the lengths of rope each man carried inside the shield on his back. They attached themselves together in groups of two or three so that, crouching as they moved over the long stretch of bridge, they would lessen their risk of being taken over the edge. At its widest, the span was more than three man-lengths across, which would allow them to advance alongside each other. Eam attached himself to one of his guardsmen, and Dathien did the same with one of the Csithian soldiers.

Dathien led the way, crouching low and scuttling with the Csithian beside him. He was a young man and properly frightened.

"Captain," he asked, "what will we find when we reach the other side?"

"Just keep low," Dathien told him.

When they were nearly to the plateau, however, Dathien and Eam and their men turned at a loud hissing sound. Looking at the mountain, they saw winged creatures gliding toward them. The bony heads had long beaks, longer than the height of a tall man, and long crests behind. The stretched wings of skin reached from the powerful arms to the legs. Dathien reckoned that the monsters were fully capable of flying away with the members of a traveling caravan—or with men tied together on a span of bridge.

He called back, "All of you stay low! Don't panic!"

But that was not possible. The first of the monsters glided low over the bridge and dropped down, snapping quickly with its beak, taking off most of the head of a man in the middle of the span. As the body twisted, throwing out blood, the soldiers tied to it loosened their ropes to get free. But a second monster caught one of them by the chest and lifted him and the others into the air above the gorge. Long jaws finally snapped the victim in two so that the man tied to him dropped, screaming.

Frantically the groups of men wrestled each other to escape from the bridge. Some tried to crawl back to the forest. Others fought to reach Dathien and Eam, who had made it to the plateau under the arch and were undoing their ropes as quickly as they could. Some tried to cut themselves free with their swords but, forced off balance, fell to their deaths.

Three men tied together were nearly dragged into the gorge by a fourth who, in the panic, had been pushed to the edge of the bridge. As he grappled with bleeding hands, trying to pull himself to safety, the others cut through his line so that he dropped away. The falling man was caught in the powerful beak of a gliding creature and cut in half. Part of him continued to spin into the mists below, the insides of him coming out and slowly spreading apart in the air, while the monster flew away with what it had kept.

"What have you done?" Eam screamed at Dathien. "What have you done?" He pulled the closest group of men to safety, then started to return across the bridge.

Dathien caught the lord prince by the neck of his jacket, yanked him backward, and pushed him ruthlessly against the mountainside. "You can't help them!"

"Remove your hand!"

"You can't help them!"

"*I'll have you killed, barbarian!*"

Dathien let him go, but he growled at Eam, "You stay alive until we find out what's in there."

"And you do as you're told. You're an officer in my army."

"Not after this."

They kept their eyes on each other as the screams from the bridge finally stopped. Behind Dathien, one of the Csithians kneeling on the plateau retched and brought up whatever he had eaten from his ration pouch.

Dathien stepped away and looked at the bridge. No one was left. One of the monsters was perched on the span, its head back, beak in the air, gulping down what remained of whomever it had caught. Still protruding were an arm and a hand with a ring on one finger. The creature snapped its neck, the arm with its hand tipped into the monster's gullet, and it lowered its head, turning to one side so that with its black eye it could watch the men on the plateau.

One of the guardsmen asked Dathien, "Will it follow us?"

"I don't know."

Eam said, "And we don't know what's in there."

"Your sister," Dathien replied. "And what other path would you take, Lord Prince?"

"You're going in first, Captain."

"And you keep your sword in your sheath, prince or not," Dathien sneered at him. "Do we understand each other?"

"Onward, Captain."

Dathien at last looked away from him and proceeded into the tunnel. Eam and the remaining seven followed.

4. Sogrul

"It feels like it's alive," said one of the Csithians.

"This tunnel?" Dathien asked.

"Yes, sir."

They all felt it. The way was cramped; most of them had to crouch to prevent their helmets from scraping the rock above, and their shoulders frequently rubbed into the walls. The tunnel was damp, and it smelled of more than rock, of more than wet earth. Where their shoulders touched the walls, the walls seemed to give. The tunnel almost pulsed, like a muscle or a neck, as though they were moving inside something as nearly alive as they themselves were.

The Csithian said, "I grew up working in the mines, and I— *Hhh.*"

Dathien and Eam turned. Dathien quickly crouched, making of himself as small a target as possible. He heard the Cisthian gasp as the last of his air left him, and then bones breaking. The men closer to the tunnel entrance began backing out. They pulled their swords free, the metal whispering.

Eam asked, "What is it?"

There was little light this far back from the entrance, but they could see something hanging from the wall, a damp white stalk or length of flesh, perhaps a plant or a tendril. Dathien had seen sea creatures with such tentacles—snakelike, unjointed arms. But this one had a bulb and a sort of mouth at the end of it.

With his sword in front of him, he moved at it, stepping over the dead Csithian. The tentacle reached for him, and Dathien chopped at it, pushed in with his sword, cut down, and pulled back.

From behind him, deep within the mountain, there came the sound of a voice rising in a howl.

Dathien chopped again, felt hot fluid jump onto his sword arm, and moved away.

"It takes a cut like a man," he said.

He stepped back, bumping into Eam, and saw where the severed tentacle lay on the tunnel floor.

"That's the head," he told Eam. "Or something with some kind of teeth. I think it ripped out the throat of your man."

On the other side of it, a guardsmen said, "It's not moving, sir."

Dathien looked at his sword arm. The substance on it was more viscous than blood, and it was gray, but although it itched slightly, it did not burn him or stain his skin.

Eam said, "Whatever's here, I'm going on."

Dathien told him, "Then keep your sword out."

Eam led the way, with Dathien close behind him and the rest of the men following. The tunnel veered to the left and lifted under their feet, rising in elevation. It widened, as well, until two men could walk abreast in it. And they saw light coming into the tunnel from whatever was ahead of them.

But before they reached the light, they spotted two more of the damp, white stalks waiting for them. One hung from the wall to their right; Eam, able to distinguish it in the dimness, shoved his sword through its head. The jaws snapped and drooled; then it slumped against the wall.

The sound of a voice came again, as though killing this thing had brought a groan from the mountain itself.

The second of them was on the floor of the tunnel and was barely a stalk. It had the mouth and the sharp teeth, however, and two black eyes like gems pushed into soft dough. This one they passed by, leaving it to snap at them as well as it could.

The light increased. They came to a wide flight of stairs, carefully went up them, and entered a small cave. The light was brighter here, and they went on through the cave into the tunnel in the opposite wall. Finally they came to the source of the light and walked onto a small open ledge.

"What sort of creatures used this?" Eam asked. "Not those things in the tunnel?"

There was no answer to such a question. They overlooked a gigantic cavern. The natural rock here had been hewn into the semblance of a temple. Stalactites and stalagmites had been fashioned into decorated columns. Idols and statues set against the arching walls resembled creatures somewhat human, with features far more distinct than the weathered pieces across the gorge. The floor once had been level, or nearly so; now, the carvings in it were broken and twisted as though the restless mountain itself had stretched the floor out of shape.

Rooted in that floor were more of the white tentacles, a thicket of at least twenty of them, some taller than a man and as round as a tree, others mere buds beginning to burst from the floor. All of them had the small black eyes; all had wide mouths with sharp teeth. What within this mountain caused monsters to grow from it like shoots from a plant?

In the middle of the floor, as though guarded by the mouthed tentacles, was a well of large diameter surrounded by a low wall.

To the right, high on the wall, was an opening that let in sunlight and air. On a ledge protruding outward from this opening stood two of the flying creatures. So this was their roost.

To the left, the cavern retreated into darkness. Piles of rubble stood in the shadows. The piles were pyramids of skulls and severed heads, some animal, some human.

At the far end of the cavern, on the other side of the moving white stalks and beyond the mouth of the well, was Sogrul—or what remained of him. There was a head. A shoulder. A portion of the left arm and hand. He was white, with no color to him at all, as white as a worm. Whatever else there was of him, trunk and legs, apparently was buried in the cave floor and the wall behind him. He appeared to have sunk into the very rock.

His eyes were open. He spoke. His speech was slurred and imperfect but understandable, and he recognized Dathien.

"You are here," the head spoke, staring at the men at the end of the tunnel.

Dathien led Eam and the other four down a wide series of steps that led into the cavern proper. They moved toward the living stalks but stayed well away from them. Dathien called to Sogrul, "What are you? You were a man. Did I do this to you?"

"I am the demon's friend now, Dathien. I am immortal. I dream. It is bliss."

"You're not even alive." He looked in every direction, eager to identify any other horrors that were here.

"This *is* life, Dathien. I see everything. I know everything. I dream. The demon feeds me. I swim in its dreams. Dathien," Sogrul said to him, "join us."

The tentacles wavered.

Dathien growled at it, "I came for treasure. Where is it?"

"There is no treasure."

"You're a pirate. All you do is steal. You expect me to believe you don't have gold and silver here?"

"I have only dreams. I feed the demon." The head inclined toward the open well. "They made it live. Their spell." He meant the figures carved into the walls. "Their demon killed them. Yet the spell continues. The dragons live. I live. Everything lives again. We swim in dreams."

Eam pushed Dathien aside and yelled at the slurring head, "Where is my sister?"

"She is here. In bliss."

"Where is she?" Eam took a step forward and tried to judge how he could evade the tentacles and make his way to Sogrul. He pulled out his sword.

Dathien read his mind and drew his own weapon. "He's mine!"

Eam faced him. "You challenge *me*?"

"I claim the pirate!"

The prince glanced at his troop but shook his head at them. Stay back. He raised his sword to Dathien. "Then claim him."

Dathien grunted and came at him. He aimed his weapon straight on but then moved it underhand, catching Eam's where the prince did not expect it. Eam backed away but brought his own sword around, striking Dathien's. And again. The two lengths of steel rasped along their edges. Dathien cursed and pressed the prince back another step, then slid quickly to his left, putting Eam between himself and the tentacles.

The heads swayed, leaning close to the lord prince.

Eam let out a howl and charged, making a wheel of his weapon and lunging at Dathien.

Dathien side-stepped him. Crouching, he brought his weapon up and nearly caught Eam through the wrist. The prince stumbled as he jumped away, fearing for a moment that he had lost his hand.

Dathien snarled at him, "Come, Lord Prince. Finish it."

Eam pulled in a breath, considered the dare—and reconsidered. He yelled at his guardsmen and the Csithians, "To me!"

Quickly the six young men drew their weapons and circled Dathien, pointing their swords at his throat, heart, belly.

"Dog." Dathien made to sheathe his steel.

"Throw it to the ground!" Eam ordered him.

"Go to hell."

The sword points leaned in.

"To the ground, Captain."

Dathien did it angrily, slamming down his weapon.

"Let him go," Eam said.

The young men sheathed their weapons. Dathien stepped away from them. He moved toward the stairs, aware that he was armed now only with a side knife.

Confident and in command, Eam eyed Sogrul once more on the other side of the moving stalks.

"Pirate! I came for my sister. Where is she?"

Sogrul's face twisted as though attempting an expression. "One of those," it said, and shifted its eyes to its right.

A mouth at the end of a swaying tentacle arced across the distance between it and a pile of skulls, took into its jaws one of the heads there, and tore into it with its teeth.

Sogrul said, "The demon eats the heart and the body. The heads and eyes are mine."

Eam looked at the stacked heads.

Halfway down this side of the nearest pyramid was Amyra, her head, upside down, with her eyes open.

She was looking at Eam.

She grinned at him and whispered, "Brother."

Eam screamed. He ran. Sword lifted, he jumped toward the pyramid.

Immediately the stalks closest to him, three of them, came at him with mouths open.

"Lord Eam!"

His guardsmen and the two Csithians pulled out their weapons and rushed to him.

Eam cut one of the tentacles and stabbed the head of a second. As he did, more of the things reached for his men. Blood flew, and all seven of them screamed as the mouths tore into them, taking them by the legs and arms.

Dathien scuttled across the cavern floor to retrieve his sword.

One of the heads caught Eam by his left leg and held him upside down. The prince tried to stab it, but another mouth clamped on the wrist of his sword arm.

Eam called to Dathien, "Captain!"

A third head settled about the prince's throat and pulled Eam's head free. It dropped to the ground.

Dathien got hold of his sword but as he gripped it, one of the heads moved at him. He jumped away, slicing with his blade as he did. Gray blood struck him in the face and chest, and Sogrul, the head of Sogrul, moaned from across the cavern.

The thing went for his legs. The teeth of it caught Dathien in the right thigh just as he came down with his weapon and halved it. The eyes fell one way, sharp mouth and stalk the other.

Again Sogrul made sounds.

"They're you!" Dathien yelled.

Sogrul hissed.

The headless bodies of the guardsmen and Csithians were being shredded by the tentacles with mouths. They passed the pieces among themselves and dropped them into the well to feed the demon, whatever was down there.

Dathien looked at Eam's head. It lay on the floor in front of him, eyes and mouth open.

The eyes moved, and the head spoke.

"Kill me! It is eating me!"

"What's eating you?"

"The demon!"

Dathien reached for the head as another sharp-mouthed tentacle tried to take it. He picked up Eam's head by the wet chin strap of the helmet and stepped away.

"Kill me!" Eam's head begged him. "Quickly!"

Stab it? Cut it open?

From the nearest pyramid, Amyra's head said, "Brother."

Eam screamed, "Kill me! Then her!"

Dathien looked through the moving thicket of tentacles.

Sogrul told him, "Go to the well. Face the demon. I will not harm you."

Eam's head screamed, "Kill me!"

"Go to the well."

"Brother."

"Kill me, barbarian!"

Dathien growled and smashed Eam's head to the floor, chopped at it with his sword, breaking it apart, cutting the helmet and face into pieces. Grabbing a portion of Eam's head by a length of its hair, Dathien swung the meat toward Sogrul and released it.

Tentacles moved for it. One caught it.

"Take him!" Dathien yelled at Sogrul.

"Go to the well."

Dathien growled. He stared at Sogrul, no longer the man he remembered, the face and the arm, everything about him colorless, bloodless. No longer a man but a thing, part earth, part demon. But the well held a secret, and Dathien was intrigued. The tentacles held back as, stepping carefully, Dathien approached the well.

There was nothing within it. It was black. Nothing. But now there was movement, light and shadow, nothing solid, nothing real, but the light reached upward, and Dathien understood what was within the well. It must reach— How far down must it reach? Yet there was treasure within the well. That was what Sogrul meant by the dreams. The dreams were the treasure, dreams in which one could rest forever, one with the demon, like Sogrul.

Dathien pushed himself away from the well.

Sogrul hissed.

A tentacle moved toward him, and Dathien jumped. He cut it, stabbed it, and Sogrul yelled in pain. Dathien roared and backed away, then in rage charged into the moving tentacles, cutting in every direction. Heavy drops of blood showered him. Quickly moving mouths snapped at him. One of the mouths caught him again in the right thigh and opened it.

He stumbled away, panting, sweating, bleeding.

"Return to the well, Dathien."

"Sogrul!"

"We are brothers."

Growling in frustration, Dathien moved toward the stairs he and the others had followed to get here. He looked at the piles of heads and skulls. Amyra was staring at him. The winged creatures at their roost watched him. And the tentacles with their mouths. And Sogrul.

Exhausted, bleeding, he yawned for air.

"Dathien," Sogrul said. "We are brothers."

He climbed the stairs quickly, turning his back on the cavern, but at the mouth of the tunnel, he looked down a last time.

The pirate slurred at him, "There are other wells."

He turned and ran into the tunnel, through the small chamber with its dim light, down the first tunnel, past the young, eyed head on the floor, over the dead Csithian youth. As he cleared the Csithian's corpse, it moved. Dathien looked at it.

The headless corpse reached for him, one arm, one hand, groping. Beside it was the young man's head. The head tried to move but, although it shuddered with the attempt, could not. Facing the wall of the tunnel, the head said to Dathien, "There are other wells."

Dathien ran. He moved onto the bridge. The air was thick and damp. He turned and, panting, looked at the mountain. It was golden in the early sunlight, beautiful, with mists rising about it.

He backed across the bridge, and as he did, he saw a monster approach from around the mountain. It glided on stretched wings, circled above him, then perched on top of the arch, the dragon's jaw. There it tilted its head to one side to watch him.

Blood dripping from him and sweat, his torn leg pulsing, Dathien waved his sword over his head. He roared at the monster, roared at it. "Here I am! I'm here, damn you!"

The monster did not move.

"I'm here!" he roared. He waved his sword, out of control. *"I'm here!"*

A wind came and nearly knocked him into the gorge. Dathien dropped to his belly and held onto the rock until the wind passed. Then he moved, crouching, into the forest at the end of the bridge.

"Stop where you are!"

Dathien held out his sword and squinted into the darkness of the forest.

"Where are the rest of them?" It was a young man's voice.

Dathien asked the voice, "You made it off the bridge?"

"Yes."

"Just you?"

"Where are the rest of them?"

"They're dead. Are you Csithian or one of Eam's guard?"

"Csithian." He came forward, revealing himself from behind broad leaves, but he kept his point up. "They're all dead? Even Lord Eam?"

"Particularly Lord Eam. Put down your weapon. I'm not going to challenge you." Dathien sheathed his own steel and moved into the cool shadows.

The young Csithian watched him. "You led those men to their deaths."

Dathien dropped to the damp ground and cleaned the blood and sweat from his face and arms and the front of him, pieces of Prince Eam and gray blood from the tentacles, and got his air back. He leaned against a weathered stone, another of those with the carvings on it nearly obliterated.

"Well?" the young man continued.

"If you're going to talk, at least make sense. Here." Dathien took from a shrub next to him one of the blue fruits, halved it with his knife, and with the point flicked out the barbed worm in its heart, the worm as white as Sogrul. He threw one of the pieces to the Csithian.

The boy tried to catch it but it bounced off his chest. He set down his sword, then thought better of it and picked it up and sheathed it. Then he took up the fruit.

"It won't kill you to eat it?" he asked.

"It's the worm in it that kills you." Dathien bit into the meat of the fruit, relishing the living sweetness of it. When he was finished, he began eating a second, holding it in stained fingers. He asked the boy, "You want another one?"

"No." He kept his distance, wary.

Dathien closed his eyes for a moment and yawned.

"They're all dead? Even Lord Eam?"

He considered that Eam's father and brothers now would surely go to war with Prince Terias. Armies would ride against each other, and two thrones would threaten to fall until one or another of those men remained sufficiently alive to take ownership of whatever was left unbroken.

Let them do it, Dathien thought. Let the galleys offshore return sail with word of the failure, and let all of those sons of theirs die. No doubt they considered it to be important.

What was important for Dathien was to be away. He himself had come for treasure, and there was no treasure here any more than there was the sister of a prince.

A light breeze touched him, and he welcomed it. He opened his eyes. The breeze lifted heavy leaves in front of him so that he saw for a moment the span across the deep gorge, the stone arch of the dragon's jaw, and the monster sitting there, wrapped in its long wings. It was still looking in Dathien's direction as though able to see him in the deep shadows.

"There are other wells."

He rose and looked at the Csithian. "You'd better come with me."

"I'm not going anywhere with you. All of their blood is on your hands. You got them killed."

"Listen to me. Nothing's safe here."

"I'll be safe. You just want to kill me, too. You're one of them."

"Come with me now or not at all. Don't follow me."

"I'm safer here."

Dathien left him and moved into the living darkness of the forest. Eventually, late in the morning, he heard the young man's screams and knew that something or someone had found him.

So many screams away in the distance, the screams of life dying, fearful, angry, damned, alone, lives exerting themselves in a final effort of sound, sound.

Dathien kept moving—wounded but no longer in chains, with blood on his hands, alive but resisting sleep. If he did not stop, if he evaded whatever might cross his trail, he would be out of the deepest part of the forest by sundown and then could reach Leja's hut, or even the river where he'd killed Sogrul, where he'd killed his brothers.

Then, perhaps, he could sleep.

The Last Words of Imatus Istum

Here is the ending of a people and our way of life. Death is everywhere, and what we trusted is gone. I remain. I place these words on the scroll that was in my hands when destruction came to Mograd, my home. My pen is a splinter of my leg bone. The leg is shattered. My ink is my own blood. My breath now comes with effort, and the world is fading and falling away from me. I will be dead by evening. I must speak of the end of my city and my people, who were cultured and loved learning but who were betrayed.

My name is Imatus Kad Istum. I was taken alive with many others when the Kunashtu came down out of the north and took our city. They had attempted this previously because our city was a prize. We were the Mogrem, and our home, Mograd, was a thousand years old and had withstood many attacks many times from great armies and eager kings as well as such barbarians as the Kunashtu. Once our tall towers and spires glowed in the sun and welcomed travelers. Caravans visited from everywhere. Our walls were old, and our singers proclaimed how much the gods loved us in proud songs that were as ancient as our stone gates. Physicians and scholars, poets and artists came to our city to learn from us. The universe was ours, and we sat in the center of it as on a throne. We were respected. The gods loved us.

We had heard that the war makers were approaching. Already they had taken other cities in a brief season of slaughter, and we expected them to arrive before winter. There was famine in the lands around us, and the Kunashtu, who rode the northlands on strong ponies, were taking from others to stay alive. This was their way. Our ancestors had defeated these riders several times before, but that was a long time ago. Now traitors among us who had been promised gold let the Kunashtu inside our walls. They opened the stone gates in the quiet of the night to the marauders.

Of course, the traitors were then the first to die. How could the war people trust such as these, who would betray their own? So their blood was the first to run on the stones.

The warriors struck at us very quickly. We were overcome, as the poet says, as are the birds of the air in a deadly storm. We wailed to the gods as our blood sprayed from sword and hoof. The pacifists and irenics, those who did not believe in war, were put to the blade like meat hanging in the marketplace. Who were we, merchants and farmers, scholars and artists, to stand up against these warriors born with knives in their fists and nursed on the blood of their mothers' breasts? It was said that the Kunasht who does not bite his mother while suckling and draw blood from the thing that birthed him is no Kunasht, and that such a babe is given to the animals to be killed or raised by them, whichever the animal spirits decide.

The healthy men among us were murdered or taken prisoner; only lesser ones such as I, good only for servitude (I have suffered from birth with a clubfoot) were spared. Of the women, the aged and the sickly were sworded. The mature were taken as concubines and chattel, the ruler of the killers assuming the daughters of our king for himself. The young of both sexes were herded into buildings and kept until needed, to be slaughtered; their flesh was used for food and the rest of their bodies for all purposes: teeth as jewelry, hair woven into raiment, bones crushed to powder to use as aphrodisiacs and ingredients for magicians' recipes.

Following the morning and afternoon of our death, the Kunashtu feasted on the cooked bones of our young men and children throughout the evening. For entertainment, the warriors—men and women both—bid for possession of those of us who had survived. Each family chief took a man or two as personal servant and brawled for the comeliest of our women. I was given to a young warrior named Agrat; I had studied books and was a poet, and Agrat claimed to love stories, so I was to entertain him with such as I knew.

Thus ended the first day of our occupation. With others who had been permitted to live, I was kept in one of the rooms of the oldest homes in our city, sleeping on the floor, never to see my own bed again. I determined that I would do everything I could to stay alive in spite of whatever our conquerors might do. Many others chose to die. They deliberately provoked the Kunashtu to violence and were struck down. Others took poison and jumped into wells to ruin the water, or leapt from our high walls to die that way. Those who survived these efforts were burned alive or fed to the wild dogs, or used as targets when the warriors practiced knife-throwing and the bow and hurling stones with their slings.

This was the world against which we had built our walls. This was the world against which our city had been an oasis—a *sumum*, is the word of desert people—a *sumum* of quiet and literature, poetry and song. Although we had indeed trained some of us in brutal skills, we were not in our hearts killers, brutes, and animals like the Kunashtu.

But all things change.

We would learn.

Let the Kunashtu feast; we changed beneath their eyes as they did. Our gods spoke to us, and we changed.

Was it justice? Vengeance? I let you who read this make the decision. Decide only what you and your own people would do had the Kunashtu destroyed your city and homes and temples and everyone you love.

The day after the storm when they fell upon us, as the blood dried upon the streets and buildings beneath a cool sun, Kunashti youth struck us with horsehide whips and commanded us to cart the bodies and parts of bodies of our families outside the city walls, where others of us were forced to dig a trench in a circle around the city. Here, we dumped the dead and covered them over with hard earth and clay and snow. Bury them deep, said our priests, who knew well what they were saying as they assisted with these unclean chores. Even as I did this, I looked for my parents and my brother, even for parts of them, but was unsuccessful. I did, however, discover what remained of a poet I had known. He was a brilliant man but possessed of a sincere although morbid desire to learn why one would take one's own life. Perhaps he had found the answer on the end of his own blade or one of those of our conquerors.

The deepest part of winter came on cold and harsh, and snow and ice covered the land and sliced the air. One day became the next, then the next, as those of us who served the conquerors became used to a new way of life, all of us doing whatever the Kunashtu demanded at any time of the day or night. At least, because of my deformity, I was spared being used for blood sport by our conquerors. It was clear that even the Kunashtu had some rude sense of honor or dignity and used only the strongest men and women available as worthy of engaging in their games. And some of us did survive these violent spectacles; when one of us did, he or she was honored by the barbarians and given prizes and lauded with songs. A few of these Mogrem, to their everlasting shame, even asked to be adopted as Kunashtu into their clans, and were granted such standing. They would be repaid for their treachery in time. Meanwhile, beyond the city walls, the remains of our dishonored dead slept in the earth, sinking into the soil that our proud ancestors had cultivated, a great ring of corpses closed tight beneath the snow and rain.

Time passed as it would for dogs or any animals, our fear and boredom interrupted only by the meals and commands we were given. Midway through the snowy season, in a tower room where I slept with others like me, the weak and bent, I began to suffer strange dreams. At first, they seemed no more than memories—sunshine-dappled avenues, the curtained merchants' bazaars, our grand buildings and temples, the palace undefiled.

But after a short time, my dreams became more distinct, vividly colored and real. I saw my old neighbors and the king in parade, my parents—my mother smiling, my father's deep-set eyes and masterly visage—my brother and his wife, and even a dark-haired young woman I had admired from afar. Her I had indeed found dead the night of the attack, and I had buried her with hands that I had dared to hope would one day caress her, which was not to be.

I was not alone in experiencing such dreams. Within a few nights, it was apparent that all of us in that old room were sharing one common dream, a vision—a visitation by the dead through the colorless fabric that separates life and death, speaking to us as we slept. It was frightening but true. We learned this when we shared what we had experienced. Our own relatives and friends were returning to us as well as they could, and with the same message: We see all. We have not left you. You are not alone. We are watching.

One evening, as I stood with Agrat in the feasting hall, Kunashti skalds recited the violent songs and dirges of their people. When they were done, Agrat asked me for my thoughts. I told him the songs were of interest to me but not as fine as the lays of my people, and that the Kunashti skalds were too drunk do their poetry any justice. Agrat was offended and became threatening until I offered the services of myself and my companions. The warriors were too jaded and drunk to object, but they threatened torture if we proved not acceptable. Hotar waved a hand, granting his assent.

I asked any of my friends and companions who wished to sing to come forward; six did, some hobbling because of their wounds. They circled the fire pit in the center of the throne hall and prayed to our ancestors and our gods, then lifted their voices in praise to the skies and the winds and the earth, chanting the early songs of our people when, wandering, we found this land rich in soil and vast in grains and grasses and so built our home here. Generations passed as we prospered, and we held celebrations throughout the year thanking the earth that fed us, the skies that nourished us, the animals that assisted us and fed us, the lakes and fishes and blooms and trees, the earth, the earth.

When they had finished their final song, the throne hall was silent except for weeping. Even Hotar, their king, and Agrat were wiping tears from their faces, for our songs spoke to them of what they knew, the wide lands that they rode on their ponies beneath endless skies, the bite of freezing winds and of ice and snow, and then of the warmth of the spring and the joy of the summer, when color is everywhere and the animals graze freely. This was the heritage of the Kunashtu as well as our heritage, and they wept like children to be reminded of the proud earth that is our home, the sweep of the skies and the fields that will last forever even as men and women pass like barley.

Agrat then ordered me to recite. As the six singers retired to their places, I limped to the fire pit, lifted my arms to the ancestors and our gods for inspiration, and began. Because the Kunashtu were barbarians, I recited to them poems of the barbaric days of the first Mogrem. I spoke of the land of the mists to the sun-dying west, and how when we found this land of water and fields, trees and plenty, we fought all who dared to take what we had built. Sorcerers came with armies, I said, and bands of raiders of the most primitive sort. Then the Mogrem proudly remade the tools of the field into the tools of war, so that with spears and axes, swords and arrows we met every attacker on the field and from our walls. The blood was more plentiful than the rains of spring. When at last we had earned the right to live in peace, we did so, and the barbarians we had fought also built villages and towns and cities as we taught them, so that all prospered. We destroyed the weapons we had forged, built tombs under the earth for the kings and queens who had led us to victory, and settled into many generations of prosperity.

It was only when the dread Kunashtu, powerful but greedy, sought to take the cities of the plains and fields that we were awakened to the fears that had led our ancestors to greatness. Each time they came to try to take us, we met them in the fields and sought peace and friendship with them, but our enemy would not listen. We would teach the great Hotar and his people how to turn to the plow and to create books for learning, but Hotar and his powerful war people were content to slay others and take what was not theirs. Our walls were strong against them, but at last traitors among the Mogrem delivered a proud people to their enemy.

But the Mogrem would not forget. Though we be made slaves, our children and our children's children would know the glories of our great days despite whatever the Kunashtu might do to us. And if we had not been betrayed, we would have risen again with weapons and fire to fight as our ancestors fought, for the heat of their lives and determination remained in our blood, unweakened by the careful years of peace.

When I was done and stood silently, looking at Hotar and Agrat, at their shield-bearers and fighters, at these powerful men and women, again the room was silent, until Hotar slapped the side of the throne chair with his hand. All of the Kunashtu then stamped their feet, raised their voices, and pounded the ends of their spears on the marble floor. I remained where I was.

When silence came again, Hotar said to me, "Your people were once great. It is too bad that your people turned from arms and warfare. You might have continued to be great. Your rage is apparent. We might have met on the battlefield, you and I. You have pleased my people with your poems of slaughter and combat." As I took my place beside Agrat, he nodded to me almost as though I were his equal, so inspired was he by my verse.

The Kunashtu were not incorrect in behaving as they did. I understood them and had declared this in my poem. They lived with the truth, the truth of the earth, the truth of the gods, which is to be one with the earth. We Mogrem had forgotten this truth. We had sealed ourselves away from the earth, content to be singers and thinkers, poets and artists, teachers and healers. The gods had sent us the Kunashtu to remind us of the first law of the world, which is that life is survival, that poems are carried in the blood, strength is the true teacher, and a dream in one hand is only as worthy as the sword in the opposite hand. Dreams alone never cut the earth with furrows or slew the enemy at the walls.

My dreams that night, the dreams my companions and I shared in our room, were the dreams that we needed then, dreams from under the earth. And even the earth trembled that night, as though our lost dead were troubled in their rest to be reminded of the truth of what I had recited. The poet may sing, the children may play, the priests may pray, but to protect them, men and women of the sword are required. Put down the sword, and poets will not sing again, or children play, or priests pray.

We had forgotten the laws of the wild in our eagerness to remove ourselves from the wild. These attackers were our teachers, therefore, our new poets, our new priests.

Spring must come soon. We felt it rising, as natural as the sweetness of buds opening to the air, as true as the morning sunlight that extended its warmth with the passing days. In our sleeping room, the others and I therefore emptied our hearts, for we knew that when the Kunashtu left our city, they would slay every one of us who remained alive, having no more use for us. But every night as the warmth of the season grew, we continued to dream in our sleep, and the dreams became powerful.

I heard loud voices now, my family and friends reaching out to me. They were as they had been in their last moments on earth. Dressed in scarlet wounds and running with blood, here was my mother, her face beseeching mercy, gashes across her face and body. There came my father, hobbling on a split foot and one arm gone, strings of meat and tendon trembling from the open shoulder. Here was my brother, once a strong and handsome man, now in death a broken thing with no legs, pulling himself forward with his arms, his wife beside him, on her belly and kicking with her feet as her head rolled beside her. I could have screamed out to die, but my beloved ones told me with blood in their mouths that in their fury and sadness they were working their revenge against the conquerors. Our people together would do what they must, as they had not been able to do when they were alive and killed in the night of terror. You spoke well, said the ghosts in my dream. Now we will serve the Kunashtu a poem done in language they understand.

This is how the great change came to be, a city once alive returning as a city of the dead, the blood of the slain everywhere under the earth weakening the very earth that the Knuashtu so proudly assumed was theirs alone. For they, too, were becoming restless as the season warmed, eager to be away from us, to be on their ponies and riding the wide plains. I wondered if some of them also had had dreams, if the ghosts of their own dead families and ancestors had come to them as they slept to tell them that soon their work would be turned against them, that there was a strength to the Mogrem that even the Kunashtu did not comprehend.

I was in the sleeping chamber when it began. All of us were preparing to settle into rest but dreading the sleep that would bring the ghosts that frightened us. I stood at a high open window and was looking byond the city walls at the great ring of sunken earth where we had buried our dead when I saw the earth move. It dropped or pulled down, then rose as things reached from under the earth, arms and faces in the moonlight, the dead climbing out from where we had put them.

I screamed, hearing myself as I did. My companions hurried to look out other open windows and saw what I saw, our dead returning, pushing up from beneath the surface of the world like blisters breaking through skin. All of us then heard further shrieks rising from every area of the city, and we saw warriors, the Kunashtu, all of their men and women and children, hurrying into the streets under torchlight as buildings began to tremble. I saw stones go loose and fall from rooftops, then many statues and columns twist and drop into the streets, striking people as they ran.

This was not all. For as the buildings came apart and as the stones of the streets and avenues sank, the bodies of our dead moved those stones aside and lifted themselves upward from beneath the earth. Those with legs walked as well as they could and fell upon Kunashtu close to them, clawing at them and biting them. Even when an invader with sword or knife removed an arm or head from one of our dead, the corpse continued as it had been, clawing at the killer, using pieces of their own bones as sharp weapons to cut and stab. The streets rippled now like waves in a pool, and riders on their ponies were thrown as the animals dropped, unable to move on the unstable ground.

My companions were now hurrying downstairs from the sleeping room. I followed them. Here was our opportunity to hurt those who had hurt us, and we were determined to do it. As I came into the street, the house behind us rocked back and forth, threatening to fall. I hastened so that I would not be crushed. Kunashtu were running in panic in every direction. I saw many holding red hands to their faces and necks, and others lying beneath fallen stones and lengths of timber, beseeching me, reaching for me, as if I would ever help them in their pain. I stepped onto the face of one of them, stamping on the nose and eyes as strongly as I could, until the blood came.

Now our great walls began to topple, the powerful walls that had withstood so much for so many generations. It was apparent that our city was falling into a great hole or crater and that I must attempt to move outside the city if I were to live even a little longer. I hurried toward the eastern wall, part of which was upright, and away from as many of the moving dead as I could.

Mobs of us circled smaller groups of Kunashtu and dismembered them as they howled, using whatever weapons they could find, tools of any sort or swords and axes taken from the dead warriors. They chopped the fallen Kunashtu as they might split wood for the fire or cut an animal for the supper table.

As I climbed over fallen blocks of marble, I saw beneath them a powerful Kunashti warrior, one of the men who had proudly killed some of our people in the contests in the palace. Now he was beneath the fallen blocks, the bottom of him not to be seen, but his chest and arms and head still there. He looked at me, daring me to approach him, and he yelled and spat at me, even as he was dying.

I killed him with part of himself, his own sharp bone torn from his arm and shoved into his heart. He stared at me while I did it. I tore the broken bone from his arm with a strength I did not know I had, and as he watched me, I forced the sharp end of the bone into his heart. I leaned on the length of bone and pushed and pulled on it, back and forth. It was proper to do this. Blood came in a stream, and still he stared at me. He lifted a hand to try to reach me. Why? Then his head tilted and he died, his eyes still open. I pulled the sharp bone from his heart and put out his eyes. What else could I do?

On I went. The ground continued to tremble and sink. Buildings everywhere collapsed, our strong structures brought down upon our enemies. I saw others like me trying to escape. They were crushed by falling stone or killed by Kunashti warriors who were themselves then attacked by the dead come back to punish them. I saw many Kunashtu, wounded and bleeding, held down by our dead people and being tortured as they had been tortured. At the end of an alley, I saw my mother, her corpse, biting out the throat of a Kunashti woman who was unable to move because the lower part of her body was missing. My mother looked at me as she did this and smiled at me. I did not understand her or myself then. My brain became mist. I saw the head of my brother's wife latched onto the arm of a man who had fallen. He struggled to remove her head, hitting it on the street stones, but he could not, so fiercely was she attached to him. These scenes were more horrible than those in my dream, yet here we were, my mother and I and my brother's wife, in the world this way.

Our library and the buildings near it had not collapsed. They were by the eastern wall. I saw some of my people go into these buildings for safety. I followed them, thinking that some of us might live past this destruction.

In the library, I saw others taking scrolls from the stone shelves, hoping in that way to preserve some of our history and culture. I did the same. I was near the entrance when the earth heaved upward, then collapsed. I was pushed outside the entrance while the others inside perished. Still I held onto some of our poetry, and with those scrolls, I continued toward the east wall, which had fallen entirely, burying many Kunashtu beneath it. They screamed, and I was glad to hear their suffering.

With some others of my people, I climbed over the fallen stones as well as I was able. It was then that a loosened block of the wall fell upon my bad leg and opened it, smashing the bone. Now I crawled. In the fields outside the city were only a very few persons who had escaped what was happening. All were my people. The corpses that had come back had made certain that none of their enemies should live, even at the cost of killing all of us within Mograd.

Now a great cold wind came. The poet says that the winds of Hell are fierce and hot, but here was a cleansing wind as cold as the top of a mountain, as cold as the dying bodies about me. Around the field, in the great surrounding ring where we had placed the bodies and parts of bodies of our dead, the world shifted and the earth dropped downward. Then then it tilted upward. The ground beneath me lifted skyward, and I felt myself sliding back toward the sinking city. I kicked with my good leg and with free hand was able to reach the wet grass of the field away from the sinking of the earth. I continued to hold in my right hand a scroll I had taken from the library. I held onto it as though it meant life itself to me. It was all that mattered to me in that moment.

I saw a few remaining Kunashtu slide down the inclined field to the crumbled walls of Mograd as if they were slipping down the side of a deep bowl. I reached this tree on a slight hill, and from here looked back to see all of my city falling in upon itself. A great depression remained in the earth. A few persons, warriors and Mogrem both, continued to climb upward but finally dropped back into the crater of collapsed buildings, the great stones sliding upon themselves and continuing to sink into the earth. There was a final tremor, the earth making thunder like the sky, and the rim of the crater collapsed. Where the city of my people had stood, there is now only a wide depression.

Evening is descending. I am no longer myself. My head hurts and spins. I am breathing dust, the dust of our city and of my people, the dust that remains from our dead enemies. I see no one else.

I am now afraid. I did not fear death before the Kunashtu came, when I wrote poetry, but everything now has changed. Life is no longer what it was. I was prepared for death in those days, but everything is now bleak and empty, cold, the skies are low, I can almost touch them, the sky is so gray and flat, and there were bodies everywhere, erupted from the earth, the dead killing the living, men, women, horses, all of life. I should never have learned poetry. We should have remained barbarians and never created a city. We should have stayed on our ponies and lived in the wild as the Kunashtu did. Our ancestors were wrong. We climbed heights, but the world remains low. Why dream? The world is falling away from me. My sight I hurt This is what the gods gave us that we call Here is death Imatus Kad ist

Aliastra the Sorceress

Count Holos stood in a corner of Fesk's shop, waiting for the woman at the counter to retrieve her goods. Pride kept Holos in the shadows; born to wealth, he had little to show for his title these days besides the vest and belt he wore, both of them his grandfather's, made for that old man by an artisan in the time when the family had land and money. The loss of this inherited fortune had been the fault of Holos's father; Count Fen had pledged his estate and securities to an expedition contracted to recover grand treasure, fabulous ancient things from the days when demigods had lived on the heights of the mountains in the westlands of Csith. But the demigods were gone now to dust, and there had been no fabled treasure; the family had lost its estate and holdings, as well as any standing it had had among the high-born of Nistadum. Holos's parents had taken their own lives for the shame of it. Their son and sole heir, finding the use of poison disagreeable and the thought of the razor's edge discomfiting, had settled instead on the notion of rebuilding the estate and thereby recovering the family's name.

Years on, he still had had no luck. Holos was not a man with talent for fortune-making. Rather, he had a gift for losing money, as well as a weakness for drink and women—which made him the equal of every scut on the street and all larceners and pickpockets besides.

"And I thank you!" Fesk smiled to the woman at the counter.

"As I thank you." But she lifted her head to the bargainer, offended by the sight and smell of him.

Holos recognized her now; it was a woman whom the tricks of time had also brought low. But he did not introduce himself. Of what would they speak? They had nothing in common now if they ever had.

When she was outside, he approached Fesk with too bold a stride.

The pawn artist looked what he was: dressed in a motley of discards and tradeoffs, as lean as an alley dog, and as keen on the scent of profit as any scavenger that lives off the meat of its neighbors.

"My lord," he said to Holos.

"Do not mock me."

"Never, sir. I do not make light of my important patrons. Have you more?"

He meant payment on the ring he held in pledge. Holos removed his purse from his belt and emptied the contents on the scarred wooden counter: four in copper, three bronze Salasan coins worth their weight, and one short gold piece.

"You have done well at cards," Fesk complimented him. "Or otherwise."

"Just give me my goods."

With a cupped hand, Fesk pulled the coins toward him and into a box behind the counter, then apologized profusely. "My lord, the price for retrieving your goods has increased."

"What?" Holos was easy to anger; since the loss of his family's wealth, he had become prone to distemper and wildness at the merest slight. Now here was this splendid thief playing a game with him, an old game, and Holos became himself on the moment. He was not a tall man but he was ruggedly built, taking after his grandfather, and any softness he had inherited had long ago been replaced with hard muscle earned by plain labor and a quickness come from tavern brawls and short back-and-forths on the street between him and men with knives and fists.

He reached across the counter to take Fesk by his shirt, as quickly as he might push out another man's eyes. "You gave me a price. Keep to it."

"Please don't hurt my fine shirt."

"We had a bargain."

"Bargains are made to be bargained, my good lord. Here is what happened. A stranger learned of the ring and offered me fifty in long gold for it."

"*You sold it to him?*" Holos nearly pulled Fesk across the counter.

"I never would do that to my friend! But to prevent him from robbing me, I had to agree to his price. I told him to return after dark. Of course, I was gone before dark, and he had moved on. So I protected you."

"And now you want fifty for it."

"Bargaining is bargaining. The price is set."

Holos released the old wolf. "Devils take you. I should kill you now and take it back for myself."

"But I have secured it in my special hiding place. It was necessary. Only myself and the ghosts of this house know its location."

"Who told the stranger that you even had my ring?"

"It is a mystery," Fesk said, frowning.

"You told him yourself, son of a pig. Or you're making this up to goad me into paying more for my family's crest."

"I agree with you that it is unfair," Fesk said, wiping his nose and regarding whatever had collected on his fingers, "but bargaining is bargaining, and I do what I can to keep body and soul together, as do we all."

"I swear by my mother's mother, Fesk," Holos warned him. "I will take back my family's ring, and when I do, I will settle with you, too, and not for gold."

"Then perhaps we should bargain further," Fesk said. "Peace on my own mother's spirit, she would not wish me to defame your mother's name. Come back to me with ten in long gold, and your heirloom is returned to you."

"I should burn your house down now and you with it."

"There is always the opportunity for that, of course."

"How do you put up with yourself, Fesk?"

"I learned long ago, my lord, never to judge myself or others, but only respect those who get through the day as best they can. Life is full of traps and tricks; how you or I manage them, that is our own affair."

Holos backed away, the perspiration of anger on him. "I meant what I said."

"Only a bit more, Count Holos. To see me through my troubles."

"You'll have troubles enough if you try to cheat me again."

Fesk nodded to him as Holos opened the shop door. "You strike a sharp bargain, my friend."

"Go to hell," Holos told him and made certain to pull closed the door as loudly as possible—all he could do, short of killing the usurer in plain view of the public byways.

The sun was setting. Holos walked the bricked street past other low shops and buildings in this oldest part of the city, far from the heights where his family's estate yet sat, a home now to parvenu merchants. Pride and honor meant nothing to such people; money and the latest gossip and fashions made them who they were, and that was little enough for this day and age.

He had not given Fesk all of his money, of course; he had kept some coins in a pocket sewn inside his vest. Now he took out a copper and stood at the board of a wine merchant on a corner, paying for a gourd to steady himself before taking up what he must do next.

"Another one, Count Holos?"

"One will do me, and I thank you."

"Good evening to you."

Night was everywhere now in the torchlit city. Holos went past taverns and closed shops and the last of the brothels, where the women sat undressed, displaying themselves in open windows and waving to passersby.

"Come and see us!" they yelled to Holos.

"My purse is empty, daughters of Tanish!"

"Come and see us!" they called to the men behind him.

To the west, where this street ended in the reckless hovels of the deep old city, a single tall structure rose above the cramped houses near it. It was unlike any of the surrounding buildings, older, a remnant from the city's foundations, and left alone while Nistadum had prospered and grown in other directions with shining towers, long boulevards, and fine temples and apartment buildings. Holos knocked upon the one door of the place that let onto the street, more an alley now than anything else.

The door was pulled open. Light struck his face. A blonde young woman, quite fetching, looked at him.

"Good evening to you. I've come to meet with your mistress."

"Does my mistress expect you?"

"I believe she does," said Holos

The young woman paused, judging him, but let him inside and closed the door.

"And which one are you?" she asked as they stood in a hallway lit by an oil lamp on a tall table.

"My name is Count Holos."

"Count—?" She smiled. "You're a count and I'm a countess."

Holos frowned. "Mind yourself!"

"Oh, and a temper besides. I'll be sure to warn my mistress."

"Announce me!"

Behind her, Holos saw a stone stairway, torchlit from above against the dimness.

"This way." The young woman proceeded up the stone stairs.

Holos followed her. She had a tart tongue, but he admired her undulant hips. "What is your name?"

She tossed her hair and looked over her shoulder at him. "Ishni."

At the top of the stepway, they went along a short corridor to an iron door. Ishni bade Holos wait as she pulled it open by a staple at one side.

Old, old, this door, this structure. The iron made sounds against the pins that hinged it, but it had been balanced so that even so slight a person as this young woman could move it.

Ishni stepped inside. "Mistress, there is a Count Holos—"

"Show him in."

Holos and the clever young woman exchanged glances; if she were eyeing him to suggest anything of importance, however, he missed it—the wine, and no food in him the day long. Holos entered. Ishni returned to the corridor and closed the great door.

The room was not angular but oval, in the manner common in the oldest fortresses and towers in Csith. Holos knew that the style had been inherited from the first families, inspired, it was said, from the earliest days when huts made of animal skins were common. As an affectation, such design had occasionally been resurrected among the fashionable, but there was nothing false to this room. It went back to the beginning of time.

Even the furniture was of another age, the divans and couches polished and kept bright, but thickly encrusted with gems and jewels, rubies and emeralds and cut diamonds, turquoise and gold that glowed, pieces done for a queen. The hanging tapestries and fine rugs displayed scenes of the gods; the oil lamps and tables were done with craftsmanship of an order Holos appreciated— and he knew good metal artistry when he saw it.

Aliastra now rose from one of those couches, putting out a hand to greet her guest.

"Count Holos."

Holos took her hand and bowed shortly. "My dear Aliastra."

She was lovely, no taller than Holos, with sparkling eyes as dark as her hair, which flowed over her shoulders and down her slender back. She was mature but lithe, vibrant, and gowned in a light thing that complimented her figure. Aliastra wore many jewels, pendants about her throat and waist and wrists, slim torques of silver and worked gold wrapped about her arms and ankles.

"I am glad," she said, "that you could answer my summons."

"I could not ignore so charming a summons."

Aliastra waved a hand. "Sit here, beside me. There is wine."

Holos sat on a heavy cushion and poured a goblet full, then leaned back. "You aren't having wine?"

"I have had my wine already, with my supper."

Holos sipped and set down his cup. "My lady, you astonished me with your summons. You are a legend in this city, but known for your solitude—although your beauty, may I say, is understood to rival that of Tanish herself."

"Charming, as I suspected," Aliastra replied, reaching with a finger to scratch his arm. "You wonder why I asked you here?"

"Naturally." Holos glanced at his arm; the goddess had drawn a little blood.

"I am lonely," she complained. "Who of us is immune to such? When I saw you yesterday at the bazaar, did you not see me?"

"I saw a beautiful woman's eyes behind a veil, looking upon me with curiosity and caution."

"I seldom go out of doors. I do not care for the world out there. But I determined to ask after you when I saw you."

"I am honored that you did so. "

"Your family is an old one. I appreciate that."

"Thank you."

"And you do not fear the rumors?"

Holos smiled and helped himself to slices of fruit in a tray on the table. "You are a sorceress!" he grinned.

"I am indeed."

"Which intrigues me," he admitted. "I imagine you conjuring spells, relaxing in dreams with ghosts, savoring a fortune in jewels and diamonds once worn by goddesses, and immune to the troubles that pester the likes of me."

"You are imaginative." Aliastra smiled.

"I depend upon my imagination these days. My title means nothing any longer," Holos told her frankly. "I am become a wanderer and a rascal and a thief, my lady. I do what I can to get through my days and nights. But your summons—why ask me to visit you when you have your sorcery and your dreams?"

"You speak so well," Aliastra said.

"I am well educated although fallen."

Aliastra rose from the divan and went to an open window, leaned on the wide sill and looked out at the moon and the stars. "You remind me, Count Holos, of a man I knew years ago. I lost him. He promised he would return to me. I await him here." She turned to face him. "When I saw you, I was frightened. You bear an uncanny resemblance to my Ormenidus. That was his name.

Ormenidus." She pronounced the word slowly, rolling the syllables off her tongue. "Will you judge me for this?"

"Never." Holos stood and went to her, somewhat unsteady because of the wine.

"Have you ever known deep passion, Count Holos?"

"I've known passion."

"I don't mean lust sated in some alley. That is for low fools and children. I mean the thing of the heart and spirit that never dies but takes you completely." She smiled, aware of herself. "I have had too much wine already."

"As you say, I do not judge you."

"You may go from whore to whore to ease your lust, but this a burden on me."

"You wish to be free of this burden."

"If only for a time."

Holos stepped close to her, looked her in the eyes, read her heart, and felt that she read his. He put his arms around her as she, too, quickly embraced him, and they held each other in the moonlight of the window, in the lamplight of her room.

Holos felt the fullness of her body. Thick warm hair brushed his face. Her tears wet his skin. He smiled.

"Free me," whispered the sorceress. "Ormenidus, free me."

When the moon was high and the sky bright with clouds, Holos pulled on his mantle and bade Aliastra good night. She lay stretched upon a divan, flushed and dreaming, naked and silver in the moonlight. Holos moved quietly downstairs.

Ishni was waiting at the door that let onto the alley.

"And how does my mistress entertain you?"

"Mind your tongue. This is no concern of yours."

"But it is, Count Holos."

"I'll have your mistress whip you. "

"And how do you know that I wouldn't like that?" Her hands were on her hips, her head tilted to one side. She was, after all, a beautiful little thing. "I know what you're after," she told Holos.

"I don't—"

"What's in your hand? Best pocket it, or you'll find that and your hand *both* gone before you get home in these streets."

"I told you to mind your tongue!"

Ishni laughed at him. "Oh, she's willing to pay the price, Count Holos. Money means nothing to her, only the search for lovers. You're not the first."

"Did you think I thought so, you little—"

"And she *is* a sorceress! Ishni whispered. "Don't be fooled by her! You've just sold your soul for a mere ruby, Count Holos, for a red stone."

"I assure you I know rubies as well as I do women's passions."

"Listen to me," Ishni told him. "I'll help you if you help me. That's all I'm saying. I can't get away from her otherwise."

Holos felt her push against him, felt her hand on his and the press of her breasts. She was trembling.

She asked him, "Did she tell you about Ormenidus?"

"Yes."

"Did she tell you that they were together before, ages ago? And that she's not a woman at all? She's a corpse. She keeps herself alive by magic."

Holos grinned. "I assure you that that woman is no corpse."

"Why would I tell you this?" Ishni asked him. "Help me!"

"Stop it. You want to be beaten again?"

"You're a fool like the rest of them. Did she cut you? Did she draw blood?"

Holos became uneasy. "Yes. She scratched me."

"Then she'll begin her work on you. Listen!"

Silence.

"There is nothing," Holos told her.

But then he heard echoes from a rising voice, a woman's voice carrying from far away, from deep within the building.

"Aliastra is not in her chamber where you left her," Ishni said. "She imagines you've gone by now. She has a room below this building where she works her magic. Can you hear her?"

"Yes."

"Then it's really very simple, Count Holos. Did you make love to a woman or to a thing?"

"You're wrong."

"Am I?"

He was holding tightly onto the ruby, but it felt warm, even hot in his hand. Holos pushed the jewel into the inside pocket of his vest.

"Open the door and go," Ishni told him. "Or follow me and see for yourself. But you'd better keep quiet if you do, or she'll kill us both."

Holos hesitated.

"Well?"

"All right."

She led him down a hallway to a door, opened it, and took a long series of stone steps wholly in darkness. Holos moved carefully behind her.

He whispered, "Light a torch."

She turned and touched a finger to his lips—no sound.

The stairwell curved, and luminescence spread upon the walls on either side—ancient hewn rock, not brick or stone. With the light came odors, the heaviness of incenses and burning woods, kyphi and sonter, as well as of decay, the stink of dead animals, so that Holos had the taste of rot and sweetness in his mouth. He coughed; Ishni, glowing as they came into the light of that place, squeezed his hand, warning him again to silence.

And as they reached the bottom of the stairwell, she leaned against Holos to whisper as lightly as possible into his ear, "Do not scream!"

Three more steps, and Holos saw.

It was a great room—a cave, a place of rock—and on the uneven floor of it and its walls had been painted signs, symbols, designs that Holos had seen in old books, even in scrolls as ancient as the land itself, but they were not marks of the gods. There were the sigils of demons and words written in the signs of old alphabets, words that been outlawed—not to be spoken, not to be thought.

Aliastra spoke them now, chanting them as the smoke from braziers moved like fog in the cave, the air of the swamp and of dead places, of the tomb and the holes in the earth where the dead were put out of the way.

For the dead were with her there. Holos had been warned, but he had to tighten himself to stop up the groan that was in him. Aliastra, staring upward, knelt naked in the middle of the floor with those same symbols painted on her body, her arms and legs, while around her moved dead things—a man's arm, the furry hand of someone else, a rolling leg—while torsos, headless, armless, legless, heaved their chests, pulling in the same air that sickened Holos.

Ishni whispered to him, "All that remains of her lovers!"

As she said it, Holos felt the pain on his arm where the sorceress had scratched him, pain as from poison, so deep that he wished to cut free his arm to release himself from the suffering. He hissed to hold back the hurt.

Aliastra did not hear him or see him or Ishni. Now she faced them, but her eyes were closed and her head tilted away as she lifted her arms and spoke to whatever things listened to such prayers.

"Ormenidus, return to me! Come to me now! Rise from thy grave and take for thyself the spirits of these dead! Dress thyself in their flesh and return thou to me! Speak with me now against those cold gods that hold thy spirit in bondage! Whisper unto them the prayers and incantations I have taught thee in my dreams, and comest thou to me! Let our days and nights be as they were in Nistadum of old! Ormenidus! Every prayer I know, I have recited in thy name! Be for me what Osuru was for Tanish when she raised the broken parts of that god's body and made him whole again! Become whole for me once more, Oremenidus! Gods of every hell and lower regions still, holy Tanish, shadows of the departed, lift him from the dead and *return my lover to me!*"

Now she leaned forward with grievous weeping as the moving legs, arms, and hands of murdered men circled her as though to comfort her.

Ishni led the way back up the stairwell and along the corridor.

"Do you see?" she whispered to Holos when they reached the door.

He was shivering, and he pressed his left hand over the painful cut on his right forearm. "She brings back the dead!"

"Yes! And she will slay you with her magic like those others as soon as she knows that the spirit of Ormenidus is not in you."

"Ormenidus—"

"The witch put him in his tomb farther back than any of us knows. She has kept herself alive since then, and young, as she was then. She uses her sorcery for that, and to bring back his bones if her spells succeed. This is the shadow on this house. Holos, leave, and take me with you! Fight her. Are you strong enough to fight the spell she's put on you and break the spell she's put on me?"

He rubbed his face, wet with sweat. "Not—tonight," he told Ishni. "I need to come back for stones and jewels. I need the money."

"I'll get you jewels, but take me with you."

"Tomorrow night," he promised her. "I'll be here."

"You'll have to be," Ishni warned him. "She has marked you, and if you try to resist, she will know it and pull you back to her. Then she will drug you and kill you and send your soul to Hell to raise the corpse she loves."

"Not me," Holos said, promising it. "She won't take me."

"Fight her."

He looked Ishni in the eyes. "You fight her, too."

"With whatever I have."

"Look for me tomorrow night. As soon as darkness comes, be here."

"I will."

He said, "I never knew such foulness could be."

"She has done things worse even than this."

Holos wished to hear no more. He went out. Ishni waited at the door, watching him go, as though she dared not or could not cross that threshold, held there by the spells of her mistress.

Walking purposefully, Holos recalled conversations he had had with his father, long before the man had squandered their wealth. Why are we even born? Holos the young man had asked, and his father, well read, had told him of philosophers and religious scholars, warriors he had known, and men and women of business, those who saw all of life in the gold coins and fine things that possessed them with their polished allure. Were any of these the ultimate truth?

Father, why are we even born?

His father had answered him, To make the choices we must make, for our choices tell us who we are, and that is the secret of life, Holos, for us to grow into what we are. You must choose one of many paths. All are available. Your choice sets into motion everything around you and touches all whom you will meet. Those are the kindred souls you require in this life.

His father had been righter than he knew, though his own choice had brought down a house that had been respected for generations.

So here now was a choice that Holos must make, and one that his father could never have conceived, to free himself from this witch—and no doubt from the other things that held him, the anger and resentment that crushed his heart like a coiling serpent.

You can be as free as you wish to be, his father had told him. All paths are available.

He was not free yet.

But he would be, Holos promised himself, and soon.

Why else had he been born?

Perhaps the thieving Fesk was righter than he knew, as well.

Holos returned to him as soon as the scoundrel opened his shop the next morning, directly after the gong sounded from

Tanish's temple on its height in the middle of the city. For believers, the gong's echo was the sign to lift morning prayers to the goddess of love, desire, and fortitude. For Holos, it was simply an alarm to rouse him from his rest, for he had been awake most of the night, worrying and cursing, staring at his wounded arm, and satisfying himself as best he could how he might fight or even kill Aliastra the sorceress.

"Yours, now." He rolled the witch's great ruby on Fesk's counter.

Fesk grinned. "My good friend, that will more than buy you back your ring."

"I don't want the ring. Not yet."

"No?"

"Give me the finest sword you have here."

"You can use a sword?"

"I'll use it on you if you don't hurry."

"No anger, no anger!" Fesk exclaimed. "We are all friends here."

As he turned to enter his back storeroom, Holos told the barterer, "And with as much silver on it as this gem will buy."

Fesk turned and smiled. "Killing demons and ghosts now, are we, with our silver?"

Unamused, Holos replied, "Yes."

The sword was a good one. Fesk claimed that it had belonged to a nobleman who had joined an order and fought under the banner of the god Isk during the religious upheavals fifty years past. Whether the claim was true or not, Holos preferred to think that the blade might indeed have some holy power to it—the better to put to death the witch who had poisoned him. Blessed silver could undo evil where even steel might fail.

Holos kept a bed in a hostel for itinerants near Fesk's shop. In the rear of the house was a yard bordered by alleys on facing sides and stables directly behind. Here, while poor children cared for the horses of travelers and homeless men and women sat in whatever morning shade they could find, Holos practiced his sword work. He had been raised in the handling of the weapon, taught skills by men hired by his father, and despite the years since then, he now managed this blade well, defining his guard postures and slicing and thrusting cleanly the air between him and whatever dreamy foe he was confronting. Soon he was sweating, and his shoulders ached; it was good to feel the ache. He was at arms again, as he had been when a young man taken on travels with his father and grandfather.

When he felt sufficiently secure, Holos asked a boy passing by to assist him, to fetch a basket of fruit gone bad, apples and pears, and gave him two coppers, one for the fruit and one for himself. When he returned, they both stood in the yard, with the boy lobbing apples and pears one at a time toward Holos, who speared them on the end of his sword or sliced them in midair. He had the boy stand near him at first, but by midafternoon, the youngster was across the yard and sending the fruit from that distance. Holos took nearly every one, to the cheers and hoots of those sitting nearby.

When a boy himself, Holos has been asked by a solider to assist him in just this way. Holos had declined; he had been too proud to spend his morning that way, wealthy as he was and interested only in himself. Now life had come around to remind him of that and to shame him.

The vaults, tombs, and mausoleums of the many dead of Nistadum were kept separate from the living parts of the city by tall solid trees with roots as thick as men and by great stone walls covered with growth. Here, in low mountains as old and brooding as gods, within a rock-cut tomb, as night fell, movement began—movement as slow as a shadow in this cave where movement had ceased long ago. On a ledge near the floor, what remained of an ancient shroud was pushed away by a hand that rose with difficulty. From the shroud fell stones and jewels left on it in memory and placed with prayers.

The witch had left those stones and jewels during her many visits to this cave, this tomb, and had pressed into the shroud still more ornaments and metal and bone devices concocted during rituals she had performed to help the corpse return to whatever life it might have.

Which now it did, awkwardly and slowly, breathing strangely as it had not drawn breath in years upon years. There was hissing as air came into the old lungs; there were noises as bones turned and muscles stretched where the bones should rightly have been dust and the muscles no more.

The thing dropped onto the rock floor of the cave, flat on its side, there among the others all enshrouded and forgotten. It pressed long fingers as stiff as wood into the cloth about its face so that it could see past the dust of it. It stretched as well as it could, working, and at last in its foolishness rose from the floor of the tomb and stood, naked but for the rags on it, the skin gray where there was skin, the hair white where there was hair.

More movement, as some among the other dead things in that cave trembled, uncertain of themselves and unaware, but animated by whatever sorcery animated the standing thing—the power of the witch, increasing over many years, more than sufficient not only to resurrect her dead lover but also to disturb others buried in the stone.

Hissing. Gasping at the air. The standing corpse made attempts at a voice, at pushing out words like detachable parts of itself, and managed only syllables, but the syllables created a name, fell from the old mouth to make certain what should have been forgotten by now, as forgotten as this lich itself: "*Ah. Lees. Tra. Uh. Al. Lees. Uh. Truh.*"

It remembered.

As though alive, it remembered.

The first to see it was a thief standing among the trees that night and giving consideration to entering the tombs or a mausoleum to take rich things buried with the bodies there. The corpse came close by him, on the other side of a strong oak. When the corpse saw the thief, it reached for him to push him out of the way or to strangle him. Boots unmoving, mouth dry, the thief felt the fingers of the thing brush his throat, leaving decay and the dust of time on him. As the figure passed on, the boots found movement, and the thief was away from those tombs, retching as he went.

The figure continued, casting before him a shadow that staggered over the stones as it came into the streets of Nistadum. Others saw it, the low of this part of the city, other thieves and doxies, as well, and they moved away from it and made signs before themselves to the gods they had been taught in childhood. *Keep it away from me, immortal ones, whatever it is, give me one more night, do not punish me more than I deserve!*

At last it reached the door that opened onto the street and pressed on it, scraping and knocking like an animal eager to be let inside.

From within came footsteps.

The door opened, and a bar of light slid across the corpse's face.

A scream.

Ishni dropped upon the threshold.

The figure moved around her, leaving dust, and slowly made its way up stone steps to the door of Aliastra's chamber. Everything was just as it had been when he had been put away years ago—walls the same, stairwell, door—

The sorceress herself, there, on the other side as the door was opened.

"Ormenidus!"

"*Uh. Al. Lees. Uh. Truh!*"

Oremenidus looked from a window of Aliastra's chamber: He said, "The Tower of Etima is gone. I would come to you in this house when its dome grew hot in the morning sun."

"Thou rememberest," she said.

She had given the corpse a brew prepared in anticipation of this night, and the fluids in that brew had improved his flesh, strengthened his bones, repaired him so that he could speak and see.

Still, he was a corpse. He turned from the window and the view of Nistadum at night, the city all new to him. He said to the sorceress, "What have you made of me?"

She was on one of her couches, dressed in finery. "My love, I dared not believe that thou wert truly gone from me. Put in thy tomb, thou wert still alive to me. Such was thy command over me and my desire for thee."

He said to her scornfully, "Do not speak in the ancient tongue, Aliastra."

"It is but the voice of our love, my Ormenidus. Ours from long ago."

He moved toward her from the window, slow movement upon movement.

Aliastra told him, "All other people are a disappointment. Each hour among them is wasted. Dost thou not see? Everything of thine I have kept here. Thy boots. Thy paints. Your lyre. With these nearby, you were with me again. They have brought thee back because they *are* you!"

"No longer, no longer," said the corpse. "Stand before me."

"At thy command." The sorceress rose from the divan. "I am yours."

"Yes," said Ormenidus. "All these years I heard you living your life...heard everything. This city and its changes. Voices, sounds, all of it. Yet I could not move. Partway alive, but still dead. I dreamed of my parents and things I did as a boy. I tried not to listen to your spells and your lovers, and I tried not to listen to the earth as it changed...hills shrinking, trees growing, life changing. It changes, Aliastra, from generation to generation, the children improving upon the parents. Did you not notice that truth while you were hidden away here in your room? I heard distant wars, felt them tremble through the earth and touch us dead there in the tomb, but I could not cry out. What if fire had come, or deadly storms? What should I do? I could hear all but not move."

Aliastra told him, "That is not what I wished!"

"And yet it was so."

"You should have told me in dreams, Ormenidus! You should have come to me with thoughts, sent me visions!"

"How?" asked the corpse. "Where is *my* magic, Aliastra? Where are *my* spells? I have no magic. I have no spells. You ached for me to join *you*. My ache, witch, was for you to join *me*."

He reached out and took her neck in his hands, pressed his fingers into her throat and bent her back, startled as she was, until the breath was gone from her and Aliastra lay silent on the floor.

Ishni awoke and pulled herself to her feet as Holos came up the street, sword in hand, and found her just inside Aliastra's house.

"The jewels," he said to her. "Do you have them?'

"Yes, but Holos—"

"I'm here for the witch." He put a hand on Ishni's shoulder to press her aside.

"Holos, he is here!"

"Who is?"

"Her lover! The corpse! Ormenidus!"

"You've seen him?"

"He's with her now!"

"Then I'll kill him, too!"

He looked up at a sound, and Ishni turned, as well.

Down the stair steps came the corpse, moving carefully until it reached the floor to stand a short distance from Holos and Ishni.

Ishni backed away. Holos stayed where he was, gripping his weapon.

Ormenidus lifted a hand to point to it. "Use that sword, friend, to undo me. I ask it now of you."

"It is for the sorceress, lich."

"Aliastra is dead. I have killed her."

Ishni moaned.

Holos said, "I don't believe you."

"It is done. She is dust."

"But she couldn't be killed. This sword has silver in it. Silver will kill such as she."

The corpse said, "She empowered me with her own magic, so how could she resist me, herself against herself, when I killed her?"

Ishni said to him, "But she loved you, and you loved her."

"No. Even then, ages ago, she kept me prisoner with her magic. Neither of us was free of her lust. There was no peace. I took my own life to be away from her, and even as I was in the grave, she continued to prison me with her skills."

"Name of the gods," swore Holos.

Ormendius told him, "Use the sword now. The silver will give me rest at last."

Holos approached, blade up, the point chest high and aimed at the monster's heart. He looked into the thing's yellow eyes and asked it, "No prayers? No words?"

"Useless," said the dead man. "Let me guide the point."

He put out his dry hands, pulled the blade toward him, and walked into it, step by step, until he sank to his knees. Holos let go of the grip, and the blade fell with the dead man, gone now to whatever finally awaited him.

For only a moment, Holos and Ishni stared at the thing.

Then Ishni said, "Enough."

"Yes, yes." Holos undid the scabbard, left it on the floor beside the sword, and gripped Ishni's hand.

They left the door open as it was, with the corpse there for anyone to see.

As they quickly walked away, Ishni showed Holos the purse in her hand. "The jewels you wanted."

"Good. Now we pay Fesk to get my ring back and buy a horse. Can you ride?"

"No. You'll have to help me."

He stopped and turned toward her, faced the young woman in the moonlight there in the street.

"We must hurry," Ishni told him. "It isn't safe here."

He pointed to red marks on her arm. "From her?"

"She beat me again today."

"Did you enjoy it?"

"Never."

"I thought not," Holos said.

Fesk got more than he had asked for, and when Holos put his ring on his finger again, he felt the price worth it, thief though the barterer was. Two streets away, he paid a horse seller two large rubies for an excellent white, a beautiful animal, and so he and Ishni were gone.

In the wide fields outside the city, the night was warm with a breeze. Holos held the reins; Ishni sat behind him. They paused to rest on the path leading north.

"Life is full of traps and tricks; how you or I manage them, that is our own affair."

True, Holos thought. So he had once more managed to evade traps and tricks. He pressed his hand on his right forearm and looked at it. The scratch had vanished, and any pain; he had noticed it as soon as they were out of the city.

He showed the arm to Ishni. "Gone," he said.

"It was an illusion. Like everything about her."

"Everything except her riches. Let me see the jewels again."

"Oh, you've seen them."

"What's the matter with you?" Holos turned and took the purse from her, then held it between his legs and dug his hand in. He cursed loudly. "Ishni, what you have you done?"

"Not a thing."

"Where are the jewels? These are...stones! Seeds!"

Ishni laughed. "I warned you before. That horse dealer will curse us when he goes to his banker tomorrow!"

"And Fesk!" Holos grinned. "I finally got the better of him!"

"And the sorceress," Ishni said.

"The corpse was right, then. She's dust."

"She's dust," Ishni told him. "And her house and all of her fine things— I was with her when she purchased them in the bazaar."

"There's nothing as exquisite as those things in the bazaar," Holos said. "She remade them. Her fine ornaments were all false, then."

"The only thing not false in that house was me."

"And I'm glad of that," Holos told her. "You're not like other women I've known."

"And I never will be." Ishni poked him on the shoulder. "So keep that in mind."

He urged the horse forward. It walked slowly under the sinking moon.

"So you don't mind losing the jewels?" Ishni asked him.

"Oh, I mind. But they were the witch's. I suppose you can't expect to hold onto something you never had. But I have my own riches back."

"That ring means a lot to you."

"It's part of my family. You have a family, don't you?"

"Not really," Ishni said. "I was left on a doorstep when I was born. Raised in a kitchen."

Holos considered that. "Then you're free to choose any path you want in this life."

"I suppose so. I never thought of it that way."

"It's something my father and I used to discuss. We make choices, and we set things in motion."

"That's a very deep and serious idea, Holos."

"It is. Does it bore you?"

"No, I'm interested."

"We make our choices, and so we touch all of the people in our lives, and they touch our lives."

"Not always for the better," Ishni reminded him.

"No. Not always for the better. But he believed that the path we choose was always for a purpose. We require those people."

"I didn't require that witch. Not her or that corpse of hers."

"But maybe it's the other way around," Holos said. "Maybe they required us."

"Holos, how far to the river? I require some sleep."

"Not much father. We cross the river, we're beyond reach of anyone in Nistadum."

"You've crossed the river before?"

"I was a thief! It was one of our tricks, get somewhere the law can't find you. But I don't care to be a thief any longer."

"No?" Ishni asked him.

"No. Time to make a choice of my own. Time to forget the past."

"Unlike our dead friends back there."

"Yes," Holos said. "Unlike our dead friends back there."

He spied the grasses along the river bank just ahead and soon had the horse on the opposite side.

Ithtidzik

Here is the story of Ithtidzik, and a good story it is. This tale was told in the old days when the Prophet Mutzutou was walking the earth. For this reason, you can tell that it holds a great moral lesson for everyone.

Ithtidzik was a student of gramarye and dark lore and evil signs. He was pupil of To'admret, the mighty and evil sorcerer of Shedra. One day, young Ithtidzik came to his master and complained, "I want no more of these weak spells and impotent gestures. Such magic as you teach me is magic enough for children or witches, but I am Ithtidzik. I swear to you by the prophets of doom that I will learn no more of this strengthless sorcery. I intend to learn all great things, every dark thing, and work mighty necromancy!"

To which his master replied, "Surely you are a fool."

"You will not teach me?" asked Ithtidzik, his bright eyes fiery and his lean young limbs trembling.

"What?" exclaimed his dark master, To'admret. "Teach you these things so that you can harm yourself like the wayward child that ties snakes to dogs' tails and frightens the dog, so that the child is bitten and dies? That would be excellent magic indeed for you to practice."

"Teach me these things!"

"Never!"

So Ithtidzik took leave of his master. He vowed to have revenge one day, and swore further that the world would then tremble when his name was spoken. He declared that the seas would rage and the skies boom and thunder and the lands come crashing together when Ithtidzik was in his anger—raving on and on, after the manner of thwarted young men.

So this is what Ithtidzik did: He thought to himself, "I will gain me the lost and secret lore of that dread book of Aszamazdus' knowledge, which was given him by the high gods, and by this book I will learn things no one else has dared." He did not bethink himself of the ireful doom that had befallen Aszamazdus, but that is because he was a fool.

Ithtidzik made his way to a single solemn tower beyond the walls of Shedra, a place that sorcerers and necromancers had used many times before and which now was reviled by the populace. Ithtidzik here made his magic and called up a powerful demon made of black fire and green smoke.

To this demon, Ithtidzik said, "Do not think that you can fill me with fear, because I have called you up by a magical sign over which you have no means to do me harm."

The demon growled in frustration, knowing that it was powerless.

"Now do this," commanded young Ithtidzik. "Give me the book that Aszamazdus owned in the ancient days, by which I may know all knowledge and so be a master of men."

The demon grumbled with waxing joy, for it knew that the gods surely doom any mortal who dares read from that blasphemous tome. So the demon gave it over, that large book, which was written in the script of Hell's fire.

Ithtidzik then commanded the demon, "Get you gone, but know that you have done me a service."

Spoke the demon: "I will be gone, but you should know that the high gods watch, young magician, and that what you undertake will be your ruin." The demon barked a laugh and returned to its right hell.

Now that Ithtidzik had this vile book of sorcery, he set himself to the task of learning all things. He stayed awake days and nights, which he had taught himself to do by way of secret lore. He burned demon-delivered oils and incenses of dragon's urine, eating and drinking naught, but learning and learning. The world passed by outside his windows. Day became night and night, day while Ithtidzik pored over his book. His beard grew long, his skin became as pale as the white flesh of a worm, and spiders built nests in the dark corners of his study. Ithtidzik never looked up but continued to learn all that he could.

Finally, one day, his mind was so filled with elder lore that Ithtidzik said to himself in dismay, "Why, if I were to learn any more of this book, my mind would not hold it, so filled am I with what I know already! Is this how the gods curse mortal men?"

He pondered the problem a while, thumbing the evil ancient tome with pages so many that, by the time he might learn the last word, the first would have been long forgotten. Then his eyes fell upon a certain passage, and Ithtidzik knew what he must do.

"If my mind cannot hold all that I must know, then I will get another mind to do it for me! Yet I cannot dare to hold ensorcelled another living man like myself, for his spirit would rebel, and perhaps he would be aided by the gods. And yet the mind of a dog or bird or fish is insufficient to hold all that I must know."

Therefore Ithtidzik took himself one dark night to the burial grounds of the citizens of Shedra and dug up a fresh corpse, which had not yet begun to rot or stink much, and carried that corpse back to his tower under the cover of night. He set it in a chair so that it faced him and said to it, "I will call you Sutyokith, and you will keep all the knowledge I now hold, so that I may learn more."

That corpse sat silent, its dried eyes in sunken sockets not moving, its bones swathed with mottled flesh. Yet Ithtidzik knew that it would do his bidding. And so, as they sat there, Ithtidzik commanded that all the dark lore that he had learned be given over to the corpse, and it was done by his will.

"Now have I outwitted the gods themselves!" Ithtidzik laughed loudly. "Here, corpse, and tell me what I call you."

The corpse spoke not; the frozen jaws did not creak or the dried lips tremble. But Ithtidzik heard what was in the corpse's mind and felt it say, "You have named me Sutyokith."

Ithtidzik clapped his hands at the marvel he had wrought. "Tell me," he demanded, "what Aszamazdus commands be done to alleviate a severe rash on the legs and hands. That was told early in this book."

And he heard the corpse's mind say to him, "This is what Aszamazdus commands: Take the juice of a *dugyak* herb and mix it with blood from a baby yellow dragon, and that will cure the rash."

Ithtidzik sighed with relief, knowing that he had succeeded, and so set himself to learn more and more from the fearsome text. And when he came upon a passage that quizzed his memory, he said to the corpse, "Sutyokith, tell me what this means." And the corpse told him.

Thus Ithtidzik began to learn again and memorize the words of Aszamazdus. And yet the time came when his mind was again filled with all that it could hold, and he was nowhere near to knowing all the secrets of sorcery the book contained. Ithtidzik groaned and said, "So it must be done again!" In the dark of night he took himself again to the graveyard and removed from the deep earth the corpse of a young woman, carried it to his tower chamber, and filled its mind with sorcerous knowledge. Then he commenced to learn more and more.

The years went by, season upon season, with Ithtidzik oblivious to the passing time. He memorized words and lines until he could remember no more, so full was his mind; then he would get a corpse and use its mind to store what he had learned, and so return to his book. This continued for years upon years, so that Ithtidzik's chamber became crowded with corpses, fourscore and seven of them, seated on chairs and upon the floor, lying on the shelves, some upon each others' shoulders, others suspended from the rafters. And still Ithtidzik had not learned all that there was in the book of Aszamazdus.

He was growing weary. He thought he heard the gods laughing at him. The chirps of birds were the cackling of witches' ghosts, and the light of the sun, the promise of Hell if he did not learn all the words of this book. More and more corpses Ithtidzik collected, so many that they filled his tower chamber and had to be shoved into a hallway, then more moved into another chamber, and still more moved into another. For a time, some corpses sat on window sills, and Itktidzik even carried the last few onto the roof, but it was a strenuous climb whenever he needed to question one of them up there. Also, there was the danger that a passing patrol from Shedra might notice the crowd of corpses high on the tower, drying in the sun, and so investigate and arrest Ithtidzik and have him beheaded. Therefore, Ithtidzik continued to pile these liches upon others in rooms already overcrowded.

The time came when Ithtidzik, having eaten nothing and drunk nothing and slept not at all for so many years, having ignored the world for the words of Aszamazdus, and having gathered about him seven score and thirteen corpses, came at last to the final passage in the book. He felt a deep power inside him—until he looked out at the stars he had ignored his entire life, and felt cravings in his stomach that he had not suffered his whole life long, and felt the blood slowing in his veins and his eyes quickly failing and his limbs growing ponderous.

Terror seized him. "By the gods," Ithtidzik exclaimed. "I am dying!" And then he thought, "But I need not die! Have I not read the entire book of Aszamazdus? Surely it contains the secret of eternal life!"

He turned to his many corpses. "I know one of you holds the secret of endless life, so tell it to me!" His brain rattled with pain as the minds of those many corpses, all at once, sought to make themselves known to him. "One at a time! One at a time!" Ithtidzik cried out, and, when the ache in his head had subsided, "Now—which one knows?" Once more, all of those corpses tried to talk to him, and Ithtidzik gurgled in pain and told them to desist.

"Quiet! Quiet! All right...now...now—Sutyokith—you were the first. I cannot remember. Did I teach you the secret of eternal life?"

Sutyokith's mind said to him, "No, not me, Ithtidzik."

"Yushtolu, did I teach you?"

"Nay, not me, Master."

"Mustothid?"

"Nay, not me—"

"Sidvidish!"

"Nay, not—"

"Yuttoskuk?"

"Nay—"

Ithtidzik grabbed his head and whimpered in fear. He ran out of that chamber and into another. "You corpses! You! Wisthiklo! Did I...did I teach you the secret of eternal life?"

"Nay, Master, not me."

"Neblis!"

"Nay, not—"

Ithtidzik clutched his abdomen and hurried into another chamber. He tripped over a sprawled lich and landed on his hands and knees. He crawled to the lich, looked into its black eye sockets, touched the cold flesh. "Shedrek?"

"Nay—"

He crawled on, coughing as his lungs tightened. "Lustokik? Nampirok? Hurry, I am *dying*! Pustukor! Lampido! Please!" Ithtidzik fell to the floor, very weak, now, his mind spinning. "Shidyuk? Krestorremnis? Thadlor—? Yit— N'nnran—"

So he died, too weak and ill to name the remainder of them.

And as he died, all of those corpses in the rooms of the tower and in the hallways dropped and decomposed into great nasty piles of old flesh and bad bones and dust. Their knowledge went away with them.

Except for one.

He was the sixty-first corpse that Ithtidzik had resurrected, and he it was who held the secret knowledge of eternal life.

Amidst the piles of disintegrated flesh and foul dust, he stood alone, dead but not dead, not alive, but undying.

The demon returned in a ring of black fire to reclaim the book of Aszamazdus. The corpse staggered to the demon and asked it, "What of me? I hold the secret of eternal life, but I am a corpse! I do not want to live! Help me!"

The demon laughed at him and returned to Hell in sheets of flame.

And so that corpse, which Ithtidzik had named Yuskudnak, though its real name had been Sedkur the wainwright, left the tower by the walls of Shedra to wander over all the earth, walking everywhere, seeing not, hearing not, speaking not, undying and unable to be killed, never stopping.

It wanders to this day.

Rhasjud's Destiny

For twenty years, the killers had ravaged the world. Not stopping for rest in summer or comfort in winter, they had marched through forest and across desert, over rivers and over mountains, down the rocky coast of the ocean at the western end of the world, and into the meadowlands of the south, murdering and moving on, stealing, setting to the torch, and moving on.

Leading them was Rhasjud. Born in the saddle, bred to the knife and the sword, one with the small swift ponies, at home in the night and the cold, Rhasjud rode before his host in the early days of men. But now—

Now, under the edgeless, colorless sky of an autumn afternoon, encamped in grassland that overlooked a wide, round valley—now Rhasjud had stopped his march. Beyond that valley lay further cities to kill, temples to plunder, women to rape. Yet Rhasjud did not move. His men were perplexed. Never had any of them taken pause, fallen behind, or quit the march, save to die. Now they had sat encamped for four days. Prepared to ride down the grassy slope into the valley, they instead were forced to loiter.

What did it mean? Old warriors toughened by years of Rhasjud's command did not care for it. Apprentices, young wolves, spat in disgust. Is this why they had joined the riders of the great killer of men?

Rhasjud, in his horse-hair tent on the wind-worn slope above the valley, drank at his table and sat silent. What did he fear? wondered his swords. Of what did he despair? Had the jealous gods cursed him for his bravery? Had his mind turned bad through damage on the field? Or had he some new plan to offer them, some bold maneuver to reason out, alone in his horse-hair tent?

Night descended on the fourth day. The rankled men settled about their campfires. They told stories, passed wine jugs, roasted meat on spits. Here a man laughed at some joke; there a youngster squealed as his elder jabbed at him with a knife, illustrating another way to cut men open. Bright stars large and small filled the black sky, like dust flung there. In the mountains to the west, a wolf released a howl that trembled. Wolves speak for wandering ghosts; their cries carry comfort to the spirits that roam the earth. The wail of a wolf is the memory of the pain these lost spirits suffered while on earth.

In his tent, Rhasjud demanded more wine. His servant entered with a jug and set it before him. Rhasjud took it but did not look at his man. The killer of killers, in his harness, sword beside him, shield beside him, said nothing. The servant moved away, quietly leaving the tent.

Outside, one high in the ranks, a concerned veteran, gripped the servant's shoulder.

"Is he taken mad, Eldrom? When do we leave?"

"Lord Bors, your honor, he said nothing to me."

"Nothing?"

"He whispers. He talks to himself."

Bors said, "Come with me," and with a hand on one shoulder guided Eldrom to a campfire close by, where soldiers sat. The warrior leaned in to rub his hands over the fire, and he spoke into the flames as he did. "Eldrom says he has quit his senses."

This was ruminated upon all around. An old wolf asked Eldrom, "How do you know this?"

"He talks to himself, your honor. How many years have I served him? The past three nights, he drinks and says nothing. He whispers. When did he ever do this? My fear— I do not know."

The fire sparked. The stars waited. Men extended callused hands toward the flames. Just as someone began to speak, a shadow moved over them. A few began to reach for their weapons, but in a moment, the owner of the shadow stepped into the circle of firelight.

He was as old as iron, as old as stone, familiar to all of them, but one who kept his own company, a veteran who spoke little and took his meals alone. Any who passed him nodded respectfully; his deep eyes told of much experience and of wisdom. At once the men at the fire moved to colder sections of stone and log to make room for this man. The old soldier seated himself and, when he was ready, spoke.

"Rhasjud is not gone mad," he said. "You men are wrong. He merely fears an injustice, an old crime. The gods do not let cruel crimes go unavenged, although their justice may wait many years, by our measure, for fulfillment."

Someone spat into the fire; it sizzled. "Explain yourself."

"You're young. The gods love young men, I know, but how many battles have you fought? I have seen everything. Listen to me.

"Many years ago, I was at this spot, on a night like this one. I was much younger. I loved to slay. Killing is the way of things. Rhasjud—he, too, was years younger. I never heard him rage more fiercely than he did on the morning after that night, as his army followed him down this slope into that valley—against his brother."

There was an uncomfortable silence.

"It is not unknown to kill one's blood-kin, but always is it avenged. Still, Rhasjud, heedless of the gods, heedless of anything save his pride, his wish to do everything—he carried that battle down to his brother's force. He defeated them in a day, and with the death of the sun, he slew his own brother. He cut his brother in half. I saw it. There the legs, twisting as they died, here the chest, the arms shorn, and the man's face grimacing in outrage. Rhasjud raped and killed his brother's wife, and killed the man's children. In his last moment, the brother cried out to the gods for revenge, even as the wolves came to carry the halves of his body away. Heedless of anything, cruel beyond allowance, Rhasjud left his brother and the family uncovered, meat for the wolves and wild dogs and vultures.

"He moved on. He made all those conquests that to you now are legendary. I myself killed many men, and in my space of time I doubtless killed those same men again, their weary souls returning in babes born on the red field, raised to slay, and taken once more by my blade. It is the circle of things.

"Rhasjud, too, killed many men. But no more brothers; he had only the one. Chiefs and princes fell quickly beneath him. But every year, on nights like this night—far away in the darkness—thunder was heard, like a storm in the mountains, the thunder of an army there—his brother's army—and then the battle cries, and the sweeping of our army down to meet it. Some of you men here know that I speak the truth. You have lived long enough, and you have heard it for yourselves deep at night as you dreamed. It has followed us, that event, the echoes of that battle between the brothers, during our marches, no matter where we traveled. Were they ghosts that refought those memories and created the thunder? More than ghosts? We never saw those armies, only heard them.

"Sometimes Rhasjud would scream in his horse-hair tent, scream at his brother and the gods, and scream at his brother's wife, the forest witch. Now he no longer screams. He drinks, trying with wine to erase the memory of his crime.

"We rode north, we rode west and south, we circled around, conquering and taking as we wished. Yet never again, till tonight, did we ride across this grassland and look down into the meadowed valley. Not until tonight. Is Rhasjud hoping at last to conquer his fear? That is how we face ourselves, as you know. We confront our deeds; we confront what we have been. Men are drawn back in this way to what they have done, but it requires bravery. Is this what Rhasjud is doing? Or is his intention greater than that? Does he wish to accomplish what no man has and confront something beyond the mere armies of men?

"Tomorrow, I've heard him say, we ride into the meadowlands, then across those farther hills to take Sudum."

His finish was abrupt. Faces gazed at him through the fire. Someone coughed. Someone else began to speak. "We will—"

"We will not take Sudum. Mark me."

From elsewhere in the camp, then, a hoarse voice cried out. Not Rhasjud's. But it called Rhasjud's name. The men at the fire turned and stared westward, where the grassy slope tipped down into the nighted valley.

In the dreamy starlight, they discerned a lone horseman galloping down the slope, into the ocean of shadows, purple and soft beneath the night, the meadowlands of the valley. And following the horseman, Eldrom, running quickly, calling after the rider, "Rhasjud! Master! My lord!"

Then other voices came. "Yonder he rides!" "I saw him go!" "Why did he leave?"

Gradually, the commotion died. The campfires went down. Voices dwindled. Rhasjud, out there in the night, did not return, nor did his servant. Men retreated into tents or reclined under heavy coverings. The moon dipped low. A few sentries took their posts, relieving others. The single oil lamp in Rhasjud's tent burned, flickered, whispered, and went out.

Dawn hesitated low beyond the trees to the east.

From the west came a low thunder, like a seizure under the earth, so dim as to be scarcely noticed. It subsided. But there came another buckling of thunder, distant pounding beneath the earth, tremors underground.

And there came sounds of trumpets far away—the wind rushing somewhere, yet the same sound as that of an army signaling battle.

The thunder beneath the earth increased. The ground lifted and settled, lifted again and slipped out from underfoot

Men moved from their tents and looked into the morning mist in all directions. Who was moving against them? Where was their enemy? What were their orders? Where was Rhasjud?

The thunder underearth began to hurt their ears. It was the familiar sensation of thousands of horses, of bronze wheels and booted feet nearby but nowhere to be seen. There was no wind, no presence, only the uncertain ground beneath them, only the mist.

Then from the valley below—

A sentry called out his master's name.

—Rhasjud's voice lifted, it was a howl, his voice reached through the fog that filled the wide valley.

That was all, that howl. The thunder continued, increasing, pounding with hoof beats up and down the sides of the slope. But no army was seen. The army was invisible, or hidden within the impossible mist. Still, there came the sounds of moving horses, the crashing of bodies striking each other, the cries of men dying and wounded, the clatter of weapons.

The men of the camp looked into the mist in the valley. Go down there? Who should ride into that swirling fog?

And they saw him then. Before them, in the sunlit haze not thirty man-lengths down this side of the slope, on his horse, emerging from the mist. Rhasjud. Or what remained of him. He had been halved. The top of him was gone. His legs were lashed to the stirrups, and his horse was washed dark with blood. As the horse reared, this lower part of Rhasjud leaned back, nearly falling from the saddle.

The horse turned and moved back down into the valley.

Then Eldrom. His body rolled upward on the grass, slipping out of the fog as though it had been kicked or pushed forward. He was covered in blood. His body had been broken in every direction, trampled by horses and crushed under wheels. It rested there until, with a final grumbling of the earth, Eldrom too rolled downward, away from sight, into the fog in the valley.

That was all. The thunder moved away, and the sounds of battle, weapons, men screaming, and horses and chariots. The morning fell silent. Birds chirruped, and the sun at last came over the trees.

The camp did not move that day. Neither did anyone go down the slope into the valley to retrieve Rhasjud's and Eldrom's corpses, what remained of them. Leave them for the wolves and wild dogs and the vultures. Talk was small and guarded. Night fell again, and no one slept.

At his fire, Bors sat with his circle of men. Some of them spoke of what the old man had said the night before. Would the spirits or the gods punish them, too, for being Rhasjud's men?

And where was the old man? He was not to be found any longer in camp.

Bors said, "I think we know who the old man was. I think he has been among us ever since Rhasjud killed him and his family. He was patient. The gods and the spirits of revenge are patient."

They heard a wolf howl.

Some of the men made signs to the gods.

"I think," Bors told them at the fire, "that in the life that comes after this one, in the land of the shadows, we must account for what we have done in this life. If we were brave and protected our families and helped our people, the shadows will be fair with us. If we have done otherwise, the shadows know how to deal with that, too. We have been witnesses to that, brothers. The night is silent now, but Rhasjud is screaming on the other side of this night, although we can no longer hear him. Let us burn his horse-hair tent and everything that was his. Let the gods watch as we destroy everything that was his."

This was done. The flames reached high and burned through the night.

The following morning, Bors and other men spoke, and a plan was agreed to. Sudum was not a rich city; why bother crossing the valley to plunder so modest a prize? Dev, to the southeast, had not been sacked recently and held better promise.

So it was decided. Armor was strapped on, campfires scattered, tents taken down, ponies buckled. On a colorless autumn morning, under an edgeless sky, the warriors left that place, galloping back the way they had come, down toward Dev and plunder.

A wolf followed them.

Blood Ransom

No one is injured save by himself.

—Erasmus, *Adages*

"There," said Tsathsimus. "There she is." He poked Androm hard in the shoulder.

"All right, I see her, I know." Androm pushed him away.

Tsathsimus was big—not fully twice the size of Androm, but in muscle and bone, nearly double the stretch of anyone else in Iron Fall Street that afternoon, as broad in the chest as he was from belt to boot. But it wasn't the size of Tsathsimus that so annoyed Androm.

"Well?" the giant grunted at him, lifting an elbow in a threat to poke him again. "Go on, Pretty Boy."

It was that, the rude comments about his good looks. How he looked in a mirror had brought as much trouble into Androm's young life as his hot temper had.

But because of his looks, Androm certainly couldn't be mistaken for either Tsathsimus or the giant's useless companion, Ishrid, who might well have been the offspring of something human mated with a rat. Ishrid wasn't much bigger than a rat, either. At least he seemed so to Androm, who'd grown to a good size in his twenty summers.

Tsathsimus was easy enough to understand, or at least he seemed so to Androm, as worldly as he was becoming, but Ishrid he hadn't yet puzzled out. The Rat was quick with a knife, but other than that, he seemed to be little more than a pilot fish to Tsathsimus' shark. They weren't lovers, at least so far as Androm could ascertain. Maybe there was nothing more to it than that they'd fallen in with each other, and life offered nothing bettered for either of them at the moment. Certainly both were trouble, but where the giant was an oversized menace, Ishrid was an irritant, an itch unable to be scratched, what with the smell of him, his piping voice, and his restless habit of performing sleight-of-hand when it was obvious that no one was entertained by his doing so.

Androm's intention was to be rid of them both before another day had passed. How he'd managed to fall in with them in the first place was something he wished to reexamine many times over in the near future.

"Look at this one," the Rat said to Tsathsimus and Androm. "Look what I can do." He displayed an upright, naked right palm, then the closed fist, and then the palm again, this time with a gold coin miraculously sitting between his life line and his Mound of Tanish.

"It'd be a better trick," Tsathsimus observed, "if that were real gold instead of wood with paint," and then he stood abruptly, nearly launching their table and gourds of ale onto the stones. He kept his eyes on the woman across the street but lifted his right hand to the knife in his belt and said impatiently to Androm, "You're gutless. Watch how it's done and grow a bone, Pretty Boy."

"Wait!"

Tsathsimus looked at him.

Androm swallowed the last of his brew, then stepped around Ishrid and moved into the street.

Tsathsimus remained standing, watching him.

Ishrid, playing with a length of twine looped around his fingers, asked, "Have you seen the one where I used this string?"

"Have you seen the one where I break your hands?"

Ishrid put the twine away.

The young woman's name was Asri. She was perhaps fifteen, Androm knew, certainly no older than sixteen summers—in full bloom, with auburn hair, well dressed, and wearing jewelry that did not disguise her status. Neither did her bearing, nor her fine clothes, nor the two servants who accompanied her. Older women, nearly as well dressed as Asri, keeping close by her as household guardians would, protective.

Androm didn't recognize them, but then, he had been employed by Asri's mother for only a few months. Neither would he have recognized Lady Liprosa, even if she were one of these two old women, but Asri he had spoken with several times and found her to be charming. Independent, too, with a rebellious-ness in her that had led her to go out of her way to spend time with a young man who, after all, was a hired hand on the estate, not someone whose company a young girl of Asri's station typi-cally would seek out.

Maybe she'd sensed in Androm's heart something similar to her own assertiveness, had caught a hint of it and, thus, the heart of a kindred spirit—two young people eager to take on the dares of the world.

As soon as Asri recognized Androm pushing his way by others milling in the street, she smiled warmly at him.

"Where have you been?" she asked. "Why did you leave?" Her openness was genuine.

It cut into Androm's heart, her sincerity, but he hadn't been able to think of any way out of this situation before now, and no ideas visited him at the moment, so he did the best he could, knowing that eyes were on him.

"I can explain," he told her, "but it would be—" He stopped deliberately and looked at the two old women.

Asri said to him, "Oh, it's fine."

"It's rather private."

One of the women told him, "We have few secrets, young man. You worked in the—"

"The stables."

"The stables."

Asri frowned at the thought of it. "You should have stayed. You in the stables. We could have done much more for you, you know."

"I'm still not sure how long I intend to be here," Androm confessed, trying to sound apologetic. "That's one of the reasons why I'm glad to see you. I'd hoped to, actually. I know you come here every turn of the moon."

"Do you?" The thought that he was familiar with her routine didn't please Asri.

Androm quickly explained. "Only because—I saw you last month. You ladies, too. I thought you might come back."

"You're being very mysterious," Asri said, less glad now to see him than she'd been a few moments earlier.

Androm told her, "I'm embarrassed. I apologize, but I am. Could we—?" He gestured toward a shop door at the corner of an alley on the other side of the street and said to the two old women, "It may not be a secret, but I'm still shy about it." And, lowering his voice, he said, "I need help."

"What are talking about, young man?"

"I think Asri might have guessed already."

She hadn't guessed already. She had no idea whatsoever what Androm was talking about. But— "A moment," Asri told the two with her. "We'll be right over there." She was intrigued and won over by his smile and his wonderful eyes, as she had been many times on the path that led past the stables.

The old women frowned and watched with doubtful expressions as Androm led the way around shoppers and past street entertainers to just inside the opening of the alley.

Asri was puzzled but joined him there.

Across the street, Tsathsimus slapped Ishrid on the back and told him, "Now. Go," as he himself entered the wine shop behind them.

The rear entrance of the shop connected to the same alley where Androm was testing Asri's patience, and a quick jog over the puddles back there and away from the many piles of manure brought Tsathsimus around a corner and only two or three man-lengths from those two.

Beyond them, in the street, the giant saw Ishrid doing his best to distract the old women with his "Look at this one, look what I can do!" and his bad sleight of hand.

Asri, hearing footsteps, turned as Tsathsimus stepped up behind her, but she didn't see him because he brought a fist down hard across the right side of her head, then hit her on the left side. She went limp, and Androm reached for her.

"Enough!" he yelled at Tsathsimus.

But Tsathsimus pulled her away from Androm and slung the unconscious girl over one wide shoulder.

The old women in the street saw it all and yelled for help. "In the alley! *There!*" They waved at a city patrolman, who was slow in looking in their direction and in making his way over the stones to them.

Ishrid, meanwhile, blocked their way however he could, but when one of the women tried to grab him by his collars, he twisted away, small and quick as he was, and by the time the patrolman reached the servants, he had taken whatever direction served him best to elude them all.

While Androm, breathing hard as he ran to catch up to Tsathsimus, managed, despite feeling sick about this stunt, to swing himself astride one of the horses they'd tethered behind the wine shop. He looked morosely at Asri, who remained unconscious.

Tsathsimus had her draped in front of him as he sat atop his own horse. He told Androm, "Don't try to get away from me," and slapped the young man's horse before kicking his own forward, away from the alley and the wine shop, away from the old women and the city patrol, away from the city of Kursai itself, past its walls and into the desert beyond.

Awaken in wonder, she had been told only a few years ago, when her mother and the other women had begun her initiation into womanhood and the craft. *Awaken in wonder before the goddess, the Mother of all women.*

Asri awakened with pain on both sides of her head, and when she opened her eyes, it was to look into darkness, so that she wondered whether this were the next stage in her initiation or if perhaps she were now dead and become a ghost. But the pain was not ghostly; she recognized her body because of it. As her stomach settled and as she gained a clearer sense of her situation, she understood that she was blindfolded and lying on a flat stretch of stone with her hands tied in front of her. She tried to move her hands; the wrists were bound securely.

"She's awake."

Asri recognized the voice as Androm's.

"I'm taking off her blindfold," Androm said.

"Leave it on." This second speaker—he was a big man, the timbre of his voice coming from the well of a deep chest.

But Androm insisted, "I'm taking it off. She doesn't need the blindfold."

A tug—and Asri was looking up at Androm and, behind him, a sky of bright stars, with well-worked stone in every direction, marble and granite. They were in an old building, in the wide, open vestibule of a temple, a ruin.

Asri realized something low in her heart. "Where are we?" she asked Androm.

"In the desert."

"Do you know what you've done?"

"Yes, I think so." He sounded regretful.

She told him, "I don't think you do. Help me up."

He did so, positioning her as well as he could against a column so that she might sit as comfortably as possible.

She asked, "Don't you know where you are?" There was nothing else this old and dangerous within a hundred leagues of Kursai.

Tsathsimus growled, "She talks too much."

Asri looked in his direction and heard him clicking stones in the darkness. Sparks flashed. Tinder caught fire and smoked, and shortly real flames burned inside a circle of piled rocks. Tsathsimus continued to add to the fire. He was, Asri saw, a giant.

She also saw details in the stonework around her, the friezes in the architraves.

Androm told her, "We're in some ruins in the desert. A temple."

"I know where we are. I thought you were better than this." She nodded toward Tsathsimus. "Who is he?"

"No names!" In the increasing light of the fire, Tsathsimus was a demon pulling free of the shadows. Large and unmistakable, he rose from a fallen stretch of stone, crossed the floor, and looked down at her and Androm.

Asri pressed herself against the column behind her but held her face up, defiant. "Stay away from me," she ordered.

He said nothing to her but, not looking away, grunted to Androm, "Bring her over here."

Tsathsimus led the way to an area of the vestibule caught in shadows where a deep well had been sunk, perhaps for water at one time, perhaps for storage. It was at least two manlengths deep. Several slabs of stone lay nearby, barely visible in the firelight.

Androm left Asri where she was but followed Tsathsimus into the shadows.

"We're going to put her down there," the giant told him.

Androm asked him, "Is it safe?"

"I've checked it. Look." Tsathsimus reached toward Androm, gripped him by the back of the neck, and at the same time kicked him behind the knees. Androm's legs went out from under him, and the giant pushed him forward. Androm dropped into the well.

He landed on pieces of old brick and broken stones, and sand and scrub that had been blown in from the desert. Furious, Androm lifted himself and stared up at the opening.

"Tsathsimus!"

He heard sounds of struggle and Asri yelling, then Tsathsimus growling at her.

In a moment, they both were visible at the top of the well, and Asri was dropped over the edge. Androm backed away and put out his arms to try to break her fall. That helped, but still, she landed on one hip and made a painful sound when she did.

"Cat!" Tsathsimus yelled down at her.

Androm saw him rubbing his wrist.

Asri yelled up at him, "I should have bitten your hand off!"

They saw him move away from the edge of the well, then heard powerful scraping sounds as whatever light they had was gradually cut off from above.

But not entirely. Tsathsimus was doing his best to push one of the stone slabs over the opening of the well, but he couldn't manage it.

"You damned cat!" he growled again at Asri, and left the stone where it was, covering half of the opening of the well.

"At least he's bleeding," Asri said.

Androm pulled out his sword and began jabbing it into the seams between the bricks in the wall. "Tsathsimus!"

Asri asked him, "What good will that do?"

"Tsathsimus!" He tried to scramble up the side of the well using his sword and his anger, his complete anger.

Tsathsimus called to him, "You're wasting your effort, Pretty Boy!"

"I'll kill you!"

Asri told him, "Stop."

Androm hit the wall with his sword and growled and wiped his hair out of his eyes.

Asri put a hand on his shoulder and told him again, "Stop!" It was an order, her tone that of a woman commanding a servant.

Androm sheathed his sword and stood against the wall. He was sweating. "Well?"

"Sit." She did so herself, settling on the ground.

There was just enough room for Androm to crouch across from her, although it was awkward, and their knees touched.

"Are you hurt?" Asri asked him. "Are you bleeding?"

"No."

"Make sure."

"I'm sure. No, my cheek is bleeding."

He felt her fingertips touching one side of his face, then the other, where he had hit his cheek. Her fingers were very warm, so warm that Androm drew away from her. "What is that?"

"It may help stop the bleeding."

"What is it?"

"It's something I learned how to do. You're really not hurt?"

He moved out of his crouch so that he could sit more comfortably, then groaned. "My ankle. It's not—" He moved one of his feet, scraping the heel of his boot on the ground. "I can use it. I twisted it, that's all. What about you?"

"I pulled something in my right leg, and I know I have some bruises, but nothing is broken."

Androm knocked the back of his head against the bricks of the wall. "Damn it. Damn it." He asked Asri, "Why aren't you angry?"

Awaken in wonder. See the world with new eyes. "I *am* angry. I'm waiting. I intend to use my anger."

"Use it now. Because I'm ready to try jumping out of this hole again. Damn it!" he swore in frustration.

Asri told him, "I'm angrier than you are. I'd hurt you if I thought it would help. I'm to blame for this."

"That's not true."

"It *is* true. I should have known better. But I like you. Why do we always think that pretty people are good people?"

"You're pretty." He said, "Pretty, pretty. And here we are." He yelled again, "Tsathsimus, I will kill you for this!"

The giant did not reply.

Asri told him, "We can get out of here, but I'm going to need your help, and I have to know whether I can trust you."

"Apparently you can't."

"Listen to me!" Another command—and now her voice was edged with anger.

Some real temper from her at last, Androm thought. "Is that how you order people around in your house?"

"It's how I order people around when they've offended me. Now can I trust you?"

"Yes."

Sounds came to them, not from Tsathsimus, not from above, but close by, itching sounds. Something moving within the earth.

"Listen," Asri said.

"What is that?"

"Spirits of the dead. They're part of this temple now. *Hold still!*"

He didn't. Androm gripped her hands, not strongly, not in anger, but simply to hold them while he asked her, "Tell me about the spirits of the dead."

Asri took in a breath. "They're attracted to blood. It happened hundreds of years ago. It's because of the women who rule Kursai. *They* own the city, not the businessmen, not these other people."

"Tell me what happened. I have to trust you, too, now, Asri."

She pulled her hands away from his. "Kursai was founded by women a thousand years ago. Longer than that. It's always been here. There was one attempt to steal it from us, but we held it. That was hundreds of years back. This temple was one of the places where we fought them. Men. They worshipped some god that's been completely forgotten. Gods don't live. Gods die. Women live."

"And their spirits are still here?"

"Yes. They want blood. When they sense blood—they try to get to it. My mother says that the spirits think it can bring them back to life."

"So you were touching me— Why? You stopped the bleeding."

"Yes."

"What are you, all witches?"

"Call us what you want. Now hold still."

But he held her off for another moment. "I met a witch after I left home. She frightened me."

"What did she do?"

"Fed me. I was starving. But she didn't hurt me. Just sent me on my way."

"We're not evil, Androm. Hold still." She reached toward his face again.

Awaken in wonder. Touch the world with new senses.

Androm felt her fingertips touching him delicately, then moving down to his chest, hovering over his heart. He said, "Your hands are warmer now than before."

Asri said nothing.

He listened to her breathing. "What are you doing?"

"Reading you."

"Why didn't you do that before?"

"Pretty, pretty. I blame myself." She sat back, moving away from him.

She was breathing heavily, getting her air, and Androm considered that it must have taken a great effort for her to do what she had just done.

Asri said to him, "Tell me one more thing. When did you come out here? You must have, to know about this storage well."

"I didn't. Tsathsimus did, obviously."

"You didn't know about this?"

"No. He tricked me. I didn't trust him, but I didn't see him doing this. He surprised me."

"I recognize him, and now I remember from where. Our doorman. Tarsu. He came to speak with Tarsu."

"Your doorman?"

"Yes. He suggested we come into the city today. My mother will deal with him. How do you know this man?"

"He knows my father. Or claims to. He threatened to kill him unless I helped him."

"Why is he with you? You're not like him, that's obvious."

"We can't help who we are."

"No," Asri agreed, and there was a change in her voice. "We can't. Androm, you told me that you left home, but you never told me why."

"My father and my uncles. They'd done things. Traveled. Served in armies. Now they run a farm. Am I supposed to stay on a farm my whole life?"

"You wanted to do something on your own, do something for yourself."

"I suppose."

She breathed a sigh, something like a laugh. "We have something in common. I take orders, too. I don't just give them. And I get tired of it, too. I've often thought of trying to leave, myself, but it wouldn't be so easy. Do something for me with your sword."

"Kill him? Gladly."

"We can pull bricks loose and some of this earth. If we make it high enough, we can climb out of here."

"It'll take too long, Asri."

"I don't think so. We have to try."

"And if Tsathsimus hears us?"

"He won't interfere. What can he do?"

"Stab us, for one thing. Drop a pile of stones onto us."

"I bit him. He's bleeding. That will attract the spirits of this place. Trust me, he'll be preoccupied. Please, just start digging."

Androm did so, pushing with his sword and breaking loose large bricks that lined the wall. As he did, Asri began piling them behind him and, with her bare hands, tore loose raw earth and added that between the layers of brick.

The work was quieter than Androm had thought it would be, and it went as quickly as Asri had indicated. Shortly the two of them were moving upward, and Androm was freeing bricks that had been at the height of his chest.

Finally, when his aching arms were nearly numb, he sat to rest. He was dripping sweat, and his throat was parched with the dust they had knocked loose. As he got his air, he said to Asri, "You can pretty much get out of here now. You don't need me. Why don't you just pull a knife on me for what I did to you? Get it over with."

"Do you think this is easy for me?"

"No."

"You're missing what's underneath. What you think is important...that's least important. Do you think we could have survived for so long doing what everyone else does? Women, I mean."

He considered her question. "No."

"You're not a bad person."

"Is that what you were doing with your hands? When you were touching my face?"

"Yes."

"What about the spirits?"

"What about them?"

"Are there really spirits here?"

"You can't have people without the spirits they bring with them."

"I'd never thought of it that way."

Asri began pulling more bricks out of the wall as Androm dug with his sword.

He warned her, "Careful, careful, or I'll cut you."

"No, you won't. Step down. Let me put these where you're standing."

They worked pressed against each other in the tight space, piling the bricks, adding earth.

Asri whispered to him, "Tell me about your mother."

"What about her?"

"Don't stop. Just tell me."

"She was... Her life was very difficult. My father is a difficult man. Why do you need to know this?"

"I want to know about you."

"She wasn't very old when she died, but she'd used up her life. She and my father used up each other's lives. They had nothing left for each other, so she died. Now he and his brothers work the farm." He told Asri, "I don't understand people who don't want to do something with their lives. Is that what you want to know?" He sounded annoyed.

She told him, "I suppose. Can we reach the top?"

"I'm not sure. Asri!"

They heard Tsathsimus howling in the darkness above them.

"What happened to him? Is he dead?"

"Liklely not. But it's the men we killed. Their spirits. They're attacking him for his blood. It's the only thing left between this world and theirs, so when they sense blood, they want it. Now can you reach the top?"

"I think so."

Tsathsimus yelled, "What did you do to me?"

They heard his footsteps, then saw him leaning over the edge of the well.

Within reach.

Androm gripped the hilt of his sword and slid it free.

Tsathsimus yelled down at them, "What did you do to me, you witch? Damn it!"

Androm pushed up with the point of his blade, aiming as well as he could at Tsathsimus's chest.

Tsathsimus howled. "Back away, Androm!"

"I caught you, you bastard!"

"You're slow, Pretty Boy! Learn to cut a man!" But he swore and moved away. "Damn it, damn it!"

Asri said, "Move quickly! Please, get up there, now!"

He did it, sheathing his sword and jumping as strongly as he could. He got his forearms over the edge of the well and felt Asri push on the bottoms of his boots with all of the strength she had. He felt the pressure on his twisted foot, but he was over the edge in a moment, up on his hands, then on one knee.

"You bastard!" Tsathsimus yelled at him, but the giant was dancing in a wild way and pulling at his chest and arm. Glowing red things, twenty or thirty of them, were jumping on him like locusts or bees.

"Insects!" Androm said to Asri, as he moved onto his belly and held his arms over the edge of the well. "A swarm...of them!"

She grabbed his hands and kicked upward, caught some toe-holds halfway up to the rim, and threw one hand over the edge.

Androm helped her the rest of the way.

"Not insects!" she panted, getting to her feet and looking at Tsathsimus by the fire. "They're jewels!"

"Jewels!"

"Stones. The spirits are in the stones."

"Gods!"

"They're drinking his blood." She took Androm's hand and pulled him as far away from Tsathsimus as they could go, heading toward the staircase that led into the courtyard below.

But Tsathsimus saw them and ran toward them. He yanked brilliant red stones from his chest and arm and flung them at Androm and Asri.

Androm yelped. One of them struck him on the side of the face and dug in, boring into where he had been cut on his cheek.

"Ha!" Tsathsimus drew his sword and ran at him. "Come on, Pretty Boy!"

"Damn it!" Androm pulled the stone from his face, and more blood with it, but got his sword out and met Tsathsimus before the giant could reach Asri. He yelled at her, "Get back!"

"Learn to fight!" Tsathsimus mocked him, slapping Androm's blade out of the way.

But Androm knew more that the giant anticipated. He backed up, then leaned to one side, dropped slightly, and came around with a swipe that caught Tsathsimus wholly unguarded. The sharp edge slipped across the giant's chest, opening a long cut that crossed the stab Androm had poked in him earlier.

"No more!" Tsathsimus yelled, infuriated.

"Stop it!" Asri said to the both of them, so loudly that the giant was surprised and missed his step.

Androm backed away from him and looked at Asri.

She moaned and almost fell to her knees, and in the cool moonlight that filled the open vestibule, Androm saw that she was covered with sweat. She might have just stepped from a pool.

"You're sick!" Androm said.

"No. It's my mother."

"Your *mother*?"

Before Tsathismus could get his balance and attack again—before Androm could turn to face him with raised weapon—

"She's here!" Asri hissed, and said to Tsathsimus, "She makes me strong!"

All of them heard horses whinnying, then hoof beats clattering on the stones below, followed by scores of boots stamping on the ground and weapons clanging, steel whispering as it was pulled free.

"My daughter!" came the loud, powerful voice of a woman.

Asri yelled, "Mother!"

Boots pounded up the long steps.

But Tsathsimus moved more quickly that those boots. Despite the red jewels clinging to his wounds, he jumped at Androm and, in a flurry of sword strokes, forced him away from Asri. Then he had his sword point at her belly.

"Stay there!" he ordered her. "And you!"—to Androm. "Drop it!"

Androm swore at him.

"Do it *now*, Pretty Boy!"

Androm threw his sword to the floor as a crowd of women, dressed in linen robes and leather boots, moved into the vestibule. In the moonlight, they might have been ghosts or ancient priestesses, holy from a thousand years ago, as old as Truth.

On both sides of them came men in leather and bronze armor, some with swords out, some with bows and notched arrows.

Mother Liprosa, like the other women, was dressed in linen and leather, but she also wore a cape and a heavy gold pendant around her throat. She held up her right hand.

Swords points dipped. Bows lowered.

"Do not harm my daughter," she commanded Tsathsimus.

He was behind Asri now, had a hand on her shoulder and his sword in her back.

Androm, helpless, stood to their left, looking from Asri to her mother. He shivered with anger.

"The ransom," Tsathsimus said to Lady Liprosa.

The lady gestured; from behind her, one of the swordsmen came ahead. He held two heavy sacks.

He said to Tsathsimus, "Look what I can do," and opened the sacks.

Ishrid's head landed first and rolled until the Rat was staring at the dark ceiling. Tarsu the doorman's head settled a hand away from Ishrid's. What had been the doorman's luxurious gray beard was neatly sliced close to the chin.

"You value your life so little?" Tsathsimus asked Lady Liprosa.

"That is my question for you," she replied.

"I'll shove this sword through her."

"No," the lady replied calmly. "You won't."

The swordsmen and bowmen stepped away from the women to corral Tsathsimus on either side.

"It won't work," he warned them, and grabbed Asri by the throat. He yanked her backward with him as he moved toward the opening that led farther into the temple.

Androm stayed with them.

"Not too close, Pretty Boy."

"You're not killing her, Tsathsimus."

"You just stay back."

"I'm staying as close to her as I can." And he said to Asri, "Whatever you need me to do, you let me know."

She couldn't speak, couldn't move her head, but she closed her eyes, then opened them as though in a signal to him.

"Young man," Lady Liprosa said, "this is no longer your concern."

Androm told her, "It *is* my concern. I'm not afraid to die."

"Don't be foolish. We're all afraid to die."

The group of them followed Tsathsimus as he backed away, Androm to his left, Lady Liprosa and the women flanked by the swords and bows. Behind Tsathsimus, the vestibule led into an open area of broken stone benches, fallen columns, and areas where the floor stones had fallen into disrepair. Shafts of moonlight, like spears, came through holes in the roof. Where the light touched the floor, red gems shined and moved toward Tsathsimus, drawn by his blood.

He saw them. "Witches, all of you," he growled at Lady Liprosa. "You don't frighten me!"

"Of course we do," she told him.

On either side of the open area, tall archways led into halls that ran the length of the temple. Here, at least, the giant could hold them off by ones and twos as they followed him and Asri. Tsathsimus saw the guardsmen to left of the women move toward the archway across the open area. Both of the halls, then, must meet in another common area farther back in the temple. No doubt they thought that they could corner him there.

Tsathsimus continued to back away, but he felt himself losing strength with each step. The jewels were on him, and he was doing what he could to ignore them, but they were painful, sucking on his blood and digging under his skin, into his wounds.

His grip on Asri was loosening, and his vision was beginning to blur.

Androm was in front of Asri, matching her and Tsathsimus step for step, and behind him, the lady, her women, and half of her guards.

Tsathsimus said to Androm, "They'll kill you, too."

Androm told him, "You're a dog. You tricked me."

"You're too stupid to know any better."

"Who's stupid now, you pig?"

"Help me," Tsathsimus said to him. "Get me out of this."

"Get yourself out of it."

"*They'll kill you, too!*" Tsathsimus yelled at Androm, and lost his footing.

He let go of Asri. She jumped away from him, toward Androm, then moved past him to her mother. The lady reached out her arms as Androm stepped toward Tsathsimus.

The giant brought up his sword; he was so weak, it cost him as much effort as hoisting a stone block might have. He whispered to Lady Liprosa, "What have you done to me?"

"We're strong together. One woman you can trick. All of us together—our power is great."

"Witches!" He groaned as he pulled the gems from his chest and, in pain, warned Androm away at sword length. "No closer,

Pretty Boy!" He turned then and ran down the hall as well as he could, hobbling, really, and leaving a trail of red drops behind him.

Gems crawled from the shadows of the hallway to drink the blood. Gems dropped from the dark ceiling to suck the blood the giant had left behind.

The hall ended in a great chamber colored red, lit red by the light of rubies, gems, bright stones that filled a great stone pit sunk into the earth. The pit was eight, ten manlengths long and nearly as wide. What had been its purpose? It was filled now with thousands of spirits, burning red stones that crawled over and upon each other, sensing blood in the room, all of them pulling toward the side of the pit where Tsathsimus stood, bleeding onto the stones.

Across from him in the chamber, the guardsmen who had followed the hall on that side now stepped into the waving red light, as dreamy as a fog, like light caught in the reflection of a deep pool.

Tsathsimus moved as far away from the pit as he could, into a corner, where, rocking in his boots, he kept his sword before him. He pointed it at Androm and the women and men behind him, and then at the guards on the other side.

One of those archers said, "Here is where you die," and raised his bow.

As did the archers behind him, waiting for the signal from their lady.

Tsathsimus bent his head back. He was dripping sweat, and his skin was ghostly in the red light, his face hollow. He was fearful.

In the pit, the gems and crawling stones raised the sound of insects as they moved upon one another, all clicks and snapping noises. They began to push up and over the edge of the pit, onto the floor of the chamber.

Tsathsimus howled, "No more!" and charged Androm.

Androm met him, sword to sword.

For all of his size, Tsathsimus now was quite weak, his vision was uncertain, and he did not have his footing. Still, Androm might have been caught by the giant's weapon if he had not been as quick as he was. Moving in, he made sure that he leaned away from Tsathsimus as soon as he could and, using a trick one of his uncles had taught him, jumped into the air as he did.

It was dangerous. He had his hurt foot to consider, and he might lose his balance when he came down.

But the maneuver succeeded. Tsathsimus' sword cut the air where Androm had been, and as Androm completed his move, he brought his own weapon downward in a cut that sliced Tsathsimus' hand from the wrist.

Hand and sword jumped away. The long steel scraped noisily on the floor stones.

Tsathsimus looked at it. He said, "That's my hand."

Androm moved in and pushed his sword point through Tsathsimus' belly, pulled back, and stepped away.

Blood pulsed from the giant's wrist and dripped freshly from his gut, where Androm had cut through his leather shirt.

Tsathsimus fell against the wall and said, "Give me back my hand, damn you." His knees bent, and he sank to the floor. He looked up at Androm, and then at the archers across the chamber.

They loosed their arrows. Seven, eight, nine struck Tsathsimus in his chest, shoulders, forehead. Two in his forehead. The giant squinted hard.

The stones were on him immediately, at his severed hand, on his wrist, inside his wrist, moving up his legs and into his belly, into his chest, into his mouth. They made little sound, but because they were so great in number, very quickly the jewels revealed the giant's bones, Tsathsimus' jaw, his ribs, the yellow-white of his pelvis.

Androm turned away and coughed, leaned forward and choked, spit up whatever was in his stomach. His eyes teared, and he showed a sweat.

When he looked at Lady Liprosa, she asked him, "Have you never seen death before?"

"I've never— I never killed anyone before. They're like maggots."

She said, "They are like maggots," and made a sign to the women behind her and to her guardsmen, all of whom turned to leave that red chamber, its light, and the sorrowful spirits trapped there.

One of the guardsmen took Androm's sword, and Androm went with them down the hall, across the open chamber and the vestibule, to the top of the stairs that led to the courtyard below the ancient temple. Before them, over the flat desert with its scrub, dawn was rising.

Awaken in wonder, Asri thought as she looked at the sky.

"What will you do with me?" Androm looked at Lady Liprosa and Asri and the women.

Asri whispered into her mother's ear. The lady looked at Androm as she listened, then told him, "My daughter has made a request, and she has the right because she is one of us. She says that she looked into your heart."

Asri told Androm, "If someone had threatened my mother, and if I thought that there was nothing else I could do to save her—Androm, I would have done what you did. I give you your life."

He took in a long breath and touched his cheek. "Thank you."

"Go home. Go be with your family. I intend to stay with mine."

"I understand."

Lady Liprosa told the guardsmen who held Androm's sword, "Give him his weapon."

Androm took it and sheathed it. He looked down the long staircase into the courtyard, then back at the lady and at Asri.

"Go now," Asri told him.

He hurried down the steps and ran into the courtyard to his horse. Shortly he was past the fallen stone blocks of the courtyard entrance and into the scrubland.

"Shall I bring him down with the bow?" asked a guardsman.

"No." Lady Liprosa shook her head. "No need. Let him be."

They moved into the morning, down the temple staircase, to return home.

Dark Goddess

In the past, the gods were in the world, and men and women knew them. Things of evil walked the world then also, with the gods and with us. Nights were haunted. Even daylight was not safe. The land was a place of haunted fens and forests where ghosts lived. At sunfall, the oceans of the early world caught fire like expanses of lava. The tall mountains of the north and west were dark with smoke from the furnaces of the high gods, forging their weapons to fight the demons of the shadows. The screams of dying giants and the shrieks of other things could be heard at midday by farmers and by travelers who kept to well-worn roads, away from the wastelands, away from the fens and forests.

The gods themselves were little better than the demons they challenged: triple-horned Ikribu and fiery Arkatu, fierce-eyed Urug and avenging Yem-yur, and the god whose name could not be spoken but was written as Omidom. And there was Yasdis, the All Mother, the hag with one eye and triple teats whose spittle had made the stars and whose defecation had formed the earth. Her mad singing had awakened humans to life; we crawled from the muck and ever since have wondered about the dark heart of life. Yasdis did not fight the demons; she lived in the shadows and, at night, crouched on the stars to watch what people were doing. Very little of it pleased her.

Warriors in those days wandered the world in bands, armed with weapons of steel and hearts of iron. Some of these killers had challenged even the demons, or so they said, and claimed to have won contests against giants, worms, and other monsters. But most of these leaders and their followers attacked cities and did what they wished with the inhabitants, feasting on whatever stores people had managed to set aside, then moving on, taking women and horses with them and sometimes cattle, whatever was useful.

Jutum was one of these warlords. He was powerful, a large man who wore harness of leather and horsehair and bronze. He carried two swords and called himself the man slayer and the blood drinker. Jutum prided himself on his merciless behavior and the contempt in which he held everyone except himself and his followers. These were the Nathgali. They always had roamed. In their stories, they never claimed to have come from anywhere; they were forever a restless people. They were the people whose hearts were sharp and who feared nothing.

Jutum and the Nathgali had taken the city of Coroth early one autumn with the intent of holding it through the winter. Coroth stood at the western reaches of a murky land that one day would be called Salasal. The city was, in fact, quite large, with many streets, tall buildings of brick and stone, and fountains and gardens. It was home to workers who were experts in many endeavors, from tanning and horse breeding to planting and farming. The strong women and men of the city had done their best to defend themselves against the Nathgali; they had weapons and were skilled in their use. Still, the Nathgali slew them. The bodies of the dead Corothans were nailed to posts set in the fields outside the walls to be eaten by animals and demons. The remaining women were kept alive and distributed by Jutum to his best fighters as prizes. Children, too, were spared, for they could be used for labor, as well as the old people, who were useful as servants.

The dying were still weeping and the dead being moved beyond the walls when Alia, the first priestess of the temple of Yasdis, the patron of Coroth, confronted Jutum and demanded that he and his followers leave the city. She was a young woman, Alia, and strong willed—slender, dark haired, and with something of the temper of her goddess. She announced that Yasdis had sent a message: The goddess would have revenge upon the Nathgali for hurting Coroth. In response, Jutum murdered all of the priestesses and temple servants, immediately cutting them down. He forced Alia to crawl naked in their blood, then raped her as women from his camp held her, despite her struggles. The first priestess, broken and dying, was carted out to the fields and dropped into the snow.

Great piles of corpses were all around, and soon dogs came, and crows, to tussle over the meat. Many of the Corothans left for dead were still alive and awake; they screamed as the dogs pulled at them, growling and dragging at them. Alia managed to avoid the dogs and crawled away in the snow. She tried to reach some trees a short distance away. She tore bloody clothes from the dead and wrapped them around her. Moving was painful because Jutum had broken some of her bones, and her face was so swollen that she could not see well.

As night came down, the first priestess saw figures moving toward her from the trees and assumed that they were the ghosts of the dead or, more likely, Nathgali searching the bodies for jewelry and money. Alia, afraid, stopped moving and lay where she was. The figures reached her, but she did not hear what they said.

Weeks passed. The people of Coroth, trapped, remained indoors, keeping by their fires and finding nourishment however they could. Rumors began that Yasdis, angered by the invaders, had kept Alia, her priestess, alive, no one knew where. Perhaps the goddess, who was slow to answer prayers, had been roused by the outrage of the Nathgali attack. Who could say? People met to share food, and whispers were passed as bowls traded hands. Occasionally, screams cut the snowy air—a woman or an old man or perhaps a child being cut to pieces for entertainment or as punishment. When this happened, the whisperers agreed: It is the goddess screaming. It is Yasdis, outraged, shrieking among the cold stars.

Soon we will hear the Nathgali screaming.

The deep of winter settled on the city. Everything was held within silence and ice and was still. Fires burned continuously in pit and hearth, but even the flames moved slowly, as though affected by the cold.

As was his method when wintering in a conquered city, Jutum had ordered that patrols be maintained day and night. His riders, therefore, toughened by life outdoors and familiar with the harsh cold of stony valleys and high mountains, did as they were told.

For several nights, the patrols were uneventful. The riders, heavily dressed in animal skins, their faces wrapped against the stinging wind, returned to their commanders to report that the Corothans cowered in their homes as conquered women and children should.

Soon, however, came the night when two riders failed to return to their stations at the stables in the northwest of the city. Men who had kept themselves warm until that time of the night went out to investigate and returned with word that the two riders had been found in pieces. Arms, legs, torsos—these had been severed by what could have been edges of steel or perhaps talons or claws.

Only parts remained, insufficient even to reconstruct one whole man from what was left of two. Surely dogs had made off with the remainder, dogs or wolves or the Corothans who hoped to frighten their masters by this surprising display.

Jutum retaliated by ordering twenty of the city taken at random and cut into pieces. The attacks stopped for two nights, then resumed for three nights in a row. One rider, a woman who answered the midnight screams so quickly that she glimpsed the attacker, reported that she had seen a shadow with a hunched back skitter away in the snow, then leap onto a rooftop. It was black, this thing, and in nighttime cold so deep that nothing wished to move, not even trained horses, the shadow had easily made the jump onto the top of the building, squealed, and disappeared.

Thereafter, attacks on the patrols ceased.

But dreams began. More than dreams. And only for the Nathgali.

Soon after entering Coroth, Jutum and those closest to him had taken residence in the palace. These were his leaders in the field, women of his camp, and Abrul, his right-hand man. Abrul was a young Jutum—tall and quick eyed and, like his master, with no laughter in him. Abrul had saved Jutum from what would have been a fatal swordstrike one afternoon when the fighting was close; in return, the man killer had awarded Abrul the status of staying at his side, and he was grooming the young man in the ways of leadership. Abrul was an excellent horseman and good with his weapons, and he was intelligent.

Tonight, in the throne room, with its roaring fire pits and decorated walls, Jutum slouched in the stone chair that had belonged to Asjur, the king whose skeleton now lay in pieces in the snow outside the city. Jutum's boots dirtied the silks of the throne. His warriors spilled wine and dropped food onto rich tapestries and cloth of gold. As the men and women drank wine and beer and demanded more, it was brought to them by old men and women who held their faces low but watched everything.

For sport this evening, Jutum ordered six of his bold fighters to challenge each other to duels. These men and women did so, attacking each other in pairs, fighting with knives and swords. Blade struck blade. Horsehide boots scuffed the floor. The fighters bent and leaned backward and forward and ducked their heads until one of the men, cut across the belly, lost his bowels and tripped into a fire pit. He screamed, with his long hair and beard on fire and his insides pushing out to be cooked on the coals. Although Jutum showed no smile, the room around him moved with laughter. Finally, the dying man, with no face remaining and the flesh on him hissing, was dragged from the fire and removed outside.

"What a pig!" one of the warriors said. "Did you hear him scream? He cries like a baby! We'll see how he cries in Hell!"

Further laughter moved around the room.

But Jutum was not pleased. He stood to leave the throne hall and nodded to Abrul to come with him. They took up heavy animal skins and strode out as men and women saluted them with raised cups.

At the end of a long hallway within the palace, past finely carved stone animals set on pedestals and beneath painted walls showing sunlit fields and animals running free, Jutum entered the room that his seers and omen readers used. The room was not large, and most of its space was occupied by stone shelves and long wooden tables. One window high up showed the night sky. Blood and oil were everywhere—on the stones of the floor, on the shelves and tables. There were pieces of bodies, both animal and human, and shards of bone that the seers cast to determine messages from watching spirits. Were there fewer bones here, to the north, meaning famine? Or did many fall to the south, meaning that fat cattle and many women and slaves were soon to be had?

Sodum, the man killer's chief reader, bowed as Jutum came in, followed by Abrul. Sodum was dressed in what the mountain people wore—deerskin and wolfskin, leather boots, a furred cape. Bones and lengths of painted leather were knotted in his hair and beard and eyebrows. A copper disk bound with a band to his forehead was his additional eye, used to see into the invisible worlds when he chanted and entered a trance.

But he would not breathe smoke or chew leaves and chant tonight. Jutum surveyed the room and saw only Sodum. He asked, "Where is Tobuth?"

He meant the old woman whom Jutum had known since his boyhood. She was perhaps Sodum's superior in understanding signs and looking into the future, and her word was perfect to Jutum.

Sodum bowed. "She left earlier. I was coming to tell you."

"Where did she go?"

"She refused to say. And she has guarded herself with a spell so that I may not follow her with my sight."

"She will die soon outside. Did she so greatly fear what she saw that she would welcome such a death?"

Sodum averted his gaze from his master's.

Abrul ordered him, "Answer your lord!"

Jutum cautioned him with a raised hand and said to Sodum, "Tell me what she saw. If she knows, you know."

"Lord Jutum, you feed me and keep me warm so that I may speak the truth to you. Here is the truth: We have angered the power that guards this city, and she means to hurt us for it. We should go. Leave this city to its people and their goddess."

"Is this why Tobuth went?"

"It is."

Jutum frowned. "My women are having dreams. I, too, am having dreams. Is it because of this goddess?"

"Lord Jutum, the dead we slaughtered have petitioned her to help in fighting us. I, too, have had these dreams for several nights. The people of this city made a pact long ago with their dark goddess. They worship no other gods. In return, they have never been conquered. Others have tried; all failed. We have angered this goddess. She who creates, also destroys. We should leave this place."

"Would you walk out into the night as Tobuth did?"

Sodum said nothing.

Abrul ordered the old reader, "Answer Lord Jutum!"

Sodum looked Jutum in the eyes. "I will die, either here, with you, or out in the cold, with Tobuth. Such a choice is no choice."

Jutum nodded but told him, "We will not die. Let the goddess send monsters and dreams. I, too, am a monster. You have heard me say many times that I mean to reach the lands of the sun in the east. When I buried my sons and daughters, I promised them that we would reach those lands. There is no snow there. No mountains. There is another ocean, and there is only the sun. I will see those lands. We will live in those lands."

Sodum told him, "We will not."

Jutum made a face but did not strike his reader. He turned to leave the room. Abrul followed him. Before going out, Jutum said to the old man, "I will be here again in the morning. Have a better answer for me."

Sodum bowed.

Jutum awakened to the sound of knives or claws skittering on the stone floor of his bedchamber. He kept his eyes open but sat up cautiously, holding a fist in front of his face in case a knife or claw should strike at him or a noose drop around his head. The skittering sound came again, this time from a dark corner, and then, after a moment's pause, from the opposite side of the room.

As he began to see in the darkness, Jutum looked at the two women sleeping on either side of him. He pushed one of them to awaken her. When she did not move, he grabbed her by the hair. He felt blood jump from her neck onto his face.

Jutum called out, "Who is here?"

There was soft laughter from the darkness at the end of his bed. "Both are dead, and it was done while you slept. You are next, murderer."

A woman's voice. Jutum recognized it as the priestess Alia, whom he had raped and who had been left for dead months ago.

He ordered her to light a torch so that he could see, but she refused. He asked Alia what weapons did she have that made such sounds as those that had awakened him, and she answered him, "The weapon is yours and mine. It is your gift from Yasdis, and you'll see it soon enough."

In fury, Jutum rolled over the corpse of the second woman and dropped to the floor. He drew a knife from his belt and whipped it around him in a circle, so that whatever was near would catch on the blade. There was only darkness.

He struck flint and stone on a low table near the skins on which he slept so that flame caught in an oil lamp. Described in the circle of bright light, Alia, dressed in rags and furs, stood awkwardly on a broken leg that had only begun to heal and with red scars still dark on her face.

Crouched beside her on the floor was the thing that had skittered in the darkness, killed Jutum's women, and awakened Jutum from his dreams. It lifted itself to its height and was no taller than Alia's waist. It was dark green, black-green, and its skin appeared to be damp, like that of an amphibian that has just pulled itself onto the mud. Its eyes were large and yellow. Its hands and feet were no more than fleshy balls with claws pushing out, like knives. When it leaned forward to rest its upper body on its fists, the thing's back was hunched; it was no more than an animal crouching. When it opened its mouth, there was more sharpness—teeth as threatening as the claws on its hands and feet.

Jutum said, "So you and your goddess have created a monster."

Alia told him, "You and I have created this thing. This is your child. You monstered me, and here is the result. It has grown quickly inside me, like my hatred for you and your people. And now it will kill you."

Faster than Jutum could anticipate, the squealing creature was in the air and on his throat. With his right hand, which held his knife, Jutum stabbed the thing. It continued to squeal but held on. With his left hand, the war chief caught hold of the squirming monster as well as he could and pushed it away from his throat.

Already he was bleeding, and he coughed blood. Jutum held the thing away from him. It wrapped its arms and legs around his forearm like some forest creature caught on a tree limb, and it did its best to bite into Jutum's tough muscles.

Jutum pushed it into the flame of the oil lamp. It squealed more loudly and released him, then jumped into the shadows.

In the hall outside, fists hit loudly on the door of the bed chamber.

"Lord Jutum! Lord Jutum!"

The man killer yelled for his night guards to come in.

As the door opened, Alia leapt away and held out her arms, calling the creature to her.

Jutum moved for it. Once more the creature sprang into the air, and Jutum struck at it again with his knife, missing it.

But as it came into Alia's arms, Jutum yelled to his warriors, "Kill them!"

Moving lengths of steel found Alia's neck and back, and shuddering parts of her dropped to the floor. The creature shrieked as it, too, fell. Then it moved at one of the guards. The guard fell backward with the thing on his throat, and more blood spun into the air. The Nathgal kicked with his feet, but now his blood was everywhere.

Jutum told the other guard to retreat into the hallway. Then he smashed the oil lamp onto the floor and followed. Jutum took down a torch from the wall, cast it into the bedroom, and pulled the heavy door closed as flames grew in every direction, fed by the oil.

Abrul arrived, weapons in hand, and stared at Jutum's bleeding throat.

The man killer yelled at him, "Never open that door!" Then he moved down the hall to see after his wounds.

Abrul, panting heavily, looked at the surviving guard, who said, "A monster. Something from the witch we killed last fall. A curse from their goddess."

****

Before dawn, Jutum, not having slept and with the wounds in his neck still seeping, went to speak with Sodum. But the reader was not in his room, only a palace servant, an old woman.

Jutum demanded of her, "Where is my reader?"

"Gone. Last night. He left this." She indicated Sodum's copper disk, his additional eye, which lay on a table top.

Jutum walked to the table, looked at the disk, but did not touch it. He turned to face Abrul and two more of his warriors, who had come with him.

Abrul asked the old woman, "Do you know where he is?"

"With us. He asked if our goddess would accept him. We had no answer for him. But he is alive."

"Where?"

"Hidden from you."

Abrul drew his sword and walked toward her.

The old woman did not draw back. "Do you think I care?" she asked Abrul. "You murdered my son and my husband and raped my daughter. Let me show you where to cut."

Abrul frowned but did not lift his sword. He looked at Jutum.

The man killer motioned for Abrul and the others to leave, and he followed them out.

The wounds in Jutum's neck continued to bleed. He ordered to him those who had tended the fallen in the field. Some of these surgeons had saved damaged fighters by the way they bound wounds or treated them with herbs, but the nature of the man killer's wounds made them uneasy.

"Why did the thing not kill you?" asked one of these healers. "It savaged your night guard."

The question was apt. The monster had been quick. Had it meant to behead Jutum, it might have done so before the war chief could have saved himself. Perhaps the goddess wanted Jutum not to die immediately but to suffer as he had made the first priestess suffer.

The surgeons who came to him were also perplexed by other aspects of their lord's condition. As the wound continued to seep water and blood, the skin around it began to darken. Jutum also developed a fever, surely the first sign that likely he would die.

He complained that light hurt his eyes, even the dim light in the small room, which had but one window. Outside, all was gray; clouds hung over the city; snow was falling; a wind had come. There was little light. Still, Jutum complained of his eyes.

When, in anger and frustration, he tried to rise from his bed and stand, his legs did not support him. He dropped awkwardly to his knees, his legs bending under him as though they were something foreign to his body. In rage, Jutum ordered everyone to leave him. All did so. The man killer lay on the floor of the small room where he had fallen, breathing in gasps, turning his face from the light, fighting his sickness as well as he could.

Under Abrul's direction, patrols were reinstated, and for the rest of the cold day, as snow fell, warriors moved through the quiet streets. The Corothans did not stir. It seemed that they, like the Nathgali, were awaiting a sign regarding what to do next. Surely, they had heard rumors of the attack on Jutum. Is that why they remained indoors?

None of the Nathgali questioned Abrul's taking on the mantle of leadership while Jutum was ill. He was granted this respect in deference to his relationship with the man killer. Let us see what the young man can do, agreed the older wolves, knowing that they were free at any time to challenge Abrul and drag him down. Abrul had spent many late nights learning from the war chief; he therefore had adequate, if vicarious, experience on which to depend. In addition, none of the Nathgali coveted either Jutum's present situation or Abrul's. Leadership sometimes falls, not on the one who steps forward to confront circumstances, but on the one who stands still while all others back away.

Abrul himself rode the streets on patrol. As he completed his circuit, early one evening, he stabled his horse in what had been business offices behind the temple of Yasdis. As he left the stables and walked past the temple, Abrul saw that its doors were ajar, great wooden doors decorated with bronze insets and set in stone jambs. He moved up the steps leading to the doors and entered.

There was little light, only what came through the opening behind him and from the broken windows high up. No lamps; no torches. Blown in through the open doors, drifts of snow covered the stones of the floor. Abrul stared at tall columns surrounding a circular altar in the middle of the wide room. On all sides stood pedestals supporting painted statues of the goddess as well as of animals, trees, serpents, birds. Some of the stonework was delicate and quite beautiful. On other pedestals, however, were carvings of monstrous things—creatures part bird and part man, combinations of serpent, horse, and spider, and misshapen ogres and demons. Abrul leaned forward, intrigued by these representations of horror.

"These, too, are the goddess."

The voice came from a corner of the room. An old man sitting in the shadows.

Abrul was unnerved that he had been taken by surprise. He had not sensed anyone here. He looked carefully into the darkness. He said, "Come out here where I can see you," and dropped his right hand to his sword pommel.

The old man moved forward. His beard was ragged, and he supported himself on a walking stick, something he had fashioned himself from part of a tree. He wore a robe and a vest and sandals. No doubt he stayed in here to keep warm. "I am no one," he told Abrul. "I'm not worth the effort of your sword. You have nothing to fear from me."

"Don't I?"

"I am in here, barbarian, because, before you killers arrived, I considered this temple my home. I loved this place. Why were you looking at that relic?"

Abrul did not answer him.

"Perhaps because of what has happened to your master?"

Abrul told the old man, "If you anger me, I will sword you for it. You know our ways by now."

"I know your ways, but I think you are better than that. I've watched you when you ride. I've seen how others act around you. I know that you are Jutum's son, or his adopted son."

"Not his son, but he teaches me. I am learning from him."

"Then he sees in you what I see. I think you are better than the people you ride with. I am a good judge of individuals. It is a gift I have."

"You're a very talkative old man. Talk to me about the monster that attacked Jutum."

"What do you need to know? By the grace of the goddess, Alia lived after your lord raped her, and the seed in her quickened and came to fruit."

"Jutum has had many sons and daughters. He never before sired a monster."

"He never before angered our goddess. We worship her, young man, not because she is one thing above others, like most gods, but because she is many things in one. She is existence itself. We know that beneath the surface of a calm lake are poisonous snakes. We admit that hidden within a beautiful sky are storms, and that beneath the green field there waits an earthquake. We understand that people crave order and purpose, yet life itself mocks those desires. This should not blind us to the beauty of life, but beauty and order should not blind us to the monsters within each of us. When beauty is provoked, monsters emerge. It is true of nature, and of life, and of us. This may be your first appreciation of that fact."

"Why are you talking to me?"

"Because I think you are a leader. I feel that you should leave our city and take with you whoever will follow you. It would be better for you and better for us. Otherwise, more horrors will be born."

"How can you live as you do, in this city, with such demons?"

"How can you live as *you* do and not realize that such demons are everywhere? They wait only for you to recognize them or provoke them. Why do you ride with your lord?"

"Because I am free to do it. I live where I wish. I follow the moon and the sun. I hunt and fish, and I watch the wind move in the trees. I kill when I need to, and I take what I need. I owe Jutum a great deal."

"Your life?"

More snow blew into the cold temple. The snow swirled on the floor, free in the manner of all snow. Abrul watched it as though the snow were as alive as wind moving through the trees.

He said to the old man, "When I was young, we were attacked by people from over the hill, from the other side of the forest where we lived. I was a boy. They left us for dead, but a few of us survived. It was winter, and there was no food. My mother was weak and sick, and only my father and I remained. Although my father tried to keep her alive, my mother died. We had no food. We made a soup and put pieces of my mother into it, and that kept us alive."

The old man told him, "You are a strong man. I have never been that hungry for anything."

"Altars and prayers did not keep me alive. This kept me alive." Abrul held out his arm and made a fist. "I will kill everyone in the world before I eat such soup again."

The old man said, "I understand. Perhaps I was wrong in speaking to you. But you have awakened Yasdis, and she has begun to weave her net of sorrowful consequences. The gods do not often move from their thrones or speak to us, but when they do, they damage us. I would rather have the gods sleep than save me from what can happen in life because they know no mercy."

"Do not threaten me."

"I would not dare to." The old man stopped at the sound of horses' hooves on the steps outside.

The great doors were pushed inward by a small company of armed men and women covered in snow and ice. The foremost of them yelled to Abrul, "Lord Jutum!"

Abrul asked him, "What of him?"

"The monster has returned!"

"It was burned to death. I saw it!" Abrul pulled his sword out and turned to the old man.

But he was gone. Into the shadows of the temple, or into the wind and snow.

"Lord Abrul!"

"Yes," he said, and, "Go, go," as he sheathed his sword while following them out.

"Jutum is still in that room. He has stayed there all day," one of the men told Abrul as they all came down the hallway.

Another said, as they approached the barred door, "If he came out, we did not hear him. We feared that he must have died. But then we heard him fighting the same monster."

"How could it be the same one?" Abrul asked. He was thinking of whatever had attacked the patrols nights earlier. There was more than one monster in this city.

He reached the door and waited, listening. He and the warriors there heard the squealing and the clicking of talons.

Abrul drew in a steady breath, then took down a torch from the wall. He held it in his left hand and, with his right, drew out his sword. "Open the door," he ordered, "but slowly."

Two men did so. They pushed free the iron bolt that held it closed. Staying well back for safety's sake, they pulled on iron rings stapled to the door.

The squealing grew louder.

Abrul held the torch in front of him to warn the creature back as well as to see inside the room. The squealing rose to a high pitch, and Abrul took a step forward.

He saw it. Shining skin. Mouth of sharp teeth. Hunched back. Yellow eyes. Wounds on the neck.

"Close the door!"

The thing jumped forward.

"Close the door!"

The two men shoved with all of their strength. Abrul dropped his torch and his sword and leaned in to help them. Together, they pushed the door closed even as one of the creature's hands reached around the edge and its claws scraped splinters from the wood. Finally, Abrul threw the bolt. The monster squealed and clawed on the other side of the door.

Abrul retrieved his sword and stared at the weapon as though marveling at it. The steel trembled in his hands. "It is Jutum."

"Lord Jutum?"

"Another trick of their goddess." He looked into the faces before him in the hall.

Behind him, Lord Jutum squealed loudly and clicked his talons on the floor.

Abrul sat all evening, alone, in the room he had taken for himself in the palace. He looked out the window as the snow fell and as the sky darkened.

Outside his door, men and women waited patiently, not intruding on his thoughts.

He considered what the old man in the temple had said to him. *You have awakened Yasdis. I would rather have the gods sleep than save me from what can happen in life because they know no mercy. You should leave our city.*

He thought about the warning Sodum had given Jutum. *They have never been conquered.*

How many before Jutum had come to this city to take it? How many of them had suffered like Jutum because of their angry goddess?

When beauty is provoked, monsters emerge.

This was not why Abrul had fought to live after his family had been killed and he had eaten parts of his own mother to survive. This was not why he had chosen to follow Jutum and the Nathgali.

You have awakened Yasdis, and she has begun to weave her net of sorrowful consequences.

This was not why Abrul had fought to live.

He made his decision and announced it to those waiting in the hall. There were other cities to be taken, and although deep winter was on the land, it was good to remember that they had fought harsh winters previously. Mere cold and ice could not conquer the Nathgali.

Then Abrul took to his bed and tried to rest. He did not sleep much, however; he thought he heard the squealing of Jutum from the other end of the palace.

In the morning, he and others who had decided to go with him retrieved their horses and mounted them. They said nothing to the Corothans who looked out their windows, watching as the Nathgali rode past. In the city square, in the cold morning, Abrul and the others then waited. By ones and twos and in small groups, Nathgali, even the roughest of them, rode into the square and took rude formation behind Abrul.

Meanwhile, Corothans came into the square, at first a few but then groups of them. Abrul saw the old man from the temple and, beside him, Sodum, dressed now like a Corothan.

They have never been conquered.

Behind them both were monsters such as Jutum had become. Not the baby, which Jutum had killed, but grown men, presumably, with shining dark skin, yellow eyes, mouths of sharp teeth.

Others have tried; all failed.

Abrul ordered the gate of the city pulled open, then said loudly to the old man from the temple, "What will you do with him?" Meaning Jutum. "Kill him?"

"There is no need for that. We have ways of keeping them useful."

Abrul lifted a hand, reined his horse about, and walked it through the open city gate, into winter. The Nathgali followed him.

Come, Death

What is the course of the life
Of mortal men on the earth?—
Most men eddy about
Here and there—eat and drink,
Chatter and love and hate,
Gather and squander, are raised
Aloft, are hurl'd in the dust,
Striving blindly, achieving
Nothing; and then they die—
Perish;—and no one asks
Who or what they have been,
More than he asks what waves,
In the moonlit solitudes mild
Of the midmost Ocean, have swell'd,
Foam'd for a moment, and gone.

—Matthew Arnold, "Rugby Chapel"

On a dying autumn day, a stranger approached the open gate of a silent town, Kurszagad. Clad in worn black garments and casting his long shadow before him—though it was a sunless afternoon—the stranger passed by a great open pit in the earth outside Kurszagad's walls. The pit was smoking, and it sent up a charnal stench sufficient to rival the fumes of the caverns of the underworld. The pit was piled with dead bodies, eaten away and burnt away, lying in contorted postures, crushed all together, with hot red patches here and there still smoking. The stranger knew what the pit portended. He entered through the open gates of the city and walked a deserted street.

The smell of death was here. Corpses were everywhere, frozen in postures of agony. The cool wind carried their smell as if it were temple incense. All was silent, save for the dark stranger's bootsteps, which carried. The bodies of the dead clogged stilled fountains, leaned out windows, perched on rooftops. All were corroded as if months old, as if already eaten by the worm. And there was no sunlight anywhere to the stranger's eyes, but only a dismal mist—the miasma of Hell's furnaces—which held as a breathless fog among the desolate buildings and monuments.

The stranger tasted the air. It was plague and pestilence, surely—but also something more within that poison. It prowled on his face, in his hair, rested on his skin—

The stranger came on. Here and there shadows of scavengers threw themselves across the stranger's farther path. He turned a corner and looked upon a wide streetway, rubbed his dirty long hair back out of his eyes, moved his shoulders under his coarse shirt. He saw a thin dog with the boils of disease on its hide dragging a lean corpse after itself into an alley. The cur eyed the stranger and growled, showing red gums and dirty teeth; it snarled a whimper. Foam dripped from its jaws, and it hurried to drag the corpse into the alley's diseased shadows. It disappeared, and its bundle, and disturbed mist followed after them.

The man glanced at the low sky. The sun was a smear behind the heavy clouds. They were dry clouds; no hint of rain, no promise of lightning; clouds dried of life as though the product of Kurszagad dissolving from existence.

There was a noise from above; the stranger looked. A corpse slid over the edge of a roof, hesitated a moment in space, slammed upon the dark street stones. A desiccated arm came free and settled to rest in the middle of the street.

The stranger came to a hostel and peered inside through its sagging door. Darkness and silence—and perhaps a meal, as well, for even he could not survive endlessly without food of some kind. He walked into the hostel, pushing the door open, and loose strands of mist moved away from him. The public room was large, with strong tables and chairs about, and the signs of combat—weapons, many with blood on them, scattered or driven into the floor, and corpses, also with weapons driven into them.

Behind the bar all the wine and beer casks had been emptied or smashed. A cat lay curled upon itself on a table in a corner; it raised its head when it sensed the intruder, moved its ears, showed crusted eyes, returned to dying. The stranger went toward a farther door, looked in, entered.

It was little more than a closet. A single candle burned in the mist, standing in its own drippings on a chair. It hollowly lighted a woman, young but aged with disease's decay, sitting on the edge of a rough straw bed in a farther corner. She was eyeing a bundle wrapped under the covers; her hands were clasped in her lap; sweat drooled down her face, streaking grime. She lifted her head as the stranger crossed the room and leaned against the wall beside her. Weakly, she lifted an object in her lap, a weapon, an old knife with a beautifully decorated hilt.

She whispered to the stranger, "I can still kill."

The dark man told her, "You are all dead of the plague, lady. Why did you not leave?"

She looked at the bundle on the bed. "My child," she said, and lowered her weapon.

"There was fighting here," the stranger said to her. "Some of those corpses are soldiers. This was not just the plague."

She waited, gathering strength, before telling him, "A sorcerer and his army came."

He told her, "I saw them farther back on the road. Three days ago. They are all dead now, too."

"Even the sorcerer? He was strong."

"I killed him."

She did not seem to understand. "You can do that?"

"Yes."

"He did not kill you? Why are you not dead, too?"

"I cannot die."

It was more than she could settle on in that moment. She placed the old knife aside and reached with thin hands to show him the bundle beneath the blankets: her child. A boy, maybe eight years old, sallow and wan, its face gray and damp, the mottling marks of death already clustered on its features, lumped upon its naked arms and chest.

She asked him, "Are you Ikribu, then? Are you Death? Come to take us?"

"I'm a man."

"Then how did you kill the sorcerer if you are a man?"

"I touched him and turned his power back upon himself. I did the same with his soldiers. They passed the death among themselves as they fell upon each other in their fear."

She returned her attention to her child; it barely breathed, its life sagged in its thin chest. "He is dying."

"Yes."

"I don't want him to die. "

The stranger could hear the mists outside, moving against the brick walls of the hostel, whispering in a voice.

"Why do the gods do this to people?" asked the woman.

"Let them die?"

"Kill us. Let us die. Allow such evil."

"The gods do not care. It's better that way for us. We have only ourselves to rely on."

"But the gods do not die."

"It is their curse. The gods are doomed to live forever."

"I don't want him to live forever," she said. "I want only for him to see his manhood. It is good to be young and strong, if only for a while."

He said to her, "I'm thirsty. Is there any water here?"

"It's poisoned, too."

"Not for me."

She didn't answer. He looked around the room and saw a bucket behind the door with a gourd cup in it. He filled the gourd and drank down thirstily. He returned to the bedside with the water and splashed a palmful of it onto the boy's forehead to cool him.

The woman sat up when he did it and gently pushed his hand away and caressed her son's forehead herself.

"My name is Akram," the stranger told her.

She seemed to recognize it. "I have heard of you. Yes. You are the Cursed One. A witch cursed you." She said again, "We have heard of you."

Outside the window, its shutters gone, dusk deepened, and the room darkened. The mist moved more strongly now as if alive in its own way. The woman heard the mist as though it crawled on feet or paws. Now it howled savagely. She felt it was the touch of Death upon her.

"What are the gods doing to me?" she asked.

"This is not the gods."

"It is you."

"Yes."

"Then kill me now. I am suffering. If you can do magic, take my life and give it to my boy. I want him to live."

The woman was seized with a wild sobbing fit. She collapsed and shivered, kicked at the air, pulled at her hair and moaned. She grabbed a length of her hair and stuffed it into her mouth to stop her whimpering, but she choked and coughed it out. She pounded at her head as if it ached intolerably.

The taper on the chair expired in a thin trail of smoke.

Akram walked into the front room. He went behind the bar and searched for food. He found three withered apples in a basket shoved onto a shelf. He took them and returned to the woman.

She had fallen still. Akram dropped to his knees beside her. He handed her an apple.

"Here. Eat."

"Let me die."

"You will die in time. Now eat this."

She was too weak to lift it to her mouth.

Akram set the other apples aside and held this one between his palms, twisted his hands, and broke the apple in half. The fruit was no longer withered; it was as fresh as if just taken from the branch. He snapped away enough for one bite and pressed it to the woman's lips.

She took it into her mouth.

He did the same with the boy, pressing a bit of apple to the boy's lips.

He did not move much, could not, but he took the apple between his teeth and chewed.

Akram gave them time to recover. He rose and walked into the public room, went to the door and looked out.

Night. Darkness. Clouds and mist. He looked up. The moon and stars might never have existed; the world might no longer be, out there.

He heard noise behind him and turned.

The woman, still pale, stood at the entrance to the closet, holding her son's hand. He stood beside her and stared at Akram.

She said, "I don't understand."

He told her, "I have taken so many lives into me, I am able to give life back. That, too, is my curse."

"The witch did that?"

"Yes. I can kill. All men can kill. And all men die. I can't die."

"But you can give life."

"I am a mystery to myself, woman. I do these things because I no longer know who I am. What can I do? What can I not do? I want to be done with it."

"Yet you saved us from death."

"Only for a time. Live out your lives as I cannot."

"What others have you saved?"

"None. I am not here to save lives. I search for the secret to end my own life. I want to return to Hell, where the witch made me what I am. I will find it."

"I have never heard of such a thing."

"No one has. Now leave this place."

"We will."

He walked to them, touched the woman's head and the boy's head.

"I have killed so many," he told them. "Let me do this for you."

The boy told him, "What shall I do now? I was ready for death."

"Always remain ready for death. But while you wait, live as brightly as you can."

"I will try."

When they left the hostel, the woman and her boy walked with Akram in one direction, farther on, away from where he had defeated the sorcerer's army, until they came to a fork in the road. There, the woman and the boy turned one way. Akram took the other way.

Soon enough, the woman and her son, tired, curled up beneath a large tree and slept until dawn, when they awoke refreshed.

Akram continued down the other road all through the night until the mists of the dead village were behind him and he could see the moon, the old familiar moon, and stars, alive once more—Akram the wanderer, Akram cursed by the witch of Khom, a mystery even to himself, Akram undying.

The Return to Hell

Gray hells, or hells aglow with hot and scarlet flowers;
White hells of light and clamor; hells the abomination
Of breathless, deep, sepulchral desolation
Oppresses ever—I have known them all, through hours
Tedious as dead eternity; where timeless powers,
Leagued in malign, omnipotent persuasion—
Wearing the guise of love, despair and aspiration,
For ever drove through ashen fields and burning bowers
My soul that found no sanctuary....

—Clark Ashton Smith, "Inferno"

"My lord? Once more I say, let me go with you."

This was the woman, Tharis, speaking to him as Akram, in his armor, his back to her, stood before his open tent and looked upon the field before him. Hundreds more tents were on that plain, with campfires alight and sentries on watch, all beneath a sky still star-filled, but with the purple of the night just now surrendering to the early pink and white of sunup.

Tharis had been his bedmate these past three years—he, the commander of this army of lost men and women, brigands, killers, the disowned, all of them outside the law. She'd known when she came to him that he was no better than those he led, but Akram had a whispered history that none in the world could challenge: he was a demon in human guise, a sorcerer, as able a fighter as the goddess of war and as quick of temper, and unable to be killed.

Unable to die.

Fighters followed him for that reason, certain that his sorcery would protect them as it did him when they took to the field or scaled walls and battlements or swung from the shrouds of sailing ships to plunder men and women as desperate as themselves. He was very old, the same age as many mountains, and as durable and unchanging as the rocks of those mountains, yet he appeared as young as anyone in the prime of years.

Akram turned to look at Tharis. A hint of dawn struck him from behind, so that she, no stranger to reading signs from the invisible world, saw that this large, dark-haired, dark-bearded warrior was outlined now with an aureole of brightness, no doubt an omen.

He asked her, "Where did you find that?"

She was holding a knife with a long blade; she had taken it from its scabbard, which lay on the carpet before her. The scabbard was a thing of beauty, sewn of good leather and decorated with jewels in the design of the moon and its stars. She stood proudly as she faced him. As tall as she was, and slender, and as naked as an animal or bird, she was fully aware that she was strong, her muscles good and practiced. Akram enjoyed wrestling with her.

Tharis told him, "A woman in camp gave it to me. She is a sorceress."

"Is she?"

"I know this knife cannot kill you, but it is powerful magic. It could hurt you. Your magic is strong, but so is this weapon. She used it against demons." She held it out at arm's length, as though warding off some moving spirit or active vampire, things up from the hells or free of their graves.

"If such as that could kill me, don't you think I'd have used it already on myself?" He went to her, stood plainly before her. "Why are you so eager to become a monster?"

"So that I can be my own master and answer to no one," she told him. "Why else be in the world? To know the things that you know. I'm not a fool. Our appetites make us what we are, do they not, my lord? We are swallowed by our own desires. I am young, but I have learned that much. I studied in Sorkendum for a year before joining this camp."

"You among the wise of Sorkendum?"

Sorkendum was the home of the Imnu Sher, the great House of Thought, a place of philosophers and scientists. Kings went there, heads bowed, to learn at the seat of women and men as learned as the kings were powerful.

"I hid in the shadows," Tharis said. "I cleaned their hallways and rooms and latrines. I tended them when they were sick. And I listened and learned. This is how I came to know of you."

"And what do they know of me?"

"One old man said that he knew you three generations ago."

"What is his name?"

She told him.

Akram shook his head. "I do not remember him. How many such have the same name? How many such have I met in this cursed life?"

"More than the stars, he said."

"More than the stars, yes."

"I dreamed recently that you are leading this army to the gates of Hell to fight the Witch of Khom herself, all this time in Hell, she and the one who did this to you."

Akram's attitude changed. His eyes became darker, as though growing shadows or by their own power diminishing the light around them. "You dreamed this?"

"Tell me I am wrong."

"Did you learn this trick, too, from the sorceress in camp, to read the secrets in souls while we sleep?"

"In Sorkendum."

"You learned much from the shadows."

"As have you, my lord."

"But have you learned not to die in battle?"

"Teach me."

"It cannot be taught," Akram said. "You wish to become undying, like me? To know this curse?"

"I wish to know what you know."

"Tharis...woman...it is more than we can endure." He placed his hands almost gently on her shoulders so that she would look carefully into his deep eyes. "You would be making a mistake. We were not made for this. Wizards and sorcerers learn this at their peril. How many have tried and been brought low like me?"

"How many have been successful?"

"All of them thought they were. And all now are haunted, as I am. Or dead at last by some sorcery or other. Tharis, here is what I have learned. Seek wisdom from the earth. It is our home. We are creatures of the earth. Turn to your Mother. Did they not teach you this, too, in Sorkendum?"

"They spoke of it, but there are greater matters to be revealed and learned from spirits."

The warrior shook his head. "No. Heed me. Draw no circles, Tharis; recite no spells; do not learn the tongues of the spirits. They are in their world and we are in ours. And they are strong. Don't you think the gods have kept us separate for good reason, the demons in their orbit and we in ours?"

"They do it to challenge us."

"To keep us safe," Akram said.

"You have fought demons, and you remain safe."

"So you surmise. Am I not cursed? Why are the demons so eager to come to us in our human orbit? Why do they not remain in their shadow world beneath us? Did they speak of that in Sorkendum?"

"No."

"And for good reason. You wish to have knowledge? Here is knowledge. I seek death because I cannot die. The demons seek life because they cannot live. Their existence leaves them ever hungry for what we are. They were cast off when the gods made the stars and the world. They are failures. They are eternal, but they know not what they do. We are their food. They seek us out blindly. They take what we have and give us favors in return, but only because they themselves have no wisdom. They are monstrous and stupid. They cannot comprehend the gods or earth or what we can do. They are jealous of us. We are their curse because they wish us only harm, and that is what they dream of, Tharis, of many ways to hurt us in their anger and their blindness. There is no wisdom in the demons, only power and strength and rage. This is what the demons give us."

"That is what I wish to have."

"I never wished to have it. I am cursed. I did not seek this. This is the power I have from the Witch of Khom. I am a mystery to myself, and the stars remain a mystery to me, but I have known Hell and the wisdom of the spirits in the shadows below this life. They have taught me only regret. I would go back if I could to another time and erase my parents from this earth so that I might never have been born. I cannot live in this life, and I cannot live in the next life. I will always be a shadow. But if I can find the witch again, dead as she is, perhaps I can be free of this damnation. No hell is greater than the hell I live in now, alone with all that I have done for longer than you can know."

She watched him. This was indeed truth that he was sharing. How much pain must he be in? Could she herself manage such pain to be, as he was, powerful but alone, subject no longer to the whims of the wicked of the world, slave-dealers and soldiers, princes and kings?

Tharis told him, as the light of the morning brightened the inside of their tent, "You are going to kill all of these who follow you."

"Was that in your dream?"

"Yes."

Akram said, "It is the only path to release for me. Since Nidyis and her sorcerer damned me, I have done one good thing in this dead life, one good thing. I saved the life of a child. And now I regret it because I wonder if I cursed that child, too. It would be a good jest if I had, if the shadows were watching as I saved that child's life, if they have followed that child and cursed it as they cursed me. Do you still wish to know?"

Tharis did not reply.

Akram told her, "Leave the camp now. These men and women go to their deaths in their armor and their strength. Do not be among them. They were born for this. Their lives are shorter than they know, and I hope to end my own at last."

He had promised those who came with him treasure beyond imagining, jewels and gems and all the gold and silver buried by kings and warlords so long ago that the secret of their hiddenness was something that only he, the undying one, remembered. Many of you will die, he had promised these men and women. You will confront strangeness, for these tombs are well-guarded with spells created by ancient schools of mages and witches long since gone. But the sorcery of mages and witches continues unless undone by someone possessed of certain knowledge. Akram claimed that he was such a one. Those who dared this adventure with him would win wealth and perhaps gain magic themselves to live long lives and master powerful skills. Such would be a life worth living.

He had led his army here, to the edge of the world—the vast, stony plains and wide grasslands in the far southern reaches of what had been the nations of Loksim and Terehem and Kostath-Khum before civil wars, conflicts, and plague had desolated them. They had passed through vast forests to reach these plains and, before that, north of the forests, deserts that reached into Csith and Tol and Setom, with their sunken tombs of forgotten kings and queens. Akram and his followers now were nearer to the southern seas than they were the desert, and nearer still to the great sepulchers of creatures from the first days of Time, repositories cut into the earliest mountains and into cliffs that even the strong seas could not wear away. Here were pathways to Hell, entrances to the underworld, open gates to that which humankind had fought against and survived for thousands of years, from the time of Taïsakul, who had rid the world of demons, to

the last of the kings of Kheba and Kustaka, after whom, foretell-
ers said, no further kings would rule or queens sit enthroned.

Here Akram would meet the Witch of Khom who had cursed
him so long ago. It had been an accident. The turning of him into
an ageless, undying man had come from no plan or treachery
but merely an error of the witch's, who had taken him into the
tomb of her dead lover Narathkor, an old soul. Here, the spirit
of Narathkor, glowing with hatred for the witch, had burst upon
them both and caused Akram to die for a moment yet afterward
remain as though alive. Betrayed, in revenge, Akram had tricked
a fool into sacrificing himself to Narthkor's damned spirit, so
that the sorcerer had returned, animating the dead man's corpse,
to slay the witch who had been his lover.

But Akram's curse remained. In those low corridors of stone
blocks and worked images, the warrior had dropped on the
instant when touched by Narathkor's ghost. Frozen and breathless, he had looked into deeps of ageless wonder full of dark stars,
seen all of Time, all of Life in its noise and fleetness—lives upon
lives turning to no purpose, covering the earth, lives teeming
within shadows everywhere, life teeming within the invisible
places that surround the world in rings and dimensions, life
teeming within animals and plants and souls, all lives at once
fighting to survive even in death, which is life of another sort.

An accident, and he had fallen and seen all, so that he was
himself no longer but instead a new man, all the lives he had lived
and all the lives he would live current at once in him. And the
teeming shadows he had seen and the spirits and movements
there, the voices and burning eyes of existences of every kind—
these he now slept with and spoke to, existed beside, so that his
life was no life, only an endless march in a great circle of voices
and darkness, with lesser lives passing before him and around
him like so many fires catching alight in the world and then going
dark, while he alone marched on.

But this past spring he had had a dream. Nidyis the witch had
come to him in a black flame, cloaked in a black mist, her eyes as
black as lost stars. As had he, she had spent the passing centuries
in despair, alone in places of darkness and cold rain and silence
only potentially real, fighting Narathkor's dark magic there as
well as she could with her mind and heart and with the spells
she remembered from when she walked on the earth. At last she
had defeated him; exhausted, Narathkor now was now a thing of
mist with eyes and a mouth but no tongue, no arms, no legs, no

shape to him. He was vapor able to see and understand, but he would never again speak, and he would have no rest for eternity. Such was the power the witch had brought upon him. Nidyis in the dream told Akram to journey southward to the end of the world and gather to him damned souls to sacrifice. Only then would his lives be quieted and the old rage of Narathkor within him solaced, so that sorcerer and witch and fighting man could rest together at last in endless solitude and let the work of life be taken on by others, the noise of it all, the raging and tears. He must come to where sorcery began, where the first evil had been born at the start of Time, and in those dry sepulchers of dead demons and old gods and devils, she would slay him at last, the final death.

His army was awakening, the hard men and women in their leather and bronze and steel, a motley of souls damned before they had been born, as scarred and toughened as wild animals. They came to the campfires and coaxed the flames to get a little warmth, for even the dying and dead appreciate warmth. They ate their coarse bread and their jerky, drank what they had in their bottles and skins and sacks, and began to play, practicing deadly cuts and wild dodges that they trusted to prevail against whatever they were to face.

As Akram watched them, his sight was drawn to movement some distance to his left—a woman, no fighter, but a camp follower dressed in long animal skins and painted with whorls and signs on her face and arms—

No camp follower, but a witch. The witch, for surely this was Nidyis in human form, her dark hair and dark eyes. She smiled as though he must recognize her after so long, and then was gone. Akram saw her move within a crowd of busy fighters and not emerge.

Gone.

"My lord?"

He turned.

Tharis had come outside to stand between him and the tent. She was dressed in whatever protection she had managed to gather on the march here, leather breeks and heavy boots, a thick blouse and a vest knotted with brass rings and even stones sewn into it as sensible protection against the sharp-edged blades that would come at her. At her side was a sword that had belonged to one of the ruffians in the camp. Days earlier, that one had challenged Akram, and Akram had cut him down. The man's sword he had taken; whatever else there was of the corpse's, he left for the mongrels of his army to fight over. Now Tharis had put on this sword, and Akram understood that she had knowledge of using such a weapon, as she did the knives on her belt and those strapped to her boots, as she did the short axe hanging against her other hip.

But these things would not protect her today. Although he regretted saving the life of one child, he would now protect the life of Tharis. She was no one uncertain to him, as that child had been, and was no damned thing, was not one of the foredamned human animals in this camp.

"I cannot let you," he told her.

"You cannot stop me without killing me." She lifted her head proudly. "Do not refuse me, Akram, please. I wish this."

He drew his sword.

She drew hers.

But he did not take a stance, only dropped the point to the ground and circled her, digging a furrow into the earth, while Tharis turned as he did it, taking a middle guard and watching him, ready for him to attack.

He did not. When he had reached where he had begun, he sheathed his sword, waved a hand, said a word.

From that furrow a circle of flames came up, green and sharp. Tharis understood.

"You cannot escape," Akram told her. "You do not have the words or understand the movements to undo this barrier. You will remain here until I die at last. Then the flames will vanish."

"I demand this!" she yelled at him. "Do not leave me to be this way!"

"Live," he told her.

"I *do* wish to live!"

He turned from her, going to where his horse was tethered to one side of the tent. He mounted it and nodded to men watching him; they lifted their horns and let out long notes. Akram pulled on the reins and directed his horse to the front, where the lines were forming, haphazard as they were, his armed riders at the fore and his infantry in the rear.

Tharis watched this, unable to do more.

Akram addressed those who faced him.

"There is our fight!" He pointed behind him, where the stony field ended at the face of a mountain, into which had been cut temples to dead gods, their tombs and monuments. "We are on no grand mission. We are here for ourselves! Do what you have learned to do and gain the riches you have been promised! The things guarding the treasure fear the day. They are creatures of the night. Dawn is what they fear, the sunlight and strong weapons." He drew out his sword and held it high. "Slay whatever comes at you!"

He turned his horse and kneed it so that it galloped down into the great field. The thousand and more behind him bellowed and shouted. As the riders gained ground, those behind ran as quickly as they could, howling and waving axes and spears.

When his army was advancing with all speed, Akram turned sharply to the left and retreated up an incline. As he did, he pronounced a phrase unknown to his army. Immediately the ground gave way beneath them. The thousand and more dropped through the air. There had been no stony field. Akram with his sorcery had created an illusion. Horses shrieked. Men and women screamed, and the noise of them went with them as they fell, metal weapons and armor crashing at the bottom of a deep ravine.

Akram looked until all were gone. He sheathed his sword, glanced at Tharis, then rode his horse beyond the incline, where a path was now apparent that led safely into the ravine. Wings appeared in the sky, the vultures and crows descending.

"Akram!" Tharis called to him loudly, as if doing so could compel him to return and free her. *"Akram!"*

Around her, the shocked camp followers gathered in knots—wounded men, lost women and children, cooks and menders and workers, those who knew how to sew up wounds and use ointments and salves, the men who traded in favors with other men, and any too poor to do more with their lives than follow others on one path or another. They sat and stood now, moaning and weeping, staring at where the army had been and where now there was air, nothing, air.

But Tharis saw the witch who had given her the knife. She came around the side of one of the tents, dressed in her long animal skins and painted with whorls and signs on her face and arms.

The witch gestured, and the green flames that encircled Tharis vanished. Where they had been there was now only blackened, dead grass.

Tharis called out her appreciation, but the woman had turned away and gone behind the tent, not to be seen.

The dead men and women and horses had quickly become ghosts, unclean, barely present, surprised at what had happened but visible to Akram as he walked among them and through them. The ghosts reached out to him to hurt him, hissed at him and tried to bite him, but he was not alarmed. He had lived so long with the ghosts and spirits of the dead that they were no more to him than anything else in the world, leaves or insects or stones, thoughts or desires or hopes.

But his horse was immediately set upon by the ghosts eager for its blood, which became misty in the air as the dying horse shrieked and kicked. The red mist was taken by the ghosts into themselves, as was the blood of all of their own bodies and that of their many horses, so that the crowd of ghosts moved as red wisps or, the glutted ones, more solidly as clots or lacy nets of floating red, men and women and phantom horses.

Akram crossed the wide ravine, ignoring all of that, moving beyond what remained of the animals and fighters, the parts of them scattered, limbs and torsos and the wet insides of them, the stink of it all. He mounted the wide stone stairs of a ruin he had seen in the dream when Nidyis came to him. Fallen columns stretched down the stairs, and parts of collapsed monuments lay on the wide porch leading to the opening of the temple, the stone heads of gods, the carven images of many things.

He sat on a broken column and set his feet on the wide porch to steady himself. He had begun to feel lightheaded, almost ill, as he approached this temple. Now he was becoming warm and feverish, as if his skin was alive on its own and wanted to be free of him. He was sweating, and his arms and legs trembled. It was the smell of death around him, no doubt, that caused him to feel as he did. But he had been in fields of death unending, with corpses piled in hillocks like tables full of meat for the predators and scavengers, and never had he been weakened as he was now. It was this place doing it to him, being here at last.

So this is death, Akram thought, and looked up as his vision began to mist over. Where there had been daylight and a sun in the sky, now he saw past that sky into the darkness beyond, into the endless night and the stars hovering like souls of ghosts.

He saw a shadow approach him from the entranceway of the tomb, a woman, the witch, no shadow. Nidyis was coming toward him, appearing as real to him as he remembered her, spirit though she was, yet as voluptuous as when she had been alive, dark-haired, dark-eyed, moving sinuously, an animal dressed in finery that itself must be as ghostly or as unreal as herself. She sat beside him and touched him, as nearly whole and complete as he was.

He looked into her eyes, shining black.

"Now we are here," Nidyis said to him.

The ghosts gathered, the men and women of his command and even some of the horses, those that had been strong in life, moving toward him and watching him and the witch, then moving on toward the entrance to the great tomb Nidyis had come from, the long line of them, all of the thousand moving to enter eternity, scarlet and misty as they were.

As they did, Akram saw a tall black mist with bright eyes looking at him from the shadows just within the temple entrance.

"Narathkor!" He stood and reached for his sword but then nearly fell, dizzy with rage.

The witch put a hand on him. "He is past all that."

Akram saw a mouth open in the mist beneath the eyes, but no sound was released. The mouth closed, unable to do more, and the mist with its eyes retreated into the darkness.

"Is that what I am to become?" he asked Nidyis.

She told him, "No. That is how I defeated him at last. He watches now and waits to eat anything he finds here. You and I are to be otherwise. We are both now free of that thing. He slew me. Now I may slay you. All you need do is ask."

Akram looked around him at the world. Rocks, stones, dry grass, corpses in every possible position of death. He had lived with these things of the earth for so long that he had come to think that they meant nothing to him, but now that even the sight of a corpse was real to him once more, he had a sense of loss, a sensation that had been gone from him for uncounted seasons. He had become so accepting of the numbness of himself, as something undead, that the remembrance of what had been true so long before, taste and sight, actual color and odors, weakened him. He was to be no more.

He raised his eyes to the sky and looked beyond it, to the darkness and the stars and constellations. He had lived beneath them for so long that he thought they meant nothing to him, but now that he was to join them in an eternity of—

What would it be?

Nidyis, touching him, felt his question.

"It will be the gift of sorcery," she told him. "The reason why we practice the arts. We might have dwelled among the mundane of this world, but we sensed there are greater things and we dared to seek them, Narathkor and I and you, as well. With sorcery, the earthly pleasures are enhanced, and as we go on, the darkness and its songs and sights take possession of us. So few in the world know this or understand it. Most fear it. What is there to fear? Release from what is known so that we may be ourselves in whatever may lie beyond? Yet there is no return. That is their fear. No return, Akram. We will float on mist, you and I and the sorcerer, being ourselves as we are, as we have become, in solitude but together, more alive that we ever were when we inhabited these bodies."

He told her, "I'm weakening, but I've never felt more alive, not on the field, never before now."

"That is the gift from which there is no return. Let others die for a while and then be reborn into the crowds and sewers of this world. We are more than that."

He removed his sword and held it out by the blade, ready to plunge it into his heart. "Say the words," he told Nidyis.

She did, and he pushed the weapon in, not feeling pain, so far away was he already from where he sat and what was all around. When he leaned forward, pulling out the blade, no blood came.

A horse approached, and upon it was a white shape, glowing star-like. He knew that this was Tharis.

"My lord!"

She slid down from the saddle and ran toward him as her horse snickered behind her, shying away, then turned to escape.

But that quickly, ghosts appeared from the air around it and sank into it, taking its blood.

They did not attack Tharis, who ran toward Akram and Nidyis and fell to her knees on the hard stone before them. Their presence protected her, surely. But it was clear why she had come to them.

"Our appetites make us what we are, do they not, my lord?"

"Teach me now!" she yelled at them.

Nidyis told her, "Child, I did not free you for this. Go away."

"I want this!"

"Leave us," Akram told her. "I am only somewhat here, and the witch and I are going. See there?"

He pointed at the entrance to the temple, where Narathkor had returned, eyes glowing within the black mist. Recent ghosts also came alongside him, ready to take Tharis if they could.

"I have this!" She removed the knife that Nidyis had ensorcelled.

Now the ghosts gathered around her, and with them other things, old demons still alive within the ruined temple, slithering toward her like serpents, crawling like animals, all the many shapes of them.

Akram and Nidyis stood and moved toward the opening of the temple.

Tharis ran after them and gripped one of Akram's arms from behind. He was colder than the night. And when he turned to face Tharis, she saw that the light she had known to be in his eyes all the years they had spent together was gone.

"Akram, what should I do?"

She looked at Nidyis.

The witch shook her head.

Akram placed his hands almost tenderly on the girl's shoulders and said to her, "You were wrong to do this."

When they turned from her again, Tharis dropped on the instant. Frozen and breathless on her hands and knees, she stared at the flat stone of the temple portico but saw through it, looked into deeps of wonder. She saw dark stars. She saw all of Time, saw all of Life in its noise and fleetness passing before her and *through her*—lives upon lives turning to no purpose, covering the earth, lives teeming within shadows everywhere, life teeming within the invisible places that surround the world in rings and dimensions, life teeming within animals and plants and souls, all lives at once fighting to survive even in death, and all to no purpose.

Tharis wished to throw up her stomach; she managed to gasp hotly. She turned and crouched, watching as the ghosts and dark creatures surrounded her and approached her. She screamed at them, "I was wrong! I was wrong!"

She looked at the entrance of the temple. Narathkor was there, the black mist and his floating eyes. Akram and Nidyis walked past him.

Tharis screamed at them, "I cleaned their *latrines*! I was their *whore*!"

They moved into the deep shadows within.

Tharis sobbed and waved the knife around her to keep the creatures there away from her, then laughed at them and pushed the knife into her heart.

Too late.

She fell to one side, the knife still in her, but her sight remained dark, and she saw stars, saw into the night, and felt lives moving through her, other people and her own lives lost to her, never to be. She felt no hunger, felt no warmth, was not alive but was not dead.

"Help me!"

Too late. The things were there now, with Akram gone, and the witch. Tharis stood weakly, managing it. She removed the knife; no blood was on it. She stared at the things that confronted her, ghosts, demons, whatever they were, all of them previously unknown to her but now with her, as they would remain.

Where should she go? What should she do? Her horse was dead. She no longer wanted this, and what should she do? She had made a terrible mistake.

Narathkor remained at the temple entrance, just within it, his eyes floating in the black mist of him, and below the eyes, his mouth.

He grinned at her.

The Passing of the Sorcerer

Ah, love, let us be true
To one another! for the world, which seems
To lie before us like a land of dreams,
So various, so beautiful, so new,
Hath really neither joy, nor love, nor light,
Nor certitude, nor peace, nor help for pain;
And we are here as on a darkling plain
Swept with confused alarms of struggle and flight,
Where ignorant armies clash by night.

—Matthew Arnold

In the early evening she knelt, just outside the walls of citied Karhum—Porissa, once mistress to the sorcerer and traitor to her people. Night was coming, the sun dying, the air growing chill. Above young Porissa, the branches of slender trees moved, fingers in a breeze. She pulled her wrap tightly about herself and once more arranged the flowers she had placed atop the sorcerer's grave—bright red blooms the color of blood just let, blue petals as wonderful as immense skies, fragile white and yellow blossoms that would, like all hopes, like strong desires, lose their promising brightness.

Noises came from inside the city. The towers and walls of Karhum were alight with festivities of celebration. Like children, the people sang and danced, joyful at being alive still. They had been delivered from a dark fate, and this turn of events moved them to rejoice. They had forgotten Porissa in their excitement, and certainly tonight they gave no thought to Camses the sorcerer.

The moon lifted, clouds passed, and the graveside flowers brightened. Porissa looked up. Stars beckoned.

Never again would she answer the invitation of such stars.

She thought she heard movement behind her—her father, no doubt, or one of his men. Porissa turned and saw no one. The breeze came again, sent by the perfect stars. It caught her long red hair and moved it around her neck and face.

Once more, with slender fingers, Porissa arranged the flowers on Camses' grave. She was reluctant to let go of those flowers. She wished to do nothing except sit beneath these trees, and she wished that the city would be quiet. She wished that everyone in the city, her father, everyone, would fall quiet, stop.

How fitting that would be on their night of celebration, to remind them of how their deliverance had been bought. But they were beyond redemption. They were what they were.

If a blossom of only a certain type appears from a tree, Camses had told her one evening when they were watching the stars high above, should we blame other trees that cannot provide that blossom? It is not in the tree to change what it is. If such a tree were to live forever, it never could change the nature of its blossoms. Certain trees, certain blossoms. Rare trees, rare blossoms.

You, he had told Porissa, are such a rare blossom.

As was he, of course.

The first words she had said to him were, "Be careful."

He had smiled—delightful smile—and asked, "Are they dangerous?"

They were in the main square of the city, and he was studying the flowers and herbs displayed along a stretch of stalls.

"Beautiful, beautiful," the seller told Camses. "For the lady."

Porissa and Camses ignored him. "Dangerous," she said, meeting Camses' eyes, "because they contain poison."

"Do they?"

"These dark blooms must be handled very carefully until they have been warmed in the sun. Then they lose their poison. Have a care if you're going to plant them soon."

"I was not going to plant these cuttings. There are other uses."

"Well, then." She couldn't turn away from his eyes or his smile. He was deceptively young looking, with a strong face, a pleasant face. His hair was long and dark, and his eyes very deep. He wore no beard or moustache, unlike most of the men of Karhum. Not from here, then, Porissa surmised, and in the same moment decided that his plain clothes—a comfortable robe, a leather vest, no jewelry, plain footwear—confirmed that he was neither of this city nor from the surrounding villages.

A few words, their smiles, and the two of them fell into step together alongside each other, leaving the midday heat of the square to protect themselves under the shade of awnings over-hanging the tables of a food vendor on a side street. As they ate, Porissa told Camses about Karhum. He had never been in the city before and was interested in its history. He was, however, well traveled, which intrigued Porissa. He was a student and, he explained, tiring at last of the limitations put on him by the scholars he had paid to teach him, had struck out on his own to learn what he could that way.

Perhaps that explained the youthfulness of his demeanor and his refreshing charm, although it was apparent that he was several years older, at least, than Porissa. Still, he certainly was not as old as her intended, Sullus.

She told Camses about her own life, restricted as it was. She had money; her father, Thalem, was a wealthy businessman and owned a great deal of property in Karhum as well as much of the pasturelands and groves outside the city walls. Her mother had died years ago, and her father, to consolidate his desire to be admitted into the highest ranks of society, had betrothed Porissa to Sullus, whose family had little money but retained an old name. Such pretense mattered to those who ruled this city.

Midday became early afternoon, and then nearly evening, as the two lingered over their plates and beverages. Porissa abruptly realized that she was late for an appointment with her father and Sullus.

She stood, took Camses' hand, thanked him for the afternoon, and promised to visit with him again. He told her where he lived; he had rented one of her father's own buildings in a poor section of the city.

As she went, then, Porissa wondered about her attraction to this student. She was sufficiently familiar with men to anticipate quite accurately what each one might say next or do, even which way they might turn their heads or how they might look at her. Men were all the same; most were thoroughly predictable. It was no trouble to read their thoughts; men held few surprises.

Except this one.

Camses was something altogether new. Porissa decided that she found Camses to be so intriguing because he was, in fact, genuine. Without pretense. How singular to meet a person so honest and open, so at home in the world.

Surely that was the nature of her attraction to him, and that reasoning settled the matter for her for several days, until she met Camses again, once more in the square, once more to share a meal and enjoy each other's company. Charming, she thought, and singularly authentic, yes, this one.

Until the accident occurred.

They were walking past the same flower stalls where they had met days earlier. Porissa was examining some of the stems as a seller placed new blooms on display. The merchant warned her not to touch these particular blossoms—

But it was too late. She had pricked her finger on a thorn of one of the black flowers. Within moments, she felt faint and sank to her knees.

The flower seller called out for a physician. Was there anyone in the square who knew how to help with poisons?

But Camses told him to be still. He bent over Porissa, examined the wound, and sucked it until he had gotten the poison and spat it out. Then he held the wounded finger between his palms while looking deeply into the young woman's eyes, so deeply and strongly that Porissa felt her fever cooling, her heartbeat calming.

At last Camses released her finger and helped her to her feet.

Shocked by what Camses had done and by how quickly he had intervened, Porissa examined her finger and saw no hint of the wound. It was as though the two of them had slipped backward in time to before she had ever touched the thorn, as though Camses had cleaned her wound and repaired the skin by undoing what had been done—an impossibility.

"Please don't blame me!" the flower seller insisted. "I warned her! You heard me!" He said to Camses, "You heard me warn her! Thank the gods you are a physician!"

Camses looked at the seller and said, "Yes."

But Porissa knew what had happened. As the curious that had gathered now separated and moved on, she pulled away from Camses, backed away from him, and began moving across the square.

Camses followed her.

When he caught up with Porissa, she turned to him and said, almost angrily, "You're no physician! What arts do you practice? Tell me."

"Are you afraid?"

"Yes! I should be dead! Tell me who you are!"

He did so.

Sorcery, she learned from Camses, as they sat in his apartment that afternoon, was not what Porissa recalled from the elaborate puppet shows of her girlhood. Children were told tales of magical dragons and men with wands flying in the air. These, Camses said, were primitive recollections of what had been in ancient times. Likely there still were some in distant mountains, in deserts, in remote swamplands who practiced human sacrifice and cannibalism and who mated with animals, the earliest forms of magic making. These would be the shape-changers and succubi and vampires. But dragons no longer existed, if they ever had. And men with wands remained the province of children's stories and were not to be found in the streets of Karhum.

Still, if Porissa were to ask her elders to tell what they knew of sorcerers and magic makers, of shamans and witches, they would have tales to tell. At least some of the old folk of the city knew his kind, Camses assured Porissa, for within their time others possessed of the secret wisdom surely had passed through their lives.

"If I announced myself," he told her, "they would shun me. You must be careful, for they will hurt you, too, if you befriend me."

"No, they won't. My father is too important. *I* am too important."

"Are you?

"I have a position in this city. I am my father's tool. So long as he can use me to barter his way to influence, yes, I am important. But what is it that they fear in sorcery," she asked, "if what we believe is not true?"

Camses led her to one of the tower windows of his home and gestured outside to the people of Karhum. "These," he told her, "do not inhabit the world in its entirety. They occupy a parcel of the world, and their concerns do not extend beyond those limits."

"They are provincial," Porissa agreed, joining him at the window. "Their imaginations are small. I have complained of this myself and been impatient with many in this city. Even if they are basically good, their limitations could be a danger to them."

Camses nodded. "They are the much-too-many. A few of them have the wit to join us here in this room, but otherwise, the much-too-many are no more than fish in an ocean or insects in a swarm."

Porissa faced him. "What has any of this to do with sorcery and your arts?"

"The secret of sorcery is that all things in the world touch together. You smile. Not that some things touch some things, but all touch all. Consider the depth of that. If I plant a stem in the earth or tear the petal of a flower, is it not possible that, by doing so, I have influenced the life of someone not yet born, someone who will live a thousand years from now?"

"Or rescue a woman who has touched a poisonous thorn? I've heard of this philosophy, but it's of no practical value. What purpose does it serve to know this?"

"The purpose served, Porissa, is awareness itself. What purpose does it serve that you awoke one day from your mother's womb and came into this life? What was the practical value of that?"

She told him, "I don't— Just to be. There is no reason! I am who I am! I'm alive, and that's enough. You're playing word games with me. I don't have an answer."

"And so with the world."

"You're playing games. This has nothing to do with who you are." She was becoming cross with him.

Camses led her to a chair and bade her sit. He faced her then and said, "There is more than one world. There are many others, and all touch together, the invisible worlds and this one."

"I have heard this argument, too."

"When these worlds touch, we have begun a new path and perhaps are creating a new world. That is sorcery."

"And its purpose?"

"To awaken to all that is and might be."

She smiled at him genuinely. "But no dragons? Or magic wands?"

He returned her smile. "I have seen none, no."

"And you have entered these other worlds?"

"It is dangerous. Words are involved, words that must be learned, and certain other things, but it is simple in its essence. The fearfulness is awakening to the loneliness of it. How many of those out there, told that they could do as they pleased, would do it if they had to cross a boundary and never return?"

"None of them would. I don't know if I would."

"They would rather believe in fantastic wonders than accept simple truths. Every man might be a sorcerer, could he right his mind. Every woman could command the stars, would she but open her heart. But to see life as it is—it is a great responsibility, and it can break the heart, not to be able to look away. And there is danger."

"Where is the place in this world or any other," Porissa asked him, "without danger? Will you show me? How you do your sorcery?"

"And what would be the practical value of that?"

"I would become your friend, even if none of them out there ever will be."

Camses assented and led her down many steps into the cellars and old tunnels beneath the streets of the city. There he had positioned brass and silver mirrors so that they caught the reflections of signs he had drawn on the rock walls and thus offered doorways into other places. He had set up braziers that burned incenses to open the mind, and he had created pools of water that returned his thoughts when he stared into their depths. In one room of the cellars, he had carved a great circle in the floor and a star within the circle. Inside the protection of this circle, he told Porissa, "I can visit other worlds and return safely. No heat burns me, no cold freezes me, no spirits challenge my soul so long as I proceed cautiously."

He demonstrated some of his arts to Porissa and, as a result, she understood why he walked alone.

Soon they became more than friends. Porissa made excuses not to be available when others invited her to their homes, and she even turned down important acquaintances of her father's when they requested her presence at city functions. Sullus, too, she avoided as much as possible. Knowing, of course, that her father and Sullus both would resort to spies and informants to track her and report her whereabouts to them, Porissa took elaborate measures to travel inconspicuously, even disguise herself until she was safely within Camses' house.

There, day or night, whenever she could manage to be in his company, they spent their time discussing philosophy and ideas of all kinds. A natural student, Porissa had found her desire to learn checked by her father's ambitions; he had groomed her to serve as his accomplice, not to develop her own gifts. She was hungry to know what Camses had learned, not necessarily the mystical arts but expression and thought of all kinds that she had not been exposed to.

Weeks passed in this way. Even when Camses teased Porissa when she misspoke comically or wrestled with some concept, she understood that he did this because he respected her, cared for her, in fact—and was falling in love with her, as she was with him.

"Perhaps we are old souls," he told her one evening as they looked out over the city from his tower window. "Perhaps we have been searching for each other for many lifetimes and at last have met again."

"Is that possible?"

"I would like to think so."

"Couldn't your spirits or mirrors tell you so?"

"Yes, if I ask them. But even if it were so and we have met again at last, why should we relive the pain that has separated us all this time?"

As their love deepened, their intellectual pursuits were exchanged for amorous evenings and soft afternoons, when they made love. Camses, as Porissa had surmised, was as gentle and caring in their shared bed as he was when they talked the night long. There was no need for him to act as her tutor in these arts, however, for Porissa had gained sufficient experience on her own. Still, Camses made her come alive and feel complete in ways that had become dulled for her. When had she become capable of experiencing such sensations and wonders? She felt new to herself. And in giving pleasure to Camses, too, it was remarkable how she felt about herself, as though she were inhabiting a new world in which only she mattered, in which she was of consequence, in which restraints and limits did not exist.

Inevitably, however, her family learned what she had been doing. Knowledge of a young sorcerer living among them had become common to the people in that part of the city, and soon everyone in Karhum was aware of Camses' presence. Dung had been smeared on the doors of his house and religious icons placed on his steps to help him find the path to his salvation. Word of the interesting stranger caught Thalem's attention; likely he had asked one of his employees to inquire discreetly about this person who was renting a house from him. No doubt, too, Porissa had become careless in her increasingly frequent visits to Camses. Someone had recognized her, or someone had told her father's spies that, yes, a tall, red-haired young woman has been seen entering that building at all hours of the day and night, coming and going according to no schedule.

Predictably, then, Sullus arrived late one afternoon, accompanied by two large bullies who served as his personal guards. He was of more than average stature but rather heavy for a man of his build. However, Sullus was well dressed in his polished, shining boots, and he had an expensively tailored cloak on his shoulders.

He rapped loudly on Camses' door. When it was not opened quickly enough for him, he stepped into the yard, surveyed the windows of the tower above him, then attacked the door again.

At last it opened. Camses, in his worn robe, faced Sullus.

Sullus barely gave him his attention but looked past the sorcerer, into the dim foyer within. "Porissa."

Camses asked, "What of her?"

"I know she's here. Send her out."

"Are you Sullus?"

"I am. Get out of my way."

Sullus took a step forward, but Camses lifted a hand, holding his palm close to Sullus' breast and the fine shirt covering it.

Sullus winced and emitted a sound. He stepped away and touched his chest. It was as hot as though it had been touched with a brand.

He sneered at Camses. "So those are your tricks. Tell her to come here."

"I don't tell her anything. She is her own person. You tell her."

"Then get her down here!"

"She'll come if she wishes to."

Sullus motioned to his companions. "Go in. Get her."

But they hesitated. Looked at Camses, who remained calm, and hesitated, not eager to be hurt.

Sullus, exasperated, took out the sword he wore at his side and lifted it so that the point approached Camses' breast.

Quickly Camses gripped it with both hands. The blade did not cut him, but as he held it, heat softened the outlines of the shining steel until Sullus, crying out, let go of it.

"We know about your kind!" he said to Camses.

"I am better than you. Take this away." Camses bent the hot blade in his hands so that it was twisted all around. He dropped it onto the stone steps.

Footsteps, then, sounded behind him, and Porissa called, "Sullus!" She took her place beside Camses and faced Sullus.

Sullus told her, "We know you've been staying here. We know about him. Your father wants you back."

"When I'm ready."

"Now, Porissa!"

"When I am ready!"

"Is that what I tell your father? Is that what I tell my family?"

She looked Sullus in the eyes. There was no warmth in her expression. Porissa said quietly, "When I am ready."

"You have obligations!"

Porissa turned away and moved behind Camses.

Camses closed the door.

"You have obligations!" Sullus called to her a second time as the door fell shut.

Inside, Camses, weakened by the effort of what he had done, moved to the stair steps and sat. He held out a hand that trembled from the exertion, looked at the hand, then rested it in his lap.

Porissa turned to him. "I don't know what to do."

He told her, "You will settle it with yourself."

"When?" she asked him. "How will I know? What am I doing?" She said it in a despairing tone, for the first time realizing what she had done to bring her to this moment.

Porissa did go, the next morning, to see her father. Thalem was not happy to see her. Angrily he made it clear that he wished her to cut off her association with this man, Camses, who of course was a charlatan who was ingratiating himself to Porissa so that he could make claims on her or her money.

Just as angrily, Porissa said hurtful things to her father, accusing him of spying on her, of not trusting her, and of using Sullus to try to intimidate Camses, whom Porissa cared for deeply. He was an honest and good man, unlike Thalem himself and unlike any of the men he did business with. Porissa announced that her life was her own, that she was returning to stay with Camses, and that if her father wished to speak with her again, he should come to that house in the lower part of the city and apologize to both her and Camses. He should not send Sullus and his violent companions or next time Camses might not be as patient with them as he had been yesterday, when he acted with restraint solely on Porissa's account.

When she returned to Camses' house, she was tearful, and she ached from the strain of having been so adamant with her father. She lay down and tried to sleep. Camses brought her wine. She became cross with him, as well, as angry with Camses as she was with herself, with circumstances, with the world.

Camses withdrew and left her to herself until evening. At twilight, he heard her call to him. Her tone had changed.

He went into her room and saw Porissa leaning on the sill of an open window, looking out at the city past the shutters.

"Camses, what is the matter with that person?"

He joined her at the window. In the street below, a middle-aged man was dragging himself along on his belly. With each lunge, he paused, gathering strength for his next effort. At last he fell still, his arms went lax, his body shuddered, and he did not move farther.

"Camses, that man just died! What happened to him?"

"I sensed this."

"Sensed what?"

Far away, from deep within the city, they heard wails of anguish.

"Camses, what is happening?"

"Come with me."

He led Porissa into the rooms below the tower. There he bade her be seated, passed a hand before her eyes, and made sounds. Porissa found that she could not move; she was sitting comfortably, she could see all that Camses did, but she could not move and furthermore felt that she did not wish to.

"For your protection," Camses explained to her, "should something occur that I cannot anticipate." He then walked around her in a circle, muttering again while dragging a staff with him, scraping a circle about Porissa on the stone floor.

Camses lit three braziers that stood before a tall mirror. He threw incense onto the coals so that the fumes enveloped the mirror. He drew a circle around himself with his staff and, from within that circle, called out to whatever demon or spirit was forming itself in the mirror, shaping itself from the smoke that moved into the bright metal.

Porissa watched as an uncertain, pointed face, neither human nor animal, pushed itself from the mirror's surface as though lifting itself through clouds or mist. It saw her, saw Camses, and moved its mouth. She understood what it said, as did Camses.

Camses asked the demon to identify the plague that was occurring in Karhum.

"It is an old scourge," the demon explained. It reported that in founding the city, the first citizens of Karhum had stolen the land from a local spirit. They had not asked its permission to build here; they had not offered it prayers or sacrifices; they frankly stole the land. This angered the spirit, which began to steal young children at night to drown them in lakes or feed them to wolves. At last the city's founders reached an agreement with this spirit; for their sin, they were bound to send a ripe soul every century to this spirit in Hell. This sacrifice had been completed regularly for many centuries, but recently the people had come to disbelieve the old, primitive stories. The city lord, Erbuk, and all of his nobles willfully defied the spirit of this land. They had been warned in dreams, and their priests had been sent troubling signs that a sacrifice must be prepared, but these signs had been ignored or interpreted incorrectly. "Now the angry spirit has placed this plague upon Karhum. Every soul is to die." This was all that the demon knew. If it was aware of more, it was bound by strong powers not to speak further or had been warned not to reveal more than it already had shared.

When the demon was finished, Camses spoke syllables to send it away. He stepped from his circle and freed Porissa from hers, balancing her on her feet as the effect of his spell dropped away.

When she was able to speak, Porissa asked Camses, "A... dream?"

"Not a dream."

Uncertain as she still was, he carefully helped her out of the deep chamber, holding onto her. And when they reached Porissa's room in the tower, Camses put her to bed so that she might sleep away the effects of his spell.

Through the night, the wailing carried in every direction as the city died—the old, the frail, children, and the strong and alert taken randomly. Those who tried to escape, leaving the city under starlight, dropped along the roadside, their lives taken by the spirit's anger even as they hurried away.

Camses in his tower turned to his old books, his crystals, and his pools of water, attempting to discover any means by which he might rescue the city. Several spells were of no help. Twice Camses made an effort to reach the spirit itself in Hell, once by means of his mirrors, then again by an incantation from within his protected circle. In the mirrors, the deadly spirit was but a fleet, black shade moving through bursts of flame. And as Camses stood within his circle, the spirit came to him merely as a voice and as a warm breeze, a warm presence, warning him to abandon the city.

"You may leave. My anger is not with you."

"If a sacrifice is made," Camses asked the old spirit, "will you then lift your curse?"

"It is too late for sacrifices. Let them suffer."

And throughout the night, Camses was distracted from his work by yelling men and the sounds of stones and bricks hurled against his house.

"Sorcerer! Come out and face us! Why are you killing us?"

Toward morning, Camses answered a weak knock at his door. On his steps was a young woman holding a dead baby in her arms. Her child was perhaps a year old, no older.

The woman said to him, "I know you can help me. Please. Take my life and give it to my baby. Please. I don't want to live. Can you do that? Can you do that?"

Camses assured the woman that he could not. But he sat with her on the steps of his house and held her in his arms as she cried, clutching her baby to her. Soon she died. Camses placed her under some shade trees in his yard. What else could he do? Then he returned inside, locked his door, and continued trying to undo the spirit's curse.

Porissa awoke midmorning. She told Camses, "I had so many strange dreams. I can't even put them into words. Where was I? Here all the time?"

"Here all the time," he told her, and, when she asked him what was happening in the city, he opened the shut windows to reveal the street below.

It was littered with corpses—all that remained of the lives of men, women, and children, and animals, as well, and birds that had dropped from the sky during the night. No insects hummed. There was no sun, only clouds, so that Porissa wondered if perhaps the evil spirit had managed somehow to kill the very sun, too.

She told Camses, "We must leave."

"And what of your father and Sullus?"

"They can take care of themselves. They can! My father has wise physicians. He and the other rich people will leave Karhum if they haven't already—"

"No one is leaving."

"They will! This city has suffered plagues before. Camses—you and I—you love to travel. We can travel. But we must leave now!"

Before he could answer her, there came the sound of pounding on the door below.

"Camses, don't answer it!"

"Of course I must answer it."

She stepped in front of him, blocking his way, and searched his face. "What is it? You've been awake all night. What do you know?"

"Let me see who this is."

"*What do you know?*"

Gently he moved her aside and went down to the door. Porissa followed him and waited at the bottom of the steps.

On the threshold was a man of her father's household, an old servant whom Porissa had known her entire life.

"Thotis?" She approached the doorway.

"My lady, your father is ill."

"Is he dead?"

"No, but he asks for you. He is grievously, grievously ill. Please come."

She looked at Camses. He nodded. "You must."

"I'll hurry back," she told him, and, to Thotis, "Have you told Lord Sullus?"

"My lady, Sullus is dead."

She stopped where she was. She said, "Of course he is. I saw it in my dream. Camses, what else did I see?"

"Go to your father. Come back when you can."

"Is he already dead?"

"No. But go to him."

Porissa returned early in the afternoon. Camses was surprised that she had come, not alone, but with Erbuk, the lord of Karhum, and several of his retinue—courtiers who tended to the lord's needs, such as carrying food and drink for him, as well the city's treasurer and three scholars.

Porissa likewise did not expect what she found when she entered Camses's tower rooms: all of his books and other materials were bundled and packed inside wooden boxes, ready to be loaded onto a cart, as though he were preparing after all to quit the city.

"Are you leaving?" she asked him, as Lord Erbuk and his people stood behind her.

"No."

"But your things?"

He regarded Lord Erbuk. Camses did not bow to him—in his life, he had bowed only to persons wiser than himself, those from whom he could learn—but he nodded to Erbuk politely.

One of the lord's servants touched Porissa and gently moved her aside so that Erbuk could advance and speak with Camses.

"I come to you a humbled man," he said to the sorcerer. "My people have been cursed, and you alone, I believe, can help us. I am prepared to provide you whatever you need to help us and to offer you in payment whatever you ask of me. Please save Karhum."

Camses asked him, "Are you prepared to give up your own life in sacrifice to save your people?"

Erbuk was surprised by this question. He admitted, "I had not thought that the spirit would ask for such a thing."

"Are you prepared to do it?"

"I don't know. I had not anticipated this. I don't know. I would want to discuss it with my priests and scholars first. Is there no other way to stop the spirit from committing these crimes? Has this demon truly asked this of me?"

"No," Camses told him.

"Then why would you ask such a thing?"

"Because if you had agreed, I would have gone to the spirit on your behalf and tried in that way to save Karhum."

"Sorcerer...tell me what I need to know to fight this evil."

"Lord Erbuk, this thing insists that for many years, your city offered it a sacrifice to keep it from delivering a curse. Is this true?"

Erbuk whispered to some of his scholars; one of them bowed to Camses and told him, "This is true."

"Why did you discontinue this practice?"

"It is an ancient practice. It had not been done for more than a hundred years. We no longer believe in such things. Surely it was superstition to continue killing young people so preposterously. Do you blame us?"

"No."

If Camses meant to say more, Porissa interrupted him. "What are you doing?" she asked him. "Tell me what this is about."

"The spirit will not accept another sacrifice. None of you is to live. The demon means for your city to die."

Erbuk groaned.

"But I believe that I can lift the curse," Camses told them, "by confronting it with my own sorcery."

One of the scholars asked him, "How is that possible?"

But Porissa anticipated what he would say—or she remembered, perhaps, her haunting dream of the previous night. "No!" she told Camses. "It will kill you!"

"I'm stronger than it is."

Porissa went into his arms and looked him in the eyes. She spoke quietly to him. "They're not worth it."

"Do you want your father to live?"

"I don't know! But I don't want you to die! We can *leave*! You can help protect me, and we can *leave*!"

"This is where all things touch together. Porissa, listen to me. I am being practical. Let me do this for you."

"They're not worth it! They hate you!" She coughed and held him more tightly as she quickly weakened. She whispered then, "No, no," realizing that now she, too, was ill.

Camses lifted her and carried her to a couch, gently placed her upon it, and touched her hair. He kissed her face and waved a hand over her, as he had when they were in the cellars and he had protected her with his spell.

Then he rose and confronted Lord Erbuk. He asked Erbuk and his scholars, "Do you know what wisdom is?"

Erbuk said, "I believe so." He turned to his retinue. "Give him an answer! Tell him what he requires!"

One of the robed men stammered, but Camses interrupted him. "Wisdom," he told them, "is faith. Tell Porissa, when she awakens, that I did this for her out of faith. She is remarkable. My price for doing this is to demand that you protect her for the rest of her life. No harm is to come to her. Let her find a husband and raise a family. And you are sworn to protect that family and those children."

Erbuk told him, "It will be done. I swear to you."

"You produced her." Camses said. "You are necessary because people like her come from people like you. You are the soil. That is all you are. She is the blossom."

"This is offensive," one of the scholars complained. "How dare you judge us? I am profoundly—"

"Silence!" Erbuk commanded him.

"Destroy my things," Camses told them. "They will do none of you any good."

"On my oath," Erbuk promised. "Young man...what you are about to do—"

"Is for her. Always protect her. She is better than you. Now let me by."

Erbuk stepped back, and his people moved away, pressing to either side so that Camses, in his plain clothes, a comfortable robe and a leather vest, no jewelry, walked by them and went down into the cellars underneath the city.

In her dream, Porissa had seen him do it, Camses among flames far away, and the angry spirit no more than a black mist, a shade, shrieking as Camses, a quick white ghost, held it down until it was no more. Other spirits came to watch; imps sat by; shadows older than Time observed the struggle. And it was done.

Later, still within her dream, Porissa stood in the room at the bottom of the tower and spoke into one of the sorcerer's mirrors. She watched as his face come to her wrapped in smoke and explained to her again why he had done it, for her sake.

It is too great a burden for me to bear, Porissa told the smoke. How can I live with this?

You faced demons, Camses assured her. And you confronted the elders of your city and shamed them. How can they live with you now? The burden is theirs.

The stars were fading. The moon was dim, low in the heavens. The city had fallen quiet at last, and the flowers on the turned earth of Camses' grave had lost their color.

Porissa heard a movement behind her—her father, yes, walking toward her, with the sun behind him as it began to rise.

He said nothing to her. He stood a distance away, respectful of his daughter, respectful of her. He was still weak, but the fever had passed, and he was alive.

Porissa stared at the faded blooms. Carefully, she tore the petal of one of them. Then she stood and looked at her father.

"He said that, by doing one small thing, by planting a stem, perhaps, he might change the world and influence lives a thousand years from now. That was his sorcery. His magic lay in wisdom. I will see him again," she told Thalem.

"Will you?"

"We spoke of it. We knew each other before now, and we will know each other again. He had faith in that."

"Do you believe this?"

"Don't you?"

"I don't know. It is difficult. I would have to consult priests or scholars."

Porissa said to him, "Aren't you weary of asking others for permission to think?"

Thalem didn't reply.

Porissa said, "I'm very tired." She walked to him.

Her father drew a hand around her shoulders, and together they walked toward Karhum and entered the city.

Patience Serves

With Areil were perhaps twenty others in the wide hall, each waiting patiently for his or her name to be called, each looking up expectantly when the heavy bronze doors were pulled open and the latest visitant led out. Looking up expectantly and listening carefully as the seneschal announced another name and took that one by the arm into the farther chamber, all gloomy and quiet as it was, and hazy with incense and candle smoke, dark with prayers, abode of the dead.

"Lady Tristania of Oll."

Areil rose gracefully to her feet and glided forward. Whispers and eyes, all around. Her rich robes unfolded smoothly behind her and rippled over the marble floor. The seneschal fixed her with his stare and declared before allowing her entrance:

"Our lord is sinking. Each penitent can be allowed only a few moments to be near his honor and whisper a prayer for him. If you expect a miracle—"

"I do not come as a penitent."

"What, then?"

"I knew his honor long ago. Before he was ever a lord. Remind him of that, and tell him that we were lovers."

Through all the morning and the long afternoon, the seneschal had admitted into the dying man's sanctum all ranks of local potentates and suppliants, businessmen, councilors, the wise of the cloth: and here came this dowager, a heartflame from his youth, to collect one last kiss or to remind him of some lingering kind memory. The seneschal was not so much touched by sentimentality as he was intrigued; into the chamber he led Areil and with a gesture summoned a servant to him. He spoke low into the old man's ear, and the servant moved then to the right-hand side of Lord Mors' bed to lean close and inform.

Across the room, in the shadows and in the light of great candles taller than men, stood physicians watching with darting eyes every labored breath, twitch, nod. And Mors' family, his sons and their wives and children, bored and restless.

The servant returned. "His honor will see Lady Tristania."

"Quickly, then. Others wait."

Areil approached on the left, her back to the physicians and the family. She looked down upon the dying man as though inspecting him. Lean and frail, now. Areil remembered him robust and arrogant. Mouth agape, now. Clenched, shivering fists netted with veins. Perspiration shimmering in the hollow gray cheeks. Surely all flesh decays according to the same law.

Areil sat in the chair that was there and leaned close. "We were once lovers, my lord."

He tried to reach with a faltering hand, turned his damp face toward her. Pain. "I can." Barely audible. "Hear only on. This side." He closed his eyes, opened them with a moist sound. "Who. Are you?"

"Who, indeed?" Areil smiled but did not raise her voice. We were...lovers."

The weakest of nods, perhaps only a trembling, and no expression.

The odor of him was the stink of the dead, not sweet. "I was introduced to you as Lady Tristania. By that name I have lived in this city for three years. But my name is Areil."

He closed his eyes.

"Areil, Lord Mors. You do not recall?" Her whisper took an edge. "We were ... children, really. You thought you loved me, but I was to marry—I know you'll remember the name—I was to marry Arin. Your father's stable boy? Ah, you remember."

The throat clenched, moving to force down a swallow, and did not succeed. The eyes remained closed, the lips open for air, the head shivering.

"Two nights before the wedding? You and four others?"

The nostrils flared.

"You ruined my life, Mors." Areil spoke quickly but carefully kept her voice low. "Arin and his family canceled the marriage, of course, when they learned of it. My family was shamed. My father didn't ask me to leave his household—he wouldn't have done that—but my family was shamed." She waited, but Mors lay still, offered nothing. "When I had healed, I left of my own accord. And you, your honor...you and your four. For you, it was jealousy and drunkenness and evil done to appease your pride. Foul, Mors. You are foul. You, the five of you, ruined my life.

Can you know what that means? I was unable to bear children. Physicians tried to help, but what could they do? What could I do? I prayed to the gods. 'Make what happened unhappen. Turn back the world, return me in time.' But that's not possible, is it? So... revenge? Hurt those who had hurt me? Revenge?"

The eyes opened.

"Revenge, yes, Mors."

The working chest. The stiffened hands, hurting skin. The pain. His eyes.

"We become what others make us, don't we? I've learned that; it is as certain as the stars. We're still ourselves, but not who we intended to be. In a moment, one person steers the entire direction of someone else's life, and we all live in each other's shadows."

The eyes closed.

"Essel was the first, when I returned. Not to my family; they never saw me again; but for him. He didn't even remember me. Were you all so drunk that night that you didn't *see* me? With these hands.... These hands, I learned, could accomplish anything. I castrated him in his own bed when he lured me there. It was bloody, and he screamed. I didn't enjoy it, Mors. And a little while later, a year, I think—Uveros. I had some money by that time, so I hired a man to kill him for me."

He didn't look, didn't respond. A wave of pain took him for a moment and Mors fought it, suffered it, as Areil waited until it had passed, leaving him breathless and awash in new sweat.

"I can't say that my heart went out of it after two bloody crimes, but I began to think about life and the future. I should build, I thought, as well as destroy. I had learned that life didn't have to happen to me; *I* could happen to *life*. Patience, I told myself. What's the old saving? 'Patience serves vengeance best.' I went to Osad and began a business enterprise. Halas was in Osad by that time. I spent six years there. I even met him occasionally at social functions. He didn't recall me, either. I had another name, of course. But I did what many would envy: I destroyed his business. Revenge comes in as many colors as the rainbow. Halas took his own life because of his failure. Or perhaps because I told him at last my true name and why I had ruined him."

Areil moved closer. "Many colors." She felt the pulse of life in him, ebbing life that yet persisted. Mors opened his eyes suddenly to shock her, but Areil met his stare without flinching.

"Twenty years passed, Mors. Long years. I sold my business. To make peace with my conscience, I sought faith and lived for a time in an abbey, and I came to think there that I had actually salvaged my soul. But the solace did not last; the abbey was on the coast, it was attacked, and I witnessed more violence. By some fate, I was not touched by this violence myself, and I've often wondered why. But when I stood in the wreckage and looked at the burned bodies and listened to the wailing of a few who, like me, had survived, I felt the old emotion reawaken in me like a dark flower that had slept for a long time, only to blossom afresh in the shadows of that violated place. I sought other answers and followed my awakened heart, and it led me to the dark arts."

Mors watched her.

"I learned many things from proud, powerful people, strong as only the willful and damned are strong. Are they evil? I think them wise in ways that others do not contemplate and can't imagine. All the signs, all the prayers, all the works they taught me. When I left them, I was old in years but made young again by my purpose, and when I slew Odis, it was by a secret means with these hands." She held them up. "I learned where he lived and I went there. Every evening, he stepped onto the balcony of his tower to view the sunset. I fashioned a doll in the image of Odis and on the last night that he came onto his balcony, I mimicked his movements with the doll, then forced him over the wall. He screamed for help as he climbed those stones against his will. I twisted the doll's head so that Odis would look to see me standing in the garden below, then dropped the doll to my feet. Odis's eyes were upon me as he fell, and in the last moment he understood who I was. Four," Areil said. "With these." Her hands, old yet delicate, finely formed.

Mors moved his lips with difficulty. His body, resisting him, made sour bending sounds as he turned his own head to face Areil. "And now. Me."

"Yes."

He smiled.

"My patience is ended, Mors. You are in great pain, aren't you?"

He bared his teeth, his grin, sharing his sophisticated appreciation of her story and of the old woman's achievements. But: "You come. Too late. Witch. Death. Reaches. I em. Brace this. Cold. Black. Ghost. I. Cheat you."

"Mors." Areil leaned very close, now. "Who do you think brought this disease upon you? The pain, the numb limbs, the black, dying flesh?"

He stared, he could not speak, he did not fear death but now he stared at Areil with fear in his eyes, fear. "Your. Curse?"

She bared her teeth, her grin.

Mors tried to laugh. but his pain was too great.

She rose then, erect, proud, a stately white-haired woman in regal dress, and surveyed a last time the frightened Mors, lean and thin and frail, every breath a challenge, his body but a vessel for his pain. The pain. To live with such endless pain.

Glaring at her, Mors moaned, "You come. Witch. To wit. Ness. Your. Work?"

Behind her, Areil heard the approaching footsteps of the returning seneschal.

"See. Me. Suffer?"

The footsteps stopped.

"No," Areil whispered.

"My lady," said the seneschal.

"No." She bent over Mors, moved her face close to his, and said softly into his good ear, "I come to complete my work."

"My lady, please."

"My curse," Areil whispered. "Why I waited until now for you."

Mors stared at her.

"You will remain as you are, Mors. Forever."

"Please, my lady!" urged the seneschal.

She turned to him and begged, "Another moment only. A last prayer?" then leaned over Mors again, smiled into his frightened eyes, pressed her hands, *those hands*, upon his laboring chest, and so quietly that only his honor could hear her, hissed at him as though murmuring devoutly, "You wish so strongly to live, my lord—"

The eyes. The clenched fists. The pain, the pain.

"—then, by all the gods I worship, live! Stay as you are and do not leave us, Lord Mors! *Live!*"

The Sounding of the Gong

"Are you prepared?" the old man asked her.

"I am."

"You speak with confidence."

"The knowing will be in the doing," the young woman said.

They were seated in the sorcerer's large garden of common trees and flowers—every ancient leaf and bloom brought back after centuries and carefully tended to, just as Seft had tended carefully to himself to remain alive this long—he, another ancient bloom.

The sorcerer was positioned proudly in his high-backed marble chair, comfortable in his leather breeks, well-worn shirt of artfully decorated animal skin, and short boots of human leather. On his left, seated in a small wooden chair, was Oma, in a light linen robe as plain as the earth, held at the waist by a leather cord. Protecting her feet were the rough ox-hide sandals that had brought her by a turning path to this place.

The late afternoon was cool and the skies, cloudy, but Oma did not miss the warmth. She watched as, throughout the garden, torches in sconces and coals in braziers abruptly came alight with bright fire, made to do so by the sorcerer with a gesture of his right hand. The flames were aromatic with delightful old scents that themselves had cost Seft much effort to revive and perfect. How he loved the old days of his distant youth.

A fine breeze fragrant with the aroma of the torches and braziers lightly fanned Oma's auburn hair.

She said to Seft, "It will take some time for me to fulfill what you have taught me."

"You will succeed. You have begun well."

"But I want you to stay longer."

"No. The time is proper. You will be fine without me." He reached to touch her hand, seated apart as they were.

"Seft, I want you to be here with me when the end comes."

"And so I shall be, in a way. We can always return to those places we once occupied, can we not? Call upon me. I will come."

"You don't care to witness the changes as they come?"

"I prefer the world as it was," said the sorcerer.

"But I will be unhappy in this world without you in it," Oma told him.

"As you should be. You are young. But come a day far from now, even this evening will take on a delightful haze for you. I myself can dwell in memories from long ago. It is one of the few gifts the gods have bequeathed us, our ability to reminisce on pleasant memories."

Oma smiled and touched his brow with the index finger of her right hand, the calling up hand in sorcery as he had taught her. It was a simple gesture but one she had used with him each time after they had made love, young sorcerer and old one, as if declaring without words that what they shared was not just of the body and heart but also of the mind and imagination.

Particularly the mind and imagination, where eternity lies, as Seft had taught her, and where he and she would continue even after the world was dead and gone, broken and sunk beneath the waves like a child's toy abandoned on the seashore, to be removed with the tide.

"We have vastness in every heartbeat, every moment," Oma recited, as she had learned from him. "We are free anytime to partake of it. Yet here are you and I, aware of this, partaking of it, while out there, all those that remain proceed with their lives as if each of them was as important as the air and the sun. So let them pass by, outside these walls. In here, we have eternity. Once the heart and mind and spirit have been opened, who can endure existence among such closed souls?"

"None of us who is awakened."

"What then is the answer, magister?"

"To do as we are doing, my student. To use these others as tools to open our way into eternity, as we would use a horse to ride the land or a chisel to carve stone."

"And this is best." She quoted the final words from one of the oldest scrolls in the sorcerer's possession, the last line of a long poem that taught wisdom and visions and the deepest of truths.

"This is best," the sorcerer agreed. "Others would use *you*, had they the chance. It is the way of this world. What shall we do with our existence, Oma, here inside these walls?"

"Elevate ourselves."

"Nature and the gods and their servants choose who is to be free in this life," Seft told her. "We have been so chosen. Let us be worthy of the gifts they have bestowed on us."

They were quiet for some time. They watched the high clouds and the moon, dim beyond flashes of light, which were the bright eruptions caused by dark things as they came in swarms, commanded by distant magicians and witches—low, dark things that were gradually covering the earth, moving to destroy all that millennia of men and women had made happen, all of it soon to be broken and drowned like that child's toy.

Seft saw that Oma was watching where the world was under utter darkness. He said, "You will be safe for some time. These takers and their demon lords on the horizon are content for now with the lands they are devouring and the slaves they have made."

"Yes." She looked away from the skies and smiled softly at him.

Seft said then, "Allow me to leave you with further advice, my student."

"Please."

"Do not attempt to revive dead lovers."

"I will not. To cause such unrest among the dead would undo my desire."

"Revive dead blooms if you wish, and visit places that once were, but only their ruins. Never seek to facsimilate any region or home you have known."

"Never, magister. Were I to do it, I would upset precise balances unfamiliar to me."

"Seek knowledge from demons and spirits and all of the dead and heretofore experienced, but never turn back time, for even the gods cannot reverse the Endless Turning."

"Never will I attempt to return time, even when tempted by powerful creatures held in pause by the gods or kept imprisoned by Nature because of those monsters' own accidents or ambitions."

"Seek wisdom."

"Always."

"Manipulate the elements at your will."

"I shall."

"Use whatever comes by your path to explore your own being."

"Nature provides me with what I need. All I need do is ask."

"All you need do is ask." He told her then, "Unlearn these lessons when your spirit is sufficiently advanced. There is danger in it, we know, but ultimately, oneness and wisdom."

"I understand."

"And finally, Oma—set me free this night so that I might move my soul onward, as I have prepared myself."

"I will do it as I have so sworn, magister."

"Charm the knife and push it deep into my heart to free me suddenly."

"As you command."

"These men will be here soon?"

"Yes. I have lured them perfectly."

"Good. When you are done with them, they will assist you as my own victims have done me throughout my career in these arts."

The last of the sun went away beyond the garden walls. Oma watched the distant lightning flashes and the demons a-wing above the world.

She asked Seft, "Do you remember the story of the blind woman who came to you, wishing to see everything of the world before the world ended?"

"I do."

"She was in despair. The cities are degraded, the farms cannot be cultivated, the seas are rising, mountains are sliding from their heights, jungles sink, the forests shudder and fall. All will be lost. But she wished to witness for herself any hints of beauty that yet remained."

"I remember."

"And you gave her sight. With your skills, you took this woman in, aware in her of something of yourself from younger days. And you gave her sight, opened her eyes, her actual eyes, so that she could see the world as it is."

"Yes."

"And when she saw the world as it is, she saw blooms that were not so bright as she had imagined. She hoped to see the sun in wide skies, but all is gray and clouded. She wished to speak with those who toiled with their hands to make fine things and listen to harpists and singers who bring light and joy into the world and meet with farmers and fishers to learn of their trades, but these people all were broken and fearful, homeless, waiting for the end of life, afraid of nightmares, visited by ghosts and demons, without families."

"This is now the world."

"And so this woman, in reawakened despair, became determined to take her own life. Not even to blind herself again and put out her eyes, but to end herself then and there. Yet you saved her from this. You reminded her that what we see is not all that is, that this world is an imitation of what exists, and that doors can be opened to greater sights, that there are marvels. That this life, which so many assume is given freely, is only intermittent and can be the beginning of true life, existence beyond this life."

"I taught her these things, yes."

"For which I am grateful, Seft. That woman thanks you once more, as I have every day since I came here. Now...put out the fires in your garden. I no longer need them to see. Where I was once blind, I see in darkness, now."

Four thieves crouched in an alley at dusk, listening to every sound, eyeing every shadow, anxious lest they be discovered. The first had served a year in a foreign army: his name was Aros, and he'd trimmed his beard in the pointed Tolian military style, intending that it identify him as a strong leader. He knew in his heart that even a dying world must offer more than he could hope to gain as a thief, but when he looked around him, he saw few opportunities for a lowborn man such as himself. He had already lost four companions in street warfare with men better equipped than he. Now he had but three men remaining, none of them his equal.

Sife, the same age as Aros, was used only to the mercenary life he had found in skirmishing against marauders and small cohorts of renegades scavenging whatever remained in abandoned cities and villages to the west. Hoke, a large man, and his younger brother, Morios, half his size, prided themselves on being the finest pickpockets in the gutters where they'd been abandoned in boyhood.

The antics of these four had long irritated the gang leaders who controlled this corner of Kelsum—that is, the dilapidated remains of what had once been that noble city. Tonight, each of the four was worth more dead than alive. They therefore shared one ambition: to steal gold from Seft the sorcerer (one of the few persons left in the city to have anything worth stealing) and thus buy their way free of the rough men who had placed a price on each of them. They were caught between the noose and the axe, as the saying went. There was good money to be made by the cutthroat who beheaded any of these miscreants; even a hand or part of the head or face would do, so long as it could identify Aros or one of his followers. But trying to steal from Seft, who was centuries old and guarded by ghosts and demons, could be even more dangerous than remaining hidden in the streets.

Only when Aros was approached by an auburn-haired woman who offered to read his fortune did they decide at last to act. She had seen him in the shadows of a ruined building and knew him for what he was, a desperate man ready to take a chance with his life. That he had companions was even more beneficial for her, she told him. She needed help. The wary young man with the Tolian beard allowed her to read her cards for him, and the outcome was promising: their pattern revealed great success in a new undertaking.

"But have a care," this beautiful young woman had told Aros. "One of you will betray the others."

"Which one?" Aros had demanded. "I'll slit his throat immediately, tonight."

"This I cannot see. That one has not yet decided on this act. It is to come."

Aros was convinced. The witch claimed that she lived in the sorcerer's house and that her movements were as restricted by him as the freedom of Aros and his men was constrained by the gang members who threatened them. When Sife asked Aros that night in the alley whether he trusted this witch, Aros told him plainly that he did.

"We have little choice, anyway. Sooner or later, we'll be found here; we can't hide forever. She'll help us as we help her. And even a witch and a sorcerer can be caught on the end of a blade when one of us distracts them."

It was the game they had played often, one of them getting the attention of their victim while the others moved in to maim or kill, then make away with the goods. As added protection, the four had asked a priest of Il-obu to bless them before they began their adventure. Il-obu was an ancient god, a trickster who entertained the other immortals, and thieves everywhere had taken him as one of their own. The priest whom Aros had located to perform the blessing was no better than the four themselves, and he did it for the price of a toss with one of the priestesses at what had been their temple but now served largely as a brothel for the physically aching. Still, a blessing of any kind was something, at least.

With the risen moon but a blur at the height of the covered sky, Aros finished the last of a pitcher of wine, cast it into the trash that had collected at the end of the alley, and tugged thoughtfully at his fine, pointed beard, then stood, nodding to the other three to do so, as well.

He told Hoke, "Take a look. Tell us if you see anything."

Hoke moved to the end of the alley and looked up and down the street onto which it opened. The shops and public houses were closed this late at night. Three men and one woman spoke at one far corner, deciding on a business proposition. In the other direction, there was a man set against a wall, sitting in a puddle, his legs splayed out before him.

"It's clear," Hoke said. "I see nothing."

Aros looked at Sife and told him and the others, "No knives. No nooses. He keeps no guards. The witch told me the way to enter without disturbing anything there."

"Even ghosts?" asked Morios.

"Even ghosts," Aros assured him. "She told me a phrase to say that will quiet all the protection the sorcerer has impressed on his house."

He explained again how they would find the one weakness in the garden wall that protected the premises, the path to take past a certain old fountain, and which door would come open when Aros said the words.

They left the alley and, watching carefully, made their way across several streets toward the area where previously the wealthy and the merely rich had kept their houses against the poor and discarded. These excellent homes, left behind when their owners escaped on wagon or boat for other, safer places, had been scavenged of all worthwhile things before Aros and his companions were even born, so gradually was the world going dark and dying. But Seft's great marble house and wealth remained, and often the four thieves and others in the city had seen fires burning through the high windows, seen tall shadows moving against those lights, and witnessed figures and strange animals, only partially solid, atop the high roofs, tilting their heads to the moon and baying or speaking incomprehensible words to the stars that watched them like many eyes.

They came to an unlit street alongside the grounds of the sorcerer's home. In the wall there, Aros easily located the opening the witch had mentioned, shadowed though it was behind tall shrubbery. The four went through, and Aros led the way alongside a stone path, all of them taking care not to touch the path itself, lest they rouse spirits that might be awakened should they do so. They reached an old oaken door set in a marble recess no higher than the top of Morios' head.

"What kind of person fits into a doorway that small?" he asked.

"Not a person at all, I'm thinking," said Sife.

Aros warned him, "Quiet, quiet," and said the words Oma had taught him.

The door did not answer.

Behind him, Sife, the suspicious mercenary, whispered, "A trick."

Morios said, "It's our chance to back out of this. I say we go."

Hoke told Aros, "It's a test. She's testing our determination. Say it louder."

Aros did so, and the door fell open like a hand unclenching. He looked inside.

Sife asked him, "What do you see?"

"Nothing. It's a room, an alcove. It's dark, but it seems all right."

The other three bent forward to clear the abbreviated entranceway and entered to stand beside Aros. Sife said that one of them should find something in his pocket to catch a light; he had flint and steel.

"No," Aros warned them. "No light. The witch said so."

"So she's the leader? Not you?"

"No," Aros replied calmly. "You are, Sife. Go ahead. You lead." He pointed ahead.

"I didn't mean that."

"What, then?"

Hoke growled, "Enough. Let's get this over with before we're at each other's throats."

"Maybe," suggested Morios, "that's the plan."

"All of you," Aros warned them. "Quiet. Now. The witch said to go to the right. Is that acceptable to you, Sir Sife?"

"Just get moving."

Aros pushed past him and stepped carefully over the flat stones of the alcove until he reached a curtain at the far end. He waited, listening, but all was silence. He pulled the curtain to one side.

They were now in a long corridor. A torch hanging from a chain at the far end indicated a hallway to the left and one to the right.

"I don't trust any of this," Hoke said.

Aros told them, "It's too late for that. Listen, now. We're here. We find the gold, and when we do, we give a third of it to the witch, and she helps us leave."

Sife showed some temper. "You never told us she's to get any of the gold."

"No." Aros looked him in the eyes. "I did not. You might not have come if I'd told you. But that's why I trust the witch."

"And who says she won't kill us then and take all of it from us?" Sife asked.

"Because we know how to handle ourselves."

"Against beggars and other thieves, yes," said Hoke. "But sorcerers and witches?"

"Sorcerers and witches are just other names for beggars and thieves. They're as human as we are."

Hoke told him, "I agree. My blade works on them like it does on anything else. Just keep going. I don't like standing here. Keep moving and you keep alive, I say."

Morios said, "That's done us good till now, me and my brother."

They moved slowly down the corridor, aware that, despite whatever the witch might have promised, they might at any time step into a trap or inadvertently bring forth elements that for now remained invisible and at rest. Still, as they proceeded in a silent column, they seemed to get no closer to the far end of the corridor.

Aros looked at his feet as he walked. Yes, his toes were clearly moving from one stone to the one ahead of it. Yet when he looked up, the torch was no closer to him than it had been.

Hoke said, "Did you hear that?"

Sife told him that, no, he hadn't.

"There it is again," the big man said. He looked at Aros.

"I didn't hear it," Aros said. "We're making ourselves worry too much. There's no reason for that."

"No reason for *you*," Sife complained. "*You* have an agreement with the witch."

Aros faced Sife. "Are you still with us or not?"

"Are *you*?"

"Sife, tell me right now, in or out, are you in or out?"

"I need the gold as much as you do, and you know it."

"Then do what I—"

Morios, at the end of the file, made a sound. All turned to look at him.

His face was pale. "Ghosts," he said.

His brother asked him, "Where?"

"Right beside you."

None of them saw anything remotely like a ghost.

Morios told them, "I can hear it. Hoke, this is the way it was when we were boys, before I killed my first person. Remember?"

"No."

"Like it was a dream. Like I could see his ghost before I even killed him."

Sife told him, "Shut up."

Hoke turned on him. "You don't talk to my brother that way!"

Aros, who had taken a few steps ahead and been watching his feet as he did it, turned to face the others. He didn't see Morios.

"Where is he?" he asked.

Sife shifted on his feet to look around Hoke's bulk and said, "Your brother's run away. Or the ghosts got him."

"Shut up, rat." Hoke looked down the corridor the way they had come. "Stay here while I find him."

Sife said, "He didn't make a sound."

"Shut up!" Hoke growled and lurched back down the corridor, into the deep shadows by the hanging curtain, out of sight.

Aros put one foot out, looked at it, pulled it back.

Sife said to him, "I have a question for our leader."

"What is it?"

"You know where you're going."

"Yes."

"And even if your witch is going to help us, she'll get the four of us out of here, correct?"

"Yes. She agreed to that."

"Then let's get going. We can catch up with Hoke and Morios on the way back out."

"I suppose we can do that."

"Of course we can," Sife said.

They heard a grunting sound from the hallway near the curtain. Aros looked at Sife.

Sife sneered and said, "All right, leader. Go ahead."

Aros swore and went.

The floor of the corridor behaved as a normal floor once more. He made progress. When he reached the curtain, the toe of one of his boots hit something.

Metal. It rattled and went silent. Aros carefully knelt to feel for it.

There was liquid on the floor; he touched it, smelled it on his fingers. Oil. The metal was an oil lamp.

He moved the lamp away from the oil, felt for the wick, produced flint and steel from an inside pocket of the vest he wore, and lit the wick. Flickering light—green light, oddly—showed the curtain to his right and the shimmering oil beside him on the floor and nothing else.

He looked back toward Sife, now a tall shadow halfway between him and the hanging torch at the far end. Sife made a gesture indicating that he meant to go on. Aros shook his head and waved with his hand. Wait. He pushed the curtain aside and entered the alcove.

Morios and Hoke were stretched out side by side on the flat stones, eyes open, not moving. Hoke was smiling. Morios's face was turned toward the wall, his mouth parted.

Aros moved toward them, hoping that they would do something, shudder, roll to one side, but they did not. He didn't speak to them. Clearly, they were dead, were simply their bodies, now.

But even in that alcove poorly illuminated with the weak green light of the oil lamp, Aros saw that the two men's shadows were pointed toward him.

Although the light was coming from behind him.

Their shadows should be cast away from them, past the tops of their heads.

Aros backed into the curtain.

The shadows of the two men followed him over the floor.

He pushed the curtain out of the way, turned sideways, went past the lit oil lamp, and hurried down the corridor.

He looked back.

The shadows were following him, side by side, touching each other but slowly coming toward him like two black puddles rolling downhill.

Aros turned away and looked for Sife.

Sife was not there.

He hurried down the corridor. The walls and stones complied now, allowing him to move quickly toward the torch.

He whispered as strongly as he dared, "Sife? *Sife!*"

As he passed the torchlight and took the corner to his left, his own shadow, lifeless, swooped around him. But just there, ahead of him, was Sife's body—and his shadow.

The thief's shadow hung upon the wall, but his body lay as solid and unmoving as those of the other two men. Sife had no expression, although his wet, open eyes seemed to be as alive as the rest of him was dead.

"Sife!"

The shadow on the wall began to stretch toward Aros, and as he stepped back into the corridor, the shadows of Morios and Hoke continued to move like liquid toward him.

And if one of these shadows touched him?

To his right was a wall marking the dead end of the corridor, but behind Aros was that other hallway. It ended in another small archway, no taller then the one that led here from outside, but it offered the only possible means of avoiding the shadow in front of him and those in the corridor.

Aros lowered his head and walked through the opening.

"So you are here," came a voice.

A woman's voice, the witch's voice.

Aros stepped into an enormous room all of marble. It was lit by braziers on tripods and other burners throughout. Along the walls were columns, each taller than two men. Atop many were carvings, statues of men and women standing erect, eyes staring, arms at rest by their sides. The eyes in each, Aros realized, even at this distance seemed moist and alive.

The witch was in the center of the great room, which echoed when she spoke. She said to Aros, "And so they have brought you here."

"Who?"

"The shadows. Your companions."

She gestured with her arms, and as she did, Aros turned. Behind him, he saw Sife, Hoke, and Morios, each standing straight up but floating above the stone floor, each wrapped in his shadow as though in shimmering fabric.

Their eyes liquid and fully intelligent, the corpses stared at Aros until they had floated past him. The witch manipulated the air around her with her hands so that each of the three lifted to the height of one of the empty columns and stood there, immobile with bright eyes, caught.

Oma then faced Aros.

"There's no gold," he said.

"No," she assured him. "No gold. We do not require gold in here."

"And the one who was to betray me?"

"You are the betrayer, Aros. You had your chance not to sacrifice your friends when the door outside did not answer at once to the words I gave you. Spirits everywhere hesitate at first when called upon to be sure of a petitioner's intent. But I saw this in you. In the cards."

"Why?" he asked, stepping forward and reaching toward the knife he kept in his belt.

"For him." Oma pointed to the far end of the great room. "Do you see?"

There against the wall was a stone altar, upon which lay the body of an old man. Before the altar was a wide triangle carved into the floor. A great candle stood at each point of the triangle, and positioned in the center of it, a great bronze gong.

"Who is he?" Aros asked, approaching Oma.

"My mentor. My lover. My guide. The man who has freed me from my life among such as you. No knives, Aros." She gestured with her right hand.

He stopped where he was. Unable to resist, he lowered his arms to his sides. The knife dropped onto the floor. Something Aros heard but could not see scampered from behind him and scuttled across the floor. It retrieved the knife, making a metallic sound, and returned the way it had come, chittering.

"That knife was protected by a blessing from a priest."

"His blessing was very weak," Oma said. "Was he a truly priest or merely lying for money? Of course, you would understand a man who would lie for money."

"And you never have," he said.

She shrugged away the comment. "Aros, what do you see in this room? Evil?"

"Yes."

"Are you afraid of what you see?"

"Yes."

Oma asked him, "Are you familiar, Aros, with the *Philosophies of Samis*?"

"No, witch, I am not."

"Have you ever looked into a fire to see the life there and to hear the flames, which are as alive as you yourself and have voices of their own?"

"No."

"And the great spells of Motis, which allow us to sleep while we visit the worlds inside us and gain wisdom from all the lives we have ever lived—these you have not mastered."

"No." He found it difficult to form words, and he could not flex his fingers.

"No. Of course not. You are thinking desperately at this moment how you might escape. You have no idea what has happened to your friends, but all you wish for now is get away from me to continue to live in the gutter."

He was able to say, "I'll manage."

"You will not manage. I have you trapped now just as if you were still outside, trapped by your fear of the criminals you live with. You would rather exist in a sewer in this dying world than dare to attempt anything finer. You look up and witness the same stars I do, and yet they mean nothing to you. Your ancestors—they mean nothing to you. Sounds you could hear if you tried... sights you might see if you dared to look...the wisdom of spirits and the illuminating dangers of speaking with demons who existed long before our lives began—these mean nothing to you. What is life without the mind and imagination and the dreams we seek to make actual?"

Aros could do no more than stare at her.

Oma told him, "*You* mean nothing. Do you understand? You and your friends...can you even comprehend what life is capable of? You squander everything. I can use your lives for far better purposes than the four of you ever could imagine. You will be the fuel to fire my dreams and imagination."

He could not speak to answer her; he could not move his mouth. Aros was unable to bend his neck or turn his head. He could do no more than stare directly ahead and watch as the witch proceeded toward the triangle.

As she did, the thief began to feel the inside of him turning into liquid; that was the sensation. He was not made dizzy by this sensation, but he felt his sense of himself begin to drift away. In a moment, looking down as well as he could, he saw the liquid sense of himself stretching out before him as his own shadow, moving away from him, shining like black oil.

He could not breathe, but he was not dead. He was solid, awake, and aware inside his body, which had become...wood? Clay? Stone? Only his eyes felt actual. He could not blink, but he could see, and his eyes remained moist.

What he saw was Oma the witch within the triangle. She retrieved a long metal wand from the floor and lifted it with her left hand. She spoke loudly as though addressing an unseen gathering or crowd. Aros could not understand the language she spoke. Then she struck the gong.

It made a wide sound that opened in an expanding wave, almost visible and shimmering, and as it filled the great room, a glow or light in some manner lifted above the dead man on the altar as though spreading massive wings.

Oma struck the gong a second time. The light increased and betrayed movement inside itself, things taking shape.

Aros felt himself being lifted into the air, and he began to float. He also heard Sife's voice within himself.

We are hers now, Sife's voice said. We will guard her and see for her into every space.

Aros thought, What have we become?

The witch struck the gong a third time.

Hoke answered him from his pedestal. We will learn many secrets to help her. Has she not shared that with you? We will go ahead of her as she investigates places outside this place. If we need to die for her, we will relinquish our souls and do it.

Who tells you this? Aros wondered.

Morios told him, I understand more now than I ever did. I am more alive than ever before and far more intelligent than I was previously. This is a gift from the man on the altar. He has taught us so much within only a few heartbeats.

The witch struck the gong a fourth time.

Now, from where he hung high in the air above the floor, Aros saw the things that were beginning to take shape in the bright light above the body on the altar.

He thought, But that man is *dead*.

Not dead, Hoke told him. Alive as we are alive. Passing along as we will pass along. But he is guarded by the wisdom he has learned over centuries.

What wisdom protects? Aros thought.

Now he heard a great laugh, the sound of a voice he had not previously heard.

The old man, the sorcerer on the altar.

Oma struck the gong a fifth time. As she did, the beings became quite distinct. They were small but powerfully shaped. They had faces, awkward and unusual faces. Some had wings of a sort, others, tails. Not fully human, but not animals. Life of a kind other than mere human life.

Aros heard echoes of speech in the voice of the old man and Oma.

Out there, all those that remain proceed with their lives as if each of them was as important as the air and the sun. Let them pass by, outside these walls. In here, we have eternity. Who can endure existence among such closed souls?

He thought, This is not fair. This is not fair. I've never made a mistake in my life.

Oma struck the gong a sixth time.

Aros settled upon the top of a column, perfectly balanced, and he watched as seven beings now circled the sorcerer on the wide altar and lifted the body, which now was a very bright green.

Oma spoke loudly in words that Aros could not understand as she struck the gong a seventh time.

A hole opened in the bright green air around the beings and the sorcerer, and the things walked on the green air, disappearing within that hole or opening, moving the body to wherever they were going so that the sorcerer's soul would be free.

Oma set down the wand and spoke further words, ending the ceremony. She looked up at Aros, where he stood all solid and moist-eyed atop his column.

"His sorcery is now my sorcery," she told the unmoving man. "I will speak to you henceforth in dreams and gestures and with incantations, and you will do as I say. All of you will."

She motioned to the many unmoving ones within that room.

"The world is dying," Oma reminded the unmoving ones, "but I shall not die, not yet, not like you. I shall witness the world's passing and then follow my teacher into brighter places. And you will assist me, all of you. I will perfect my sorcery. I will live my life within this room, and you shall watch me do it. And you shall have no lives of your own because you will serve me for as long as I wish. Know, however, that I understand your pain. I, too, have been in pain. You were in pain that you did not recognize. I have freed you from that abominable pain. Answer me when I speak to you."

She heard the voices of all those unmoving souls reply to her at once.

We will serve you, they agreed.

Oma turned and left the great room, going into farther places within the sorcerous house that was now her house, and Aros heard her voice and the sorcerer's as clearly as though the thief had been present himself the previous day, overhearing them as they discussed the end of the world, musing on those who yet hung onto life in a sinking world.

"What shall we do with our existence, Oma, here inside these walls?"

"Elevate ourselves."

"Nature and the gods and their servants choose who is to be free in this life. We have been so chosen. Let us be worthy of the gifts they have bestowed on us."

Aros understood now that he, too, and Sife and the others, all of them here, had also been chosen.

I was in such pain, he thought.

Now I am finally free, freer than I ever dreamed I could be, and I see everything. Let me be worthy.

The End of Days

As a breath on glass,—
As witch-fires that burn,
The gods and monsters pass,
Are dust, and return.

—George Sterling, "The Face of the Skies"

1. Refugees

Night—and the sky to the west was bright with storms as whatever had been under that sky came to an end. Nour glanced at the fiery clouds through the broken doors that led to the veranda, where his wife stood, just outside, hands resting protectively over her belly. He returned his attention to the papers on the library table but told Silene, "Whoever was here, they saw it coming."

"Then they escaped." She closed her eyes as a breeze lifted, cooling her against the heat.

The noise of powerful movement intruded—the walls of a great city falling, or a mountain sinking—and they both felt its echoes rolling beneath their feet, the flat stones of the veranda and the library floor shuddering, the furniture in the library sliding.

Nour walked out to stand by Silene and took her hand as he looked to the west. They had been a couple for nearly a year—a long time, given the dangers they and everyone else faced. But they loved each other and were determined to live, this tall, dark-haired, dark-eyed thinking man and his slender, fair-haired wife, now pregnant, whispery life within her.

Thunder. When the dark sky blossomed again with fiery light, they saw flying things within the clouds, demonic things soaring.

"Silene?"—her brother, calling from around a corner of the villa.

"We're here!"

Edric came onto the veranda. Like his sister, he was light-haired, but stocky and heavily muscled, his arms and neck thick.

Edric had not removed his armor in days, and he had no intention of relaxing now, not with his fighters as tired as he was, dried blood still on them, their wounds fresh.

He told his sister and Nour, "My rider must be dead by now. It's time we kept moving. Did you clean up?"

"We found a wash bowl," she told him. "I'd have changed clothes if there were any here. They took what they needed." She was in her heavy blouse and skirt, all she had now, and Nour, unshaved, in his breeks, torn shirt, and vest.

Edric surveyed the library as though sensing something.

Silene asked him, "What of the others?" She meant the families and other refugees being escorted by her brother and his company.

"They've rested. That's sufficient. They want to keep moving."

Nour said, "Whoever lived here, they calculated by the stars. They saw Serenthal and its army."

"Hame tells me that they're following us." He noticed Nour's scowl. "You do not trust him?"

"I am undecided."

Hame was a sorcerer. Not yet old, of medium build but already white of hair and beard, he was one of many who practiced the arts of his heritage against the dark things that were returning. He had sworn an oath to Edric to assist as he might, as did many of his kind these days, helping any surviving refugees. These practitioners of the old, alert senses had no love for the demons that sought ruination, yet the tools of their ways brought them often into contact with such sinister forces, so that Nour wished to keep his distance from this man. Hame was not evil; Nour understood that; and any weapons were good weapons to use against the monsters, whether steel and bronze or arcane and invisible.

But Nour's concern was for Silene and the child. And though he knew that Edric was concerned also for his sister's safety and that of the baby to come, still—as a military man, Edric took his advantages where he found them, including an alliance with those such as Hame. Nour understood, but he would not himself have sought out humans of the old arts no matter how desperate he might become.

He told Edric, "If they're following us, then what is your sorcerer's advice?"

"Others of his kind are aware, and they're between us and Serenthal. I'd hoped my rider would tell me their location. They are with other refugees—"

"Lord Tor," Silene said.

"Yes."

"Are he and his group dead?"

Edric told her and his suspicious brother-in-law, "Hame says not."

"His raven tells him so?" Nour asked.

"Yes. Do not," Edric said, his voice changing, "distrust the souls of the dead and the arts of the sorcerers assisting us."

Silene took his hand, and Nour apologized. "It is difficult to trust anyone today, Captain."

Edric told him, "I quite agree. Which I why I rely on the mages. We have few others to help us reach Surkad."

Surkad. Serenthal's capital city thousands of years ago, and now the city that all refugees sought, intending from there to board ships that were sailing out to sea in hopes of finding safety in other lands. Edric wondered if any of them, in fact, the thousands seeking escape, would manage to reach the old city on the coast, fighting as they were against the things crawling up from the earth and coming down from the skies. If they did not, if Serenthal and its army of things prevented them, or if any of a thousand other monsters came at them, that would end this adventure. And even if the child, his sister and Nour's child, were born alive, the only hope it could have would be to be born away from here—on one of the eastern islands or, better, one of the ships they heard were raising sail daily. Every night, as Silene went to sleep beneath the evil stars that now governed heaven, Edric knew his sister whispered to the babe inside her an old poem, as if the poem were a charm:

Sleep tonight by fires bright, though monsters be, we will be free.

People had been whispering this prayer for hundreds of years as the monsters returned to take back all lands at last, the creatures that human beings had put down again and again, had sent back into the earth, set afire, banished with spells. Where were the spells now to defeat them? Where were the heroes to put them back into the earth?

My men and I are the only heroes left, Edric thought. *Small men losing, strike by strike. But perhaps that does indeed make us heroes, to fight what cannot be defeated.*

One of the men of his command, coming through the empty villa, called for him. "Captain!"

Edric waved him onto the veranda.

The soldier saluted. "Sir, your rider."

"What does he say?"

"Dol Nem has fallen."

"There." Edric nodded to the western sky.

"Yes, sir."

"The third city this month. They hurry. So must we. Tell our company."

"Yes, sir." The rider saluted and went to do it.

But Silene moved into the library, a place of momentary peace. Even by lamplight she could tell that the artwork here was superb. Frescoes and sculptures, inlaid mosaics on the floor and the table tops. "Whose home was this?" she wondered out loud. "This is exquisite work."

Nour looked at one of the cushioned chairs in the room. "He sat there, I imagine. Admired his art for the last time. Had a cup of his best wine. Listened to the thunder coming."

Edric stepped out of the fine library and into a hallway, where everything was dark.

"Give me a lamp."

Silene fetched one from a side table in the library and handed it to her brother.

He took it with him down the hallway, making a sound as he went, the oil lamp pushing a screen of yellow light ahead of him and around him. He stopped when he entered a farther room.

"Yes, here."

Nour came behind him, followed by Silene.

Not turning, Edric said, "Not for her eyes."

Silene coughed, smelling now the death here and the oddly sweet odor the monsters carried, something in their hides or fur or skin.

Nour stepped behind Edric to see.

There was the rich man, what remained of him, a head with its eyes gone and the rest of him ripped away down to the bones, the meat and everything the demons had eaten. Not the blood. His blood was everywhere, and that of his wife and a servant woman and three children, all of them young. The girl's face was beautiful; she would have been a princess or a queen in another life, Nour thought. Now she was inside something's belly.

Nour asked Edric, "Are they still here?"

"No. You could smell them if they were. We move now. We can rest tomorrow. Put this place behind us."

2. The All-Night

The monsters and their darkness had begun moving once more
two generations earlier. Before then, the world had been quiet
for some time, the monsters at rest or gathering strength. Still,
after centuries of their gradual encroachment, the world—the
continent of Attluma, their home—was by now largely diseased,
under darkness, in shadows, become wasteland and swamp.
Nothing on the order of nations or kingdoms had persisted; these
had collapsed into city-states, which in turn had become villages,
their populations diminishing, people of one tongue or another
dying out, those of common heritage all dead.

The darkness had been born when the land itself had risen
from the ocean at the beginning of Time, the monsters and their
strength as intertwined with the earth as human beings themselves were. Unsteady had been those millennia when warriors
and kings, traders and workers, dreamers and poets had created
islands of order in every direction, life expanding. Yet the All-
Night, long prophesied, had come finally to reckon the balance,
to undo what humanity had done for so long. For scholars, the
beginning of human history was legend, and the accomplish-
ments of kings and the tides of empires, an endless scroll; but
such magnitudes of time were as nothing to the monsters of the
dawn, were no more than vanishing heartbeats; and so, timeless,
they were returning to feed on humans again and reawaken the
darkness that had birthed them, the Night.

The northern territories and nations by now were all sundered,
the people there slaves or food for the things that had returned,
Kossuth and Dalmur, Oam and Queen Ritris, creatures wormy
and deadly, holding evil shapes so as to stay on earth in a manner
peculiar to them, existing according to their own ways—and
those ways foreign to men and women used to daylight and all
that is nourished in the sun. The rocky shores of the far west
already had begun to fall into the ocean, as had the farthest of
the southern lands. A few outposts remained inland and had
adopted the names of the mighty nations that once had homed
them: Csith, Setom, Tol, Samdum.

Along the eastern seaboard, in what had been Khom, wealthy
and resplendent in its time, what remained of humanity were
moving in long trails to launch themselves east upon an ocean
that likely had no end but that promised no shadows. Some in
what had been Lusk and Kormistor and Miskor in the west had

done the same, building great galleys and ships as their ancestors
had done to go out upon the seas there. Hope is what boarded
them on those vessels, and hope steered them, perhaps into the
jaws of other monsters, perhaps into new lands of sun and life.

In Khom, it had been Edric and Silene's grandparents who
had felt the world shudder as the things began to move upon the
earth once more, traveling east with their plagues and creatures.
The grandparents had told the children how it had been, the skies
darkening, the earth opening to swallow villages. Their generation had been the first in a century to do what the ancient heroes
had done: take up arms to defend home and family against the
reborn evils from the start of history. They and their companions
had trained Edric's parents and Edric and Silene in the use of
weapons and the necessary military skills.

"Long away," the grandfather would say, in a phrase of his.
"Long away the monsters were, and now they are come back. We
must do what we can."

He was killed by them, and the grandmother, too, eaten alive
as Edric and Silene and their patents watched. Then the parents
and their children had joined the thousands of others making
toward the sea and the ships there, many of them dying as they
fought the things that chased them, or succumbing to illness or
injury, as had Edric and Silene's parents. History and memory
died as men and women and their children died, but others
remained, almost nameless, forming groups, making pacts,
convening societies, swearing bonds, taking oaths to defend one
another until whoever remained might at last have the chance to
be free of the dying world.

They had come ten leagues in three days, a hard march for Edric and
his company of two hundred and the men, women, and children
who traveled under their protection. All were weary of fighting
whatever came at them—groups of young witches and sorcerers
claiming to be allied with the dark things but who were killed
as easily as anyone else; sweet-smelling genuine creatures from
beneath the earth; living vines and plants with teeth; misshapen
animals and shadowy creatures that had not yet matured into true
monsters but would do so now that they were up from Hell and on
the earth, breathing air, eating flesh; and bandits and free riders
out for themselves in a world that was going undershadow at last.

As they marched, Edric ordered some of those on foot ahead to
scavenge for food, although the steady heat that held the world

together within its solemn haze had meant the end of many things, animals and plants both, that armies and families had relied on for sustenance. Only small game was to be had now, no fish, little fruit. Vegetables and roots that grew in the ground could be used, as well as animals that burrowed there, but these things barely sufficed to feed a company of fighting men and those in their charge. Birds could be taken if one were skilled with a bow, although there was always the danger that something high up would not be meat on the wing but rather a demon, and fast to turn and attack whoever had aimed a bolt at it. But it was that or starvation. Many times, Edric's company had seen half-eaten corpses alongside the road or in the fields they passed through, and the teeth marks on the bones were not those of wild animals.

These men and women, determined to reach Surkad and the coast, might have been the last people in the world who depended on one another and had not yet turned on the weakest of themselves. Wolves did that, and raiders and bandits and the ghouls they had fought, shadows that in the night would attack anything alive. Would the men and woman of Edric's company be reduced to that? Rather would I fall on my sword, said several of the proud fighting men and women. Or rather would I kill and cook and devour any demon that I can kill. They are made of meat the same as I am. But those were words. The meat of the evil things of the earth was poison; they had heard stories of those who had so partaken and died soon after or gone mad. In any case, they were not yet faced with utter desperation. But soon now, perhaps.

Soon.

Edric, on his horse at the head of his column, saw no signs that anyone had taken this route before them, human or not. The sun lifted, only slightly less dim than the obscurity around it. The land around them was flat and gray, nothing but scrubland and thin woods. The sun continued to rise, and this was day for them, a twilight distinguished from midnight only by the fact that it was not utterly lightless.

The company remained watchful for edible plants, and the good archers among them brought down rabbits. That boded well, that they were heading into territory had not been cleaned already of its rabbits and rodents.

Edric lifted a hand, calling a halt to the advance. Nour, on his horse with Silene seated in front of him, came alongside him.

Edric said, "I smell it."

Silene said, "I can, too, now."

The captain signaled for a man of his infantry to come ahead and serve as front walker, to scout; that one did so, spear held out in front of him, sword loose in its scabbard. He proceeded cautiously, looking in every direction as he advanced, then halted at a series of sounds.

Just within the wood line was an old man in torn attire of hide and wool, now bloodstained, as he was himself. With the long knife in his right hand he repeatedly stabbed the corpse of a monster that lay before him, almost in his lap. There was not much left of it; it appeared to have been a human-sized thing with furry forearms and forelegs, perhaps horns or bony growths of a sort from the back of its head arching forward over its brow. The remainder of it was a ruin. With each punch of the blade, the old man reached into the corpse with his left hand, then wiped the bloody fingers and palm on his own face and arms.

"It killed my boy," he said, perhaps aware that others were present, perhaps not. "It killed my boy."

Beyond him, among the thin trees, Edric and his front walker saw the corpse of a young man bitten in half, the flies already on it.

The captain ordered his man to back away; both returned to the column.

As Edric mounted his horse, the young man asked him, "Why, sir, does he smear himself with the blood of the monster? I've never seen that before."

"He thinks it will protect him from other monsters," Edric said. "But in my experience, it does no good."

3. Poetry

By midday, exhausted, having had no sleep during the night, the company found that the woodland thinned, opening onto wide flat fields and rocky terrain. They found no villas or mansions in which to bivouac, but when, late in the afternoon, they came to a gulley with a stream of fresh water nearby, Edric called a halt to the march. There had been no further thunder since last night, nor signs of monsters or other things; neither had they spotted marauders or free roamers, at least none in numbers adequate to make a challenge.

Edric led his horse to water at the stream, as did the fifty others who had managed to keep their mounts alive and service-able. Twenty under his command volunteered to spell each other at the perimeter; the remainder of his infantry rested where they were and began building fires and setting up lean-tos.

Nour brought his and Silene's horse to the stream. Helping her dismount, he walked her to the security of a slight delve, little more than a rock overhanging other rocks, but it helped to cut the hot wind when it lifted. One of the other women, the wife of a marcher, came by to leave a bit of cooked rabbit for her—for the baby. Eat, eat for the baby.

Nour built a fire near the overhang and shared with Silene water he had gathered in skins from the stream. The horses all around rested, showing no signs of sensing danger. The sun began to drop. Twilight deepened. The day cooled as much as could be expected. Nour took down the blankets he carried in a roll behind his horse's saddle and put together a makeshift tent, the lean-to that Silene had slept in for weeks. He unrolled a blanket to serve as her bed, then sat beside her, loosening his sword in its scabbard.

It had been one of his father's, and the scabbard was patched and bloodstained. Nour, lover of books and poetry, had learned to use that weapon and had killed, so far, two men with it as well as a small, jumping thing, a monster or demon or animal of some sort. He liked having the sword.

One of Edric's close companions, a middle-aged woman dressed in armor and as hardy as the rock overhead, came by to look after Silene and Nour. She was still wet from having washed the smell of dead monsters from herself and her weapons.

"You're the captain's brother-in-law."

"Yes."

"Is she well?"

"She rests," Nour told the warrior. He stood and walked with her so as not to awaken Silene with their conversation. "How are you called?"

"Esta. My name is Esta."

"I've seen you fighting. You were born for the sword."

Esta shrugged. "Born for it, and then nothing but practice. But sooner or later I'll make a mistake. Don't we all?"

"I will before you do," Nour told her. "I wasn't born for battle."

"You're a poet. You're the one with all of the books we're bringing along in one of the carts."

"Not that many. We used to have more libraries and books in this land than there are stars."

"And where are they now?" Esta asked, but then, "I mean no disrespect."

"Warrior, I like to think that they are in here." Nour tapped his chest, meaning his heart. "If we have learned any worthwhile knowledge and remembered any poems, then we carry them with us."

"Well said."

"Esta, let me ask you. What are our chances? Can you guess?"

She told him, "We may face further danger as we approach Surkad—if it still stands. But we're not alone. Many companies are doing as we are, following paths to get there or to other places that may be of help."

"As Edric has said."

"Yes. But the monsters are everywhere. And Serenthal would be pleased to destroy the city so that it can rebuild it as it was in its time. It was king there. Even the demons have their kings and queens."

"I think of the legends that say others have sailed east and found wonderful lands of plenty. Truly lands of the gods."

"Perhaps."

"Unlike here," said Nour, and it was the poet in him speaking now. "Everything here returning to the monsters as if humanity had never happened. Is this how Nature is? These things are the opposite of us, yet they exist like a disease set loose upon us. They suffocate us with their shadows and darkness. It's too much for me to imagine that everything we as people deemed right and good will become the opposite but still exist. It should be against Nature, such existence as theirs."

"Existence is all, my friend," Esta told him. "Why? Do you think life has meaning?"

"I do."

"I do not," Esta said. "We fight to live and do what we can by the moment. That is all. We do it, Serenthal does it, the monsters do it."

"Warrior, that sounds like a hopeless existence to me."

"You're a poet. A person of thought and books."

"Yes."

"I have also read books and thought many thoughts. What of it?"

Nour told her, "I have been considering these monsters since they first came back to take the world from us. Esta, do you know what the monsters do not understand? Here is my thought—that life is worth living because we work. We strive. We are curious. We reach beyond ourselves. When did the monsters ever do that? Serenthal and Kossuth and all of these things born when this land came out of the darkness—when did they write poems of love to their children? They have no children. When did they ever put down thoughts to guide others far from now? Are they curious to know anything beyond themselves? They are like the grossest animals, these things. They have no sensitivity. They are merely appetites and strength. That *is* existence, and that's all that it is. Do they have love? Esta, have you felt love?"

She hesitated before answering, but then admitted to this poet, "I lost my partner years ago. She was my life."

"What about her? Would you tell me? It is the details that we revere."

"I remember her teeth, her smile. The color of her hair. She used to make fun of me, but I liked the color of her hair, how it glowed in the light. And she had the finest legs. Strong legs. But she had a temper."

Nour said, "I remember the trees on my parents' land. Each a different color, their crowns proud, the colors changing in the autumn. Birds, too, in all of their colors, and each with its song. This is what I mean. Do you see? My father's laugh. My mother's eyes."

"And the monsters have nothing like this. Perhaps you're right."

"The monsters will take this land and kill many of us. So be it. They made this world. We have tried to live in it, but it is their land, after all. Let them have it. Even the gods have surrendered to them. We will have new lands. New gods. No monsters."

"Because we are human."

"Yes. Like the early heroes and the best of us. As it was."

"You have helped me with my thoughts, poet."

"Have I?"

Esta told him, "It reminds me of a memory. When I was small, I saw a city from far away. It was magnificent, as if the gods lived there. Shining, with lights burning like stars, the way cities used to be that we heard about, big and good. I wanted to walk to it, even if it took me all night, and enter that city. Then my uncle told me it wasn't a real city. The monsters created it. It was an illusion. The demons made it to trick us, he said, and anyone who went there would be trapped. Now I wonder if we ever did have cities like that."

"We did. And we will again. We are human. We work and we strive. Dream, even."

"Poet, thank you. I will think about this."

"As you use your skills."

Esta laughed, genuinely. "Yes! As I use my skills."

Three of the scouts on the perimeter came in and told Esta, "We heard nothing and saw nothing. Perhaps we will have a quiet night."

"A good night for thinking, then." She walked past them to take her place at the edge of the camp.

One of the three asked Nour, "For thinking?"

"We were discussing ideas," he told them.

"Oh."

"And poetry."

"Poetry," said the scout, and went to get his rest.

4. Sorcerers

The attack came just before dawn—not Serenthal but a small army of marauders and renegades assisted by monsters, things once human but now transformed, aligned with Serenthal and moving ahead of it to secure land that once was claimed by that dark king. They came from the northwest in a rush, some of the marauders on horseback, the others on foot, and the things with them on their flanks, the better to catch any who might try to escape that way.

Edric ordered the families with him and those not under his command to climb to the heights of the rocky gulley. The men were to protect the children and any women with child—Silene was not the only pregnant refugee—for these were the generation to come, the children and unborn who must live.

Edric and his troops formed a front, a wide crescent with their backs to the gulley, advancing as the invaders advanced. Nour helped Silene and some of the weaker ones nearby move up the rocks to the safety of the gulley height, where there were trees and boulders to provide possible protection, whatever might come. Nour removed his sword and held it at the ready, and Silene kept her right hand on the hilt of the long knife she had at her side. It had been useful for cutting meat and stripping bark from plants to get at the edible meat of them; now she would use it as well as she could against whatever came at her. She settled into a position against the bole of a tree and looked at Nour. Their eyes said the things that need no words.

Nour stepped in front of his wife to shield her as Hame came up alongside him, helping a woman and child climb ahead. Then the sorcerer turned to watch as the attackers came forward across the field.

Nour asked him, "Will you fight?"

"Yes," Hame told him, not looking at Nour, and then, "There."

He pointed to his raven, on the wing and coming toward him, flying ahead of the attackers. The sorcerer pressed a hand to his forehead and closed his eyes tightly.

Nour felt heat come from him, the sorcerer's hand and face flushing with warmth.

Hame opened his eyes, dropped his hand, and told Nour, "Others are coming."

"Monsters."

"No. Like me. And fighters."

Nour saw them now on the horizon, past the moving army of attackers, behind them but coming quickly, fighters on horseback, in their motley armor, and the others—sorcerers—in skins and leather, on foot to use the power of the earth, waving wooden staves and metal objects, magical art.

As Hame's raven returned to him, speaking in its language and settling on the limb of a tree close by, the attackers and Nour's company met on the field. The mounted fighters clashed first, Edric at the lead, and Silene saw her brother's sword take two heads immediately, a man's and a woman's, whose horses then ran unguided as the bodies slumped and dropped. The man beside Edric was taken by a spearman, who pierced him through, but as he fell from his horse, Edric reined about to face the attacker, a large man who pulled out a sword to defend himself. Edric's sword and his met; both swung at each other several times, their horses moving awkwardly; Edric ducked neatly, brought up his blade, and freed the renegade's sword hand. Glove and weapon dropped to the grass as Edric came around to behead him. The protective metal collar the renegade wore prevented the sword from removing his head entirely, but Edric had cut well enough that the head dropped to one side and lolled there, hanging by a length of red muscle, bouncing with the movement of the horse, the eyes staring at the world sideways as the blood poured down.

Across the field, Edric's fighters dealt swiftly with the monsters that came at them. This surprised Nour as he watched, but Hame explained the awkwardness the things exhibited.

"It is the bargain they made," said the mage. "These people were weak. To be transformed by sorcery is to clear away your soul and take on something waiting to be again on the earth. Those people were foolish to make such a bargain."

"But they can still hurt us," Nour said. "They have fangs and claws and teeth, and that one has wings."

It was a scaled thing as large as a wolf cub, once a woman but now a monster with wings of gray skin that flew into Edric's company and managed to wrap those wings around the head of one of his fighters. That man dropped his sword in trying to pull the thing free, but already the creature's clawed feet had ripped through his throat, and he dropped, all red. But a woman near him sworded the winged monster as it began to fly off, halving it, so that the two parts of the scaled body dropped to the grass, the wings shuddering.

Other monsters leaped and crawled, and where they managed to claw or bite the defenders, those victims fell with swollen legs or arms, poison taking them quickly. Still, these damaged souls were awkward, as Hame had said, and moved strangely once they had killed, so that swords and spears finished them. The stink of them then clouded the field, but dead they were.

"Let me fight!" Nour said, beginning to move.

Silene objected. "Wait until your sword is truly needed."

"There is blood to be spilled!"

But Hame told the poet, "Your wife is correct. Your time is soon."

"You know this?"

"I do. Let me guide you."

Edric's company still outnumbered the renegades, but damage was done not only by the monsters and the mounted attackers and those on foot, but also by the sorcerers with them. From their height in the ravine, Nour and Hame counted five of these people, three to one side of the advancing attackers, two on the other.

One of the sorcerous women in the field, her leather armor brightly painted with magical signs, screamed a word and shoved one end of her staff into the earth. A shimmering wall of light rose from the grass, as if the moon's reflection on the surface of a lake had come into existence. The shimmering wall was neither silver nor white but as clear as water. The witch directed this shining wall toward Edric's company, so that it moved like a winding serpent over the field.

The fighters nearest the witch were caught quickly and encircled in cocoons of cold light. They screamed, their faces visible beneath the shimmering light holding them, but their screams could not be heard. When they fell, they were crushed within these cocoons and left dead as the light about them dissolved into mist. Laughing, the woman with her staff then directed her icy wall to move onward into the jostle of fighters.

From where he stood, Hame growled and lifted his own staff and waved it, making a sign in the air. At that gesture, his raven took wing and flew swiftly toward the sorcering woman, who saw the bird, heard its cry, but too slowly made a sign to protect herself. The wall of shining light turned back toward her like a running animal, so that in a heartbeat, she was herself wrapped in her own suffocating cocoon.

One of the sorcerers nearby came to assist her, but Hame's bird shrieked again. At the sound, the witch stumbled into the sorcerer, and the cold shimmering wrapped about him, as well. In the confusion these two caused as they fell, the line of marauders near them was disrupted. These fighters panicked, and Edric and those with him moved in, cutting off the legs of any on horseback and chopping at the men and women on foot.

Nour told Hame, "This is the time!"

"Go," the sorcerer told him, pointing with his staff to the west of the field.

Twenty of the attackers, unhorsed, had gathered there in a knot so that they could defend each other as Edric's men and women came at them. As one or two fell, the others closed together and held their ground with swords and spears.

Nour hurried down the side of the gulley and ran toward them.

Silene asked Hame, "Will my husband live?"

The sorcerer did not answer, but with his staff commanded his raven, floating high above the fight, to circle close to Nour and follow him as he ran. When a young man came at Nour with a spear, the raven spoke, and Nour, alerted, moved to one side, avoiding the spear thrust while turning to cut his attacker down the back, opening him along the spine.

Silene said, "Sorcerer, you have saved my husband's life."

She pressed a hand to his shoulder in thanks but then quickly removed it; Hame was hot to the touch.

He said to her as he watched the fighting, "There. They have arrived."

Now two groups of support came in on the flanks of the renegades, some on horseback, most of them running or hurrying as they could. Clearly several of these were not sword or spear fighters but sorcerers.

Silene observed the sorcerers as they met and fought in the field. She saw the air turn colors between these people and watched as they moved their arms in gesticulations, or with daggers drew designs in the air. One or the other of these mysterious people would then die, pulled into the sky to be torn invisibly into pieces, raining blood, or drawn into the earth to suffocate, or simply fall, breathless and unmoving, wrapped beneath sheets of glowing color.

Several of the attacking sorcerers made signs toward Edric's fighters and dropped them. These men and women fell onto their backs and caught fire from their chests. They screamed as they died, but the unnatural fire consumed them swiftly, turning the men and women as black as charred wood. From the burnt corpses rose pieces of them, bits of black, which moved high into the air and, at the command of the attacking sorcerers, dropped like hurled missiles into the line of Edric's men, the bits of black pushing through faces and armor.

Silene gripped Hame's shoulder in her panic. "What are they? Name of the Mother, what are they?"

"Souls," Hame told her. "They remove the charred souls from the burned bodies to use as weapons. More than life is gone from these people. They are now lost to us forever."

"Not my husband, Hame, please, please!"

Three of the flying bits of black came toward Nour, and as they did, he lifted his sword to defend himself.

It was unnecessary. He saw now another sorcerer, a black man dressed in leather and skins, wave a dagger at the bits of dead souls to catch them on fire, so that they became ashes in the air. Then the black man engaged one of the sorcerers who had created the charred souls. He approached this man while cutting the air with his dagger. The attacker was not near the black man, but he was wounded despite the distance between them. He waved his arms in gestures of defense, but as the black man sliced with his dagger, the sorcerer was cut as if the blade itself were doing it—face cut to the bone, hands severed, stroke after stroke across the chest of him, and finally the piercing of the heart, the black man pushing forward with his dagger to the chest, so that the other sorcerer, grinning in fear, felt it move through his heart, and he dropped.

Nour, wordless, sword at his side, stared at the black man.

The sorcerer said to him, "Hame is with you."

"Yes. On the rise." In awe of this man, he lifted his sword to point behind him.

The black man said then, "We have known each other many lifetimes, he and I. So I have come."

The engagement in the field was now ending. The attackers who remained alive were riding away, defeated by Edric's company and the sorcerers and other fighters who had come to their aid. But that knot of renegades remained, more of them now fallen, but all of them determined to kill as many as possible before going to death themselves.

Edric, on foot and colored with the blood of those he had slain, now approached this group. Ten of his men and women came with him; as with their captain, the gore of battle covered them. Nour hailed Edric and approached him as the black man watched from where he stood.

One of the men huddled in the knot said to Edric, "Any of you we kill is cursed. We took an oath to our masters."

"You're lying. Your masters damned you, not us," Edric told him. "Defend yourselves."

There was a moment's pause, as the renegades spoke among themselves, perhaps encouraging one another, perhaps saying words of dark prayer. Then they broke their knot, the fifteen of them that remained, and came at Edric and the others.

"To the death!" one of them cried.

"For my ancestors!"

"For the gods of darkness!"

The work went quickly, and Nour joined in. Imperfect as he was, he found himself untouched by sword strokes or spear thrusts and was able to kill two of the renegades himself. Yet it seemed as if his sword was guided. He knew where to strike and when to guard as though he were a veteran of the field.

When the fifteen lay dead, fallen and crumpled or in pieces, with none of Edric's company wounded, Nour looked toward the black man, who had remained some distance away. His thought was of how this mage had used his dagger just before, magically moving the weapon to undo his enemy, and he said to him, "You assisted my arm."

"I did."

"Why?" Nour walked toward him.

The sorcerer did not answer immediately. He surveyed the field. "Your company has largely survived," he said. "This was what we wished."

Nour looked upon what remained of the morning: warriors of all of the companies tending to each other's wounds as the surviving marauders rode free or ran away, many of them escaping the last of the arrows and bolts from the archers among the ranks of Edric and the other commanders. The fighters walked their horses from the field, and some of them led two horses, their own and that of one of the fallen. Cries of despair were few, and they came only from men and women who had joined the fighting but were not themselves trained for such work: refugees eager to assist but unprepared for the violence they had faced. All now left behind the corpses of the renegades to be eaten by the crows—or by things under the earth that would sense the dead as food and so break through the ground with fangs and tentacles to drag the corpses with them into their burrows.

Nour told the black man, "You have not told me why."

The magicker put out his right hand, indicating that they should walk together toward the others returning to the gulley and the high ground, and he told Nour, "I have assisted many of you. It is my vow. But more than that—I sense the poet in you."

"You guided my arm because I'm a poet?"

"Why not? Look about you, young man. Look upon the many fighters and killers. We will always have fighters and killers. But poets? Dreamers? I myself was a dreamer once. Do I astonish you?"

"You do."

"Your songs and words are the root and flower of humanity. Trust in this: We of the arts are the other half of you. We are the life you sense but seldom engage. Those of you who dream—you give voice to what is deep within all of us."

Nour said, "I thought of all of you as workers of evil."

"Then you now recognize the truth," said the black man. "The least of us align ourselves with the seekers of darkness, as do the least of you who are ignorant of the arts."

Nour told him, "You have touched me. Sorcerer, you assisted me and saved my life when you did not need to."

"I saved the life of a poet. And your wife will have need of you."

"Because she is with child? You know this?"

"There are few things of stronger sensation than those of a woman with child. Nature proclaims it. Those of us so sensitive are as aware of such life as we are of coming storms and the work of other mages."

"I have much to learn," Nour said.

"You need not learn. It is sufficient to be respectful. You are respectful of Hame, are you not?"

"I will try to be." Nour gave the black man his hand and told him his name. "And my wife is Silene. Or do you know that already?"

The sorcerer took his hand. "I am Mimset. It is the name I have assumed. It was the title of an old spirit who taught me when I was young."

"Mimset, I am honored to know you."

They walked toward Edric and the others. Although he was some distance away in this crowd, Edric nodded to Mimset as he would to someone he recognized.

Nour noticed and asked the sorcerer, "You know my brother-in-law?"

"The captain and I met months ago, when he was fighting with his company in the west."

"He does not speak of that to me or his sister."

"It is just as well. But I have great respect for him. All of my kind do. He is a man to trust."

"He is, indeed," Nour agreed, and looked now for Esta in the crowd of fighters around them. He did not see her and mentioned her to Mimset.

Mimset told him, "I knew her, too, from the clashes in the west. She fell early in the fighting today."

"This happened?"

"It did. She is now with the woman she loved and with her ancestors. So goes it." He made a sign.

Nour told him, "We spoke only once. She was noble, I think. A good person."

"Yes."

"Sorcerer, wherever she is, I prefer to imagine that she is in a bright city somewhere, a good, bright city with the lights burning like stars, the way cities were when the world was free and when we ourselves were still free."

Mimset told him, "She may be in that city. Lighten your soul, my friend. We have work to do. We are needed."

5. Betrayal

Among those who had come to assist Edric and his company were Lord Tor and his fighters, whose numbers had been halved in just those few days since Edric had last seen his friend. Tor, strong and weathered, told Edric and the others assembled that evening that Serenthal had sent ahead several groups to clear the creature's road to Surkad.

"We were ambushed in a steep decline," Tor told Edric. "I blame myself. My people were nearly dead of thirst, and the pool was just within those rocks. But the things surprised us despite my scouts."

"Even Rass the Singer could not assist," said Mimset, looking at Hame. He meant an old sorcerer known to both and to many others besides. "A mage tricked his mind. Sent ghosts to betray Rass with their lies, leading him into the trap."

"I felt him die three nights ago," Hame said. "His songs were always welcome. This is a loss."

The addition of Tor's hundred fighters and those of companies led by a veteran named Sessa and by a young fighter called Ored swelled Edric's company to nearly three times the size it had been. Sessa claimed many victories to her credit; she had been a commander for three years and had fought in hard contests against warriors and demons sent first by Azuth, a demonic prince in the southlands, and then advance parties of Serenthal, the dark lord. These engagements she had survived. Ored was not so seasoned but he had veterans with him who swore to his intelligence and ability in the field. That men of such experience would follow so young a leader spoke well of him.

The hundreds of fighters and refugees settled into camps for the night, with Sessa, Ored, Tor, and Edric ordering their watches all around. As the warm darkness deepened, the sky to the north blossomed with light, and soon there came shocks under the earth, rolling in waves, and further brightness in the sky.

Even as the earth continued to shudder and the sky to brighten with evil, Hame took aside Mimset and Edric and the other commanders and spoke to them privately. Then he passed his staff to Mimset to hold for him and asked the black man and the five other sorcerers who had so far survived to join in an activity he held in the center of Edric's camp. The captain, his sister, and Nour stood close by Hame, while others in the camp gathered in a wide circle around them.

The sorcerers, too, then stood in a small circle of their own. Nour found them fascinating to contemplate. One was a woman with skin a pale yellow and curiously shaped eyes; no doubt she was from the far west, where tribes and villages of such people were said to live, but for her to have come so far east was intriguing. What knowledge had she sought to bring her so far from home? Two of the others were not unlike Hame and Mimset, older men, both of them white skinned, silent in their dignity, and marked with deep tattoos on their faces and arms and with symbols on their leather garments. The fourth sorcerer, also a woman, was short and dark haired, not slender, and with the darkest eyes Nour had ever seen. He had to look away when she settled those deep eyes on him. He wondered why Hame trusted her. The fifth was a man as young as himself, slender, not tattooed or marked with any signs, but dressed simply in plain woolen robes. All five had staffs with them, which Nour understood to be of assistance not only in this world but also of aid in reaching into the invisible world. The length of a staff marked the area that protected each mage within his or her area as the signs on it, pronounced carefully, allowed the staff to reach into those other places like an arm reaching into someplace unfamiliar.

Hame knelt, drew a number of large sticks from a pouch draped from his shoulder, and threw them onto the ground. He said a spell and waved his hands over the sticks. Soon enough a small fire came, blue-flamed, and hovered above the sticks, not consuming them as an ordinary fire would.

Nour saw by the light of the blue flames that there were markings on the sticks, symbols carved into them. These were tools, then, and not at all sticks of common wood, as he had first thought them to be.

An image appeared in the blue flames. At first dark and undefined, it soon revealed itself as the miniature image of a walled city, with vast structures broken and towers fallen. The city was dark. A haze lay over it. Its population was seen to be people in chains being whipped by demonic things of hair and wings and hoofs. Faces opened in screams that could not be heard. Writhing bodies were torn in half by powerfully muscled monsters, who cast what remained of these victims into pits where wild dogs and other things fought for them.

Unable to remain silent, Nour said, "Is this Hell?"

The image shuddered, then dissolved into the blue flames.

Hame stood and told Nour and the others with him, "This is Surkad as it stands. We are too late to defend it. This is the movement we felt moments ago. My raven returns even now from the northeast to confirm what we have been shown. Serenthal and its demons and assistants have broken into the city from the north." He turned to look at Nour, only a small distance away. "Yes, my friend. This is Hell."

The refugees spoke to each other in despair; their voices lifted loudly, gaining momentum like a surf coming onto a rocky shore. Some of them moved away to go to their fires or their tents, dismayed.

Hame then asked Mimset to return his staff. The black man did so and returned to where he had been standing. He and Hame shared a look. Immediately Hame reached out his staff, pointing it toward the young sorcerer, as Mimset took several steps back and pointed his own staff at him, so that the young man was unable to move, caught between the two older magicians.

"Do not interfere," Hame warned the other four necromancers. "This man is not one of us. He serves Serenthal."

The dark-haired woman let out a sound. "He fooled even me!" she exclaimed. "How powerful is he?"

Hame told her, "Sufficiently learned to compromise our trust in him. Even I doubted. But my raven returned to me only a little time ago and whispered to me the truth. This imposter is here to trick us into doing as Serenthal wishes."

The dark-haired woman and the others stepped away. Nour, watching, had thought that if any of them might have been a traitor, it would have been this woman. Surely he was no judge of these people.

One of the old necromancers asked Hame, "Shall we raise our staves against him, as well?"

"Not yet, friend. Let me ask him, and I free him to speak if he so wishes. Why have you done this?"

The young man said nothing but stared with hatred at Hame.

Hame frowned. "No doubt you felt that serving the dark lord is a worthy goal, despite the poison that will erode your soul and take lifetimes to cleanse. Whatever you have been told or promised, know that you are in error."

Now the young man found his voice, saying certain syllables that he had been taught would harm all of the sorcerers present. But Mimset leaned ahead with his staff to push the head of it, carved as it was with a powerful symbol, into the trapped magician's back, who grunted in pain and showed sweat.

Mimset said to Hame and the others, "He is lost. He knows what awaits him from us as well as from his lord for his failure. Let us end this."

Fear showed in the young man's eyes.

Hame lifted his voice to address the gathered refugees, the soldiers, and the commanders. "What we are about to do is of our arts. It will harm none of you. You saw violence on the field today, yet you may avert your eyes from this if you wish."

The young man whispered, "I made an error."

"You did indeed, my friend," Hame told him. "But how can we release you and trust you?"

The sorceress with the fine yellow skin said to him contemptuously, "You were a fool."

Hame said, "Now."

The remaining four moved so that they completed a circle around the young man and stretched out their staffs to touch him. Hame did the same with his staff.

The young man's head snapped back and his face contorted with fear, the muscles stretching. His gripped his staff as though unable to release it, but in a moment, it burned in his hand, becoming a length of ash, which shattered.

Silene, watching, made a sound, and Nour took hold of her to block her view. Many of the others there also turned away, men and women both. Mothers hastened their children from the crowd. Others watched in fascination.

Light grew around the young man, and an odor lifted. He was not on fire, but the light took on a blue tinge, like the flames that had enveloped Hame's thrown sticks. The young man dropped to his knees, his face still stretched with pain beneath the color, and he pushed out on his belly as if preparing to crawl away.

His body slumped and went still, yet the sorcerers kept their staffs pressed upon his body until, shuddering, the corpse released a shadow or a phantom—the spirit of the young man, which did indeed now try to crawl to freedom, moving awkwardly.

Edric whispered to Nour, "Nothing will be left of him."

The sorcerers pressed their staffs into the blue spirit as though into a chalky substance, and it began to crumble. The distorted expression on the face remained until near the end, when the head dropped and shattered on the flattened grass of the earth beneath it.

The sorcerers lifted their staffs.

One of the old men said, "So few of us remain, and here is another who gave himself to the dark lord. I remember when I was young. All I wished to do was learn. Now time and events have brought me here. I am tired of memories. There are too many memories. I no longer trust them."

6. Serenthal

Deep into the night, commanders and sorcerers met over maps drawn in the dust by firelight to come to decisions. What did Serenthal know already about them and the other refugees? The creature had taken his ancient capital city and would continue to expand its influence to the borders of its ancient kingdom. Remaining as a single force presented a single target to the demon and its followers. The four commanders therefore determined to move east separately with their fighters and refugees, each guided as well as possible by the sorcerers who would accompany them. Hame, of course, wished to remain with Edric and his company, and Mimset proposed to travel with them, as well.

A middle-aged man from Ored's company stood and said, "I have been on the trail for months, moving away from these monsters and from this demon, Serenthal. I know what the demons are. I can identify the men and women who live with the demons like pack animals, and they are no better than pack animals. But what of Serenthal? Will I know this demon if I see it? What should I know?"

Mimset told this man and the others there, "I confronted Serenthal a year ago when he first came up from Hell. This was to the west, where he had been defeated and returned to Hell ages ago by the early heroes and the sorcerers who assisted them. I fought Serenthal; I was as close to the thing as I am now to you, sir. Because it had just risen to the earth, it was not as strong as it is now. It has devoured many of us since then and is the mightier for it. When I fought it, it was taller than I and seemed to be made of a gray, oily substance, like sap or tar. It has strong arms and legs, and a head like that of an animal, all snout and brow, and orange eyes that glow. It could speak, although its utterance was in an old tongue, and I know few words of that ancient language. Still, Serenthal was able to send four of its human followers against me. These I slew without hesitation, and then I sought to kill the dark lord itself. I used my staff to wound it with fire I had conjured, but it used an old trick, gesturing with its claws, and nearly set me on fire myself. I therefore took protection among high rocks and tried to use castings and other weapons against it, but I could not prevail. I therefore escaped from Serenthal and its new servants, the people drawn to it and the monsters that had come up from under the earth with it, and I was fortunate to survive. I have this to show you as a reminder of the thing's power."

Mimset lifted his left arm and pulled down the sleeve of his garment; his black skin showed a bright pink line from wrist to elbow.

"It is painful to this day," Mimset said. "It was good that I wasn't poisoned. And this wound is nothing. Within days of my encounter, I heard that Serenthal had grown to twice the height I witnessed and was drawing to itself followers by the hundreds. Many of these brought victims with them, warriors they had killed and their families, to burn alive at feasts or go into the creature's belly. Now everything that surrounds Serenthal goes black and lifeless. It has done this to Surkad. Demons thrive in darkness as we do in sunlight. This is no land for the living. Only the dead wish to be here to work their ways as they learned to do in Hell itself. We should hurry."

Silence contained everyone there. As the eastern horizon softened with daylight, such as it was, one of the old sorcerers said in a sad voice, "Has it been only a year since we sat in the sun and hoped that, perhaps, the demons and monsters had done whatever they meant to do, and that we might own at least part of our world in safety?"

No one answered him.

The question answered itself.

In the early morning, through the shadowed land, the four commanders moved with their companies south of Surkad, with sensible distance between them but all going east toward the coast. Edric led his group closest to the dead city, within sight of it.

What they saw from their hilltop were fallen walls and collapsed towers, some of the smaller buildings still on fire or smoking, and the surrounding land burned down to blackened earth. Piled onto the dead earth were thousands of bodies, all of them showing evidence of mutilation, torture, fire. And surrounding what had been the city were stone altars and obelisks carved with symbols of darkness. From poles thrust into the ground flew banners with Serenthal's sign upon them, the black star. Death and worse than death—anyone who might go near what had been the city would be enslaved or immediately slain. Such was the law in lands under darkness. Here was the creature from the beginning of history, building its power to succeed for a thousand years by swallowing souls and spirits and bodies as it pulled them to it, killing as much as it could. Things that return from death require the sacrifice of constant deaths to ensure their continuance on the earth.

Edric's company camped that night in the wooded hills just past Surkad. They lit no fires, and those chosen to guard the perimeter stood in pairs, thinking that such a strategy might provide an extra portion of protection. Hame and Mimset also stood watch, one at each end of the wide camp, their senses alert. But when it is determined to do so, evil can find the crack in any floor, the loose stone in any wall.

****

Shadows. Mist. Moving up the hillside.

Silene awoke to a groan. Not her own—a woman sleeping beside her let out the deep sound as she reached wildly, clutching Silene in her nightmare.

The woman gasped, unable to breathe, as Silene opened her eyes and saw dark green light clutching the woman's feet and legs, dragging her. The woman lost her grip on Silene as she was pulled across the grass.

Silene took out her knife and, on her knees, scrambled toward the light. It stretched like a rope or root, pulling the woman between the trees. Silene lunged, driving the knife twice and then again into the green light.

The green light shrieked.

The woman found her air and gasped. The green tendril of light released her and pulled away as Silene stabbed it once more. It emitted a further shriek—*How?*—as a staff emerged from the dark and pushed into the light, reducing it to ash.

Mimset.

Silene looked up at him as the sorcerer lent his hand and arm to the woman who had nearly been killed. She sobbed powerfully and hugged Mimset as others all around came awake, freed their weapons, called to Mimset and now to Hame, who was just coming across the camp.

Nour, fully awake, hurried to his wife. "You killed it."

"No," she told him. "It was Mimset," and asked him, "Will she live?"

"Yes." Mimset allowed the woman to move into the arms of a man who came for her, and he told Hame, "They have just begun."

All along the hillside below them, they saw through the trees and bushes green lights erupting spontaneously from the earth. And below the night's dark clouds came flying things, demons or empowered humans, uttering mewling sounds, directing the stretching green lights to move up the hillside.

Horns sounded—Edric's command to arouse the entire camp. And the captain himself appeared now, followed by others of his troop, all on horseback.

"The refugees are to move farther south at once," he told Hame and Mimset. "Is Serenthal sending troops against us, or is it all sorcery?"

"Sorcery," Hame replied. "That was the word its spy sent him. Mimset and I know what is to be done. Can you lend us horses? And a small guard?"

Edric turned to riders nearest him and ordered ten of them to stay with the magicians and two of them to give up their mounts. "The remainder of us," he called out, "move south. Leave behind whatever we must, but get these people to the coast!"

He reined away then, not even glancing at his sister or Nour, who heard him yelling to his trumpeters to unleash the signal alerting the other commanders to do as he was doing.

Nour asked if he could be of assistance to Hame, but the wise one told him, "Not here. Not now. Take your wife. You will be needed at the water."

Silene led him away by the hand, and they hurried through the camp, Nour pausing briefly by the wagon that held his and Silence's possessions to take several blankets, but not even a single scroll or book.

We carry them with us...

As they moved on, bumping into others doing what they could to hurry away, both looked back to see Hame and Mimset riding alongside each other, staffs held high, with Edric's fighters escorting them front and back. The sky above them glowed with a green light reflected against the dark clouds of the evil coming up the hillside. The sorcerers' staffs burned with a blue glow.

"What can they do?" Nour asked, breathing heavily as he ran.

A woman behind him said, "Look!" and pointed.

Within the green air of the sky, the flying things attacked each other with claws and teeth, and fell to earth entangled to be burned by the tendrils writhing on the ground.

"How?" Silene asked.

The woman told her, "I can guess. I have learned. A little." She was herself somewhat breathless as she hurried but explained in gasps that, to defeat a sorcerer, even a thing as ancient and strong as Serenthal, one turns the sorcerer's strength against it.

Nour remembered what Hame had said about the demons and creatures they had fought on the field. *"It is the bargain they made. These people were weak."*

Serenthal's followers were weak. This was how Hame and Mimset could use Serenthal's sorcery against him. Turn his weak followers against themselves and at least gain time that way, manage to give the fighters and the renegades a chance to make it to the water's edge.

As they cleared the height of the hill, Nour, the woman, and Silene, and the others with them looked back and saw an army of fighters aligned on the hillside—hundreds, thousands of them.

"Where did they come from?" a man asked.

"They are not real," said the woman who had studied the arts. "They are trees and stones. They are illusions. The sorcerers have created them to distract the dark lord's creatures."

"Because they are weak," Nour said.

"Yes. But do not doubt it—Serenthal will come after us yet. Quickly, now."

7. Away

"I'm glad I've lived long enough to see this," said the woman next to Silene. "There are the ships at last."

They were crouched behind the ruins of a broken wall within a deserted village. It had not been demons that destroyed the village; Time had done that. But any sense of safety or home this place had once provided remained to comfort Silene and the woman next to her and the others alongside them, perhaps forty souls—other women, young and older, and their children, and young men and their fathers and uncles, desperate and worn nearly to the bone, but armed with knives and old tools and stones.

"If a demon can be killed with a rock," one of the young men had said before the light of day came, "it will see what *I* can with a rock."

Not all of them trusted the sight of the ships. "A trick of the demons," one of the older men said. "Serenthal doing to us what the wizards did to it."

"No. Those sailors are as real as I am," someone else said. "And the wind. And the scent of the waves. And those other sails coming up from the south. We'll be free."

Horses coming, the sound of them approaching from the north—Hame and Edric, Nour with them, and thirty others on foot or atop their mounts.

Silene rose and ran to Nour as he dismounted, hurried to hold him—he was certainly no trick of the demons—and others at the wall did so, as well, reaching for their loved ones.

"We still have time," Edric told them.

Hame, leaning on his staff, as tired as any of them despite his strength, said that Serenthal had left Surkad and was moving now with columns of fighters and slaves and whatever monsters of it that remained from the destruction on the hillside.

"It is determined to slay or take anyone between it and the coast. Destroy the ships. Bring down darkness from the skies and call up further evil from the earth. It might well manage it. My raven insists that the thing is eager to take as much life as it can before it rebuilds its capital."

The raven appeared, flying quickly from the northwest, to circle above them, then land atop Hame's staff.

"We could move farther south," Edric told those around him. "Serenthal has no desire to intrude upon the lands there."

Nour explained to Silene, "We may gain time that way. But other monsters command those places. We would be caught between Serenthal and more evil if we did."

"We are caught between them now," she said.

Mimset now came toward them, accompanied by the dark-haired sorceress and one of the old wizards of Sessa's company, for all of the commanders' groups had met during the night, alerted by Hame's raven, and aligned themselves along the hills and the rocks overlooking the coast. All would now make the trip down to the ships, filling up the morning and hoping that Serenthal and its army would not arrive before all had boarded the sails awaiting them.

Mimset told them, "Some of their captains have ridden the waves before now and set others ashore on the islands to the east. The mages there protect them from any evil. They remain under darkness, but the horizon to the east is clear."

Edric said, "That horizon, whatever it delivers to us..." He paused. "I will say this. Any of you who wish to remain here and hide from the demons however you can...we will not ask you to risk sailing to the east."

The woman next to Silene grunted a laugh. "Oh, yes," she said in jest. "After what we have endured, sailing to the horizon is terrifying."

Many others chuckled.

"We have faced death so often," said someone else, "death and worse than death—I will damn Death before it damns me." He looked at Nour. "Am I right, poet?"

Nour called upon old words he remembered from the books he had had to leave behind. "We must look Death in the face," he said to those there. "We stay alive every moment we can, even as we stare into the abysm of Hell itself. We keep every moment so that our lives are an affront to death. We should be so full of life that the strength of our living gives Death pause and makes Death shudder in doubt."

Voices rose, and the hands of many pressed his shoulders in thanks for his words.

Edric said to them all, "This is a good day. I am proud to have commanded you."

Hame told him, "Your command is not yet complete, my friend. Let us lead these good people down to the shore and the boats, and we will say farewell at last to this evil."

They did indeed fill the morning, the lines of them moving down from the fallen village and the trees and rocks to take their places in the skiffs and longboats that oared them out to the great galleys and merchant ships resting under the dark clouds of midday. But as Edric and his sister and Nour stood on the wet beach, assisting those who awaited the next round of returning longboats, thunder came from above, the skies to west cracked with green lightning, and a powerful wind moved down upon them, stinking with the odor of all of Hell.

"There," said Mimset, and pointed with his staff.

Over the rocks to the west and down through the trees there, bent with the wind and breaking, now, under the strength of that wind, came hopping things and crawling things and fliers, humans transformed into gray, oily skinned beasts with wings. Behind them hurried Serenthal's army of fighters, men and women eager to take lives to feed the black spirit that had mastered them.

And then came Serenthal itself, and even Mimset drew in a breath, for the thing was far more than what he had faced previously, and it had grown so as to amaze all of those on the shore. It was as tall as any tree, and its animal face with burning eyes peered down through the black mist of midday. It was now a thing serpentine and muscled with many arms. Its claw hands plucked its flying servants from the air and shoved them into itself, pushed these living things into its chest and belly and thighs, so that it absorbed them. They sank into Serenthal as though being pulled into a jelly or clay. From its torso and thighs and some of its arms protruded the hands and heads and the legs of those so taken by the thing, the parts of them not yet enveloped by its moving muscles and stinking flesh. So this thing existed, risen from the earth and deriving life from all that it took into itself, increasing itself in this way.

"What can we do?" Some of those on the shore jumped into the surf as they were, not waiting for the longboats, instead swimming out to the ships beyond the surf.

But Mimset and Hame and the other sorcerers hurried along the shore to confront Serenthal and its monsters, forming a front to face what was coming. They stabbed their staffs into the ground and thereby raised a wall of light, a shimmering like any reflection on the surface of a river or lake. The wall bent before the strong wind, but it held. Bits of black sent by Serenthal, dead souls, that dropped into the shining wall fell apart. Flying monsters that moved into this wall became ashes that blew away on the strong wind.

Serenthal roared. Its roar was an animal sound, more than animal, something produced originally in Hell, unlike any sound heard before on the earth. And it continued to approach on its powerful shining legs, pulling into it more of its demons and crawling things.

Edric and the other commanders now aligned their fighters just behind the sorcerers, so that any of Serenthal's warriors who flanked the mages and approached the beach that way could be met with weapons.

And there were many who did—crawling monsters that had to be stabbed and left to writhe on the rocks and brown grass, flying things to be brought down by arrows and bolts, and fully armed warriors, men and women in leather and steel and bronze, practiced in the ways of combat, whom the commanders and their fighters met full on, as they had the renegades on the field of battle days earlier, using their weapons as they needed to, chopping, cutting, blade on blade, so that the stones on the beach and the brown grass were soon dressed in blood from both sides of the fighting, and men and women crumpled, curled into themselves and moaned, or dropped lifeless in their weight.

Serenthal's sorcerers now moved against the wall of light, pushing against it with their artistic gestures and their own staffs, and one of them managed to breach the wall in the middle, where the dark-haired woman was taken by surprise. The light emitted by her staff twisted like a sheet of parchment, and she was brought to her knees by the man who faced her. She died there, burned alive, as Mimset, beside her, met her attacker with his own staff and cut the man through the chest.

But weakness has been found, and the crawling things and the other sorcerers hurried to that breach. Ored and Lord Tor and their fighters came around to confront them. Young Ored himself, on foot, used his steel against one of the sorcerers. He killed that one, but in pushing his sword through the mage, he was himself taken alive by green flame and died there. Tor, mounted, moved his sword in all directions, killing enemies quickly until a spear found him and pushed him from his horse. On his back on the ground, he was found by a crawling thing that sank into his head and chest and ended him that way.

Sessa ordered half of her fighters to retreat down the beach to protect the refugees there, the hundred or so who remained, awaiting the empty longboats returning from the ships. The fighters did so, encircling Nour and Silene and the others.

The shining wall of the guarding sorcerers weakened further. The two old men were slain, each of their staffs meeting the weapons of Serenthal's mages. The yellow-skinned woman then was killed, stepping in front of a fighting woman to meet one of the dark lord's warriors. She killed that one but was herself cut through the throat. Hame saw this and ordered Mimset to hurry down the beach to help protect the last of the refugees.

"I would do better to assist you here!" the black man yelled above the noise of battle.

"Remember our oath! We assist them first of all!"

Mimset told him, "I will perform a rite in your honor!"

"In the next world if not here! Hurry!"

Mimset went, going with Sessa and the twenty with her, the last of her company, all of them determined to help those on the beach.

Only Edric remained, himself and those few with them, for the beach now was full all along the rocks and grass with the dead and more dead, sorcerers and fighters, as Serenthal, the gigantic thing, continued forward. Hame's raven, which had moved among the demonic flying things and killed some of them with beak and claw, now approached the dark lord. One of Serenthal's claws caught it and crushed it and pushed the body of it into its chest.

Hame said to no one but himself, "So it is, my friend," and walked steadily toward the approaching Serenthal.

Edric saw him and cried out. "Hame, to the shoreline! To the shoreline!"

But the wizard did what he was determined to do, approaching the resurrected demon. As Serenthal reached down for him, Hame pushed his staff into the thing's claw. For the first time that afternoon, Serenthal bellowed in pain. All the strength of Hame and the dead sorcerers assisting him was contained in that thrust, and Serenthal knew it.

The dark lord then grasped Hame with another of its claws and pulled him up toward him, face to face, dying sorcerer and hellish evil, before pushing Hame into its mouth to destroy him that way.

Edric charged forward.

On the beach, Silene saw him do it, and yelled loudly. She tried to move past the fighters before her, but they held her where she was. So she saw her brother, as proud and brave as he had ever been from boyhood till now, strike at the dark lord, leg and claw, until man and mount were caught in the thing's flesh and pulled into it, Edric's right arm the last to be taken in, his sword dropping from his numb hand before it disappeared.

Nour pulled the screaming Silene with him into one of the last longboats as Serenthal watched them go, the last of the fighters, the last of the refugees. The thing's monsters moved up and down the shoreline before him, feasting on the fallen, its remaining fighters stripping the dead of their weapons and armor. Serenthal itself now lifted its great animal head and roared to the dark skies, where lightning flashed sickly green, coloring the clouds and the land below. It raised its arms in victory and howled again as the last of the boats moved out on the waves.

Sessa watched, and Mimset beside her, and Nour and Silene alongside them, seated in the rocking boat.

Silene was shivering in such agony that Mimset told Nour, "Support her."

Nour did, holding onto his wife, and Mimset pressed a warm hand to her wet hair and said a word. At that, Silene's head drooped and she fell into a sleep, and remained asleep as Nour and others gently hoisted her up to the decks of the *Moon*, the ship saving them.

Three days out, the *Moon* dropped anchor at a small island on which hundreds of others waited to greet the survivors. Coming onto the shore, one mother found her two children, taken from her earlier in the rush to save whomever could be rescued. Friends greeted friends and, soon, mourned the loss of others they had known. The skies above remained dark, but not so dark as those they had escaped, and no demons flew down at them from those heights and no monsters swam out to attack them on their island.

Mimset that evening stood on the warm shore and watched the waves roll in quietly to splash against the rocks. Friendly, he thought, the waves and those rocks, so different from the beach they had escaped. He did not weep. Sessa came up beside him and touched his shoulder, and the black man lifted a hand to cover hers. Together they saw that the place they had escaped was in view, tall trees visible and shuddering in a wind, rocky heights still to be seen under black skies that yet glowed with green fire.

Nour and Silene approached them and stood with them.

Silene said, "Sleep tonight by fires bright, though monsters be, we will be free."

"And so we are," Sessa told her.

"But we lost many," Nour said.

"But not all." Mimset pointed. "There."

Above them flew a bird, black and powerfully winged, which approached them and circled above them, then came closer.

Mimset reached out with his staff, and the raven lighted on it, great wings moving still, brilliant eyes watching the four of them.

"Hame," Mimset told the three.

"Truly?" Silene laughed at the thought of it.

But the raven let out a sound and flapped its wings, so that all of them knew it to be true.

"And he will guide us east," Mimset told them. "There are new lands for us. So our friend tells me."

"New lands with no evil?" Nour asked.

Sessa shook her head. "There will always be evil."

Mimset agreed. "On these ships are those who will indeed turn toward the dark. It cannot be avoided. The new lands will be a home to those who practice such works. It is in our nature. But the land will not be born in evil. That has occurred already, and it will not occur again."

"And will there be new gods?" Sessa asked.

"We will create them and worship them," Mimset told her. "They, too, will belong to the new lands. So it is with us. Evil, and gods, and new horizons."

"And poetry," Nour said.

Mimset smiled. "And poetry. To give us hope."

The next day, aboard the *Moon*, they were sailing east toward the new horizon. The skies above brightened, the darkness falling away, and clear seas waited before them.

Author's Note on the Stories

To date, I have written 24 short stories and novelettes set on the island-continent of Attluma; *Tales of Attluma* contains 16. (In addition, there are two novels featuring the character Oron and one featuring Akram.) Six of the remaining eight stories concern Oron; five of these appear in the collection *Death in Asakad and Other Stories* (published by Zebra Books in 1983 as *The Ghost Army*), which Pulp Hero Press plans to reissue. The sixth story featuring Oron, "The Shadow of Dia-Sust," appears in the anthology *The Mighty Warriors*, recently published by Robert Price. The novella "Engor's Sword Arm" was published in 1994 by Morgan Holmes, DPM, and is still available. The novelette "Shadow-born, Shadow-taken" appears in the e-anthology *Artifacts and Relics*, published in 2013 by Christopher Heath and available online.

Interview with the Author

How did these stories originate? Did you have a plan for world-building the continent of Attluma?

There was no plan at all. I wrote the first story in my freshman year of college; this was the fall of 1970. I'd read the Conan the stories, of course, and the Ballantine paperbacks reprinting Clark Ashton Smith's stories were beginning to appear, so those were my inspiration to write stories as enjoyable as I found those. The first one had an opening scene similar to the opening of "Black Colossus," so I was already going for this Gothic, sinister feeling. I continued to work on that one while I wrote other stories and gradually got my footing, at least well enough to be published in the fanzines of the early seventies. But no one in those days thought of "world building" in the mechanical sense we think of it today, or at least I didn't. The term didn't exist then, so far as I know. I simply wanted to write these stories as well as I could.

The fanzines of that period were critically important.

That's where my generation of fantasy and SF writers got our start. There were digest magazines on the stands then, but most of the action was in the fanzines, which really carried on the tradition of the pulps. *Fantastic* published the Lin Carter and Sprague de Camp pastiches of Conan, which I didn't care for at all, and occasionally some other stories, which I did like, but I was of a different mindset. And I went back and forth between writing horror stories and these fantasy stories, but there was no market then for horror short stories other than the fanzines. I probably placed as many horror stories with those editors as I did the fantasies.

Most of my stories appeared in Gordon Linzner's *Space & Time*, which was like the *Weird Tales* of that period. It reliably published good stories by good writers. I placed some with *The Diversifier* and a couple with *The Literary Magazine of Fantasy and Terror*, but the others turned me down. So that's how you find out the kind of writer you are and who will welcome your work. Gordon had taken a number of my stories by the time I got the idea of writing the novel *Oron* in the summer of 1973. That was when I came up with Attluma as a backdrop for the novel because I wanted it to be an epic, and Oron and his army would be conquering a lot of territory while Kossuth the demon was spreading his destruction over even more stretches of landscape. The stories I'd written up to then pretty much fit into this milieu, as did the other fantasies I continued to write afterward.

Did developing this background affect how you approached these stories afterward?

To a degree with some of them. Attluma clearly echoes the name Atlantis, which is deliberate. Also, I created the background as an homage to Howard's Hyborian Age and the environments Clark Ashton Smith had created for his stories—Poseidonis and Hyperborea, Zothique. Initially the concept was that Attluma was a battleground between human beings and the forces of darkness, which periodically over thousands of years rise up from the underworld and try to take control of the continent. Thus you have Oron, a classical-style hero, fighting Kossuth, the agent of chaos, to try to maintain order and stability for humankind.

Later it occurred to me that, rather than having the demons being the interlopers on human ground, perhaps the human beings are the interlopers against the demonic forces. So Attluma then becomes something created by evil or contrary forces, and human beings are fighting them to hold the land for themselves. Eventually, the forces of chaos will win, but they will then fight among themselves and collapse at some point, devouring each other, and the human beings either will go down with them or leave for other places. That's the idea behind "The End of Days," for example.

The gods are usually remote in these stories or, if they do get involved, as in "Dark Goddess," it's in some disturbing way. "The Generosity of the Gods" has the gods appear, but it doesn't do the human characters much good. The gods are tricksters and lagely just want to be left alone.

But not every story seems to fit into that chaotic framework.

No. Some of the heroic stories have that feeling in the background, this sense of doom or ultimate loss, but most of them came about because I had an idea I wanted to explore or I was inspired in some way. What I think are the best of the stories take place between just a few characters who are in trouble or cause some sort of trouble and then have to manage it. The story turns on the people involved. "The Passing of the Sorcerer" is one of those. "The Return to Hell" is another like that, and "The Sounding of the Gong." But some of them are their own neat little stories just as they are—"Descales' Skull," for instance, and "Ithtidzik" and "Patience Serves."

Given that there is a trajectory to the history of Attluma—a beginning, middle, and end—should the stories be read in a certain order?

Not really. A few of them, to my mind, belong near the end of the history—"The End of Days" and the two Akram stories and another one that's been published separately, a novella called "Engor's Sword Arm." The ones that are a bit lighter in tone or construction I see as belonging to the earlier part of the history. "The Generosity of the Gods" is one like that—written before I wrote *Oron*. And "Feasting Shadows," which I originally wrote as a horror story in a contemporary setting. But the order in which they're presented in this collection is fine. It follows the general order in which they were written.

You've mentioned that you recast or rewrote a number of the stories. Why, and which are they?

I reworked some of them and rewrote a couple because, in rereading the original stories, I wasn't satisfied that I'd really gotten into what worked with them or gotten into what the story could deliver, the idea or concept behind it. "Dark of Heart" was originally written as "Dragon's Jaw and Twin Pillars" and was a serviceable little story about a barbarian leading a prince into the mountains to retrieve his sister, who's been stolen by a wizard to sacrifice to a demon-god. That's the one I started during my freshman year of college. It has some good scenes—man, I was so young when I wrote that—and some tension, but it comes down to being a pretty basic s&s story. When I looked it over, I saw that I could treat the sorcerer as a character who's based on H.P. Lovecraft, a visionary or dreamer who's content to live in a fantastic environment and basically survive solely inside his head, largely divorced from reality. Dathien is Robert E. Howard, this vitalistic, powerful presence who's all about physicality and living in the present. So I set them up to bump into each other.

"The Return to Hell" originally was too dreamy. Just goes off into nothingness, although I was trying to make a comment on our inevitably being taken back by the cosmos or eternity depending on what sort of trouble we'd gotten into while we were alive. Didn't work. This version does and more clearly ties into the events of *The Shadow of Sorcery*, the Akram novel. "The Sounding of the Gong" was also that way; the set-up and then the denouement or payoff wasn't as strong originally as it could have been.

With "The End of Days," I didn't like the writing style; I was experimenting back then, and some of my writing was pretty bad. With the original "The End of Days," for instance, I got in way over my head. I wanted to write a kind of epic in which two friends wind up fighting each other as the world ends, and one dies fighting the demons while the other joins the company of sorcerers who will survive the destruction of Attluma. But the current version is superior—it's a much better story, very grounded and gritty, and it still has that epic feel. The characters are solid and the situation they're in is very dire. And the writing is much better. I wish I could have written all of these stories back then as I have here, but I didn't have sufficient practice and life experience.

Most of these stories, though, I should say, I revised only to push them ahead a step or two to get a bit more out of them. There was still more story there. "Aliastra the Sorceress," for example, and "Blood Ransom" and "Dark Goddess" and "The Last Words of Imatus Istum." "Rhasjud's Destiny" I tweaked a bit. And a few I barely had to do anything to—"The Generosity of the Gods" and "Ithtidzik" and "Patience Serves." This is the way these stories should have been all along.

Funny thing about "The Generosity of the Gods." It was the second or third fantasy story I wrote, and Gordon Linzner accepted it for *Space & Time*. After some time went by, I asked him to send it back and not publish it because I wasn't happy with the way I'd written it. He did it but was very surprised by the request. How many authors ask to have a story sent back that's been accepted for publication? Turns out, I realized later that Gordon was right; the story was fine as it was. I'd gone off on some tangent experimenting with how to write fiction or develop a style or something. Those stories I've wound up reworking, but "Generosity" is fine just as I wrote it in 1971 or 1972.

Do you foresee writing further stories set on Attluma?

Oh, yes. My latest, "Twin Scars," just appeared in *Warlords, Warlocks & Witches*, and I plan to write more as the spirit moves me or inspires me. There's room to get a few more stories out of Oron and certainly Dathien. And the witch and young fighter in "Twin Scars" could no doubt go off on some adventures. But for now, I'm finishing *Sometime Lofty Towers*, a novel, which takes place in some indeterminate middle period of Attluma's history. The story addresses colonialism in its own fashion, in that two mercenaries who had fought in what are called the Border Wars are hired by a wealthy woman to help her continue her brutal expansion into the Westlands, the hereditary lands of the *kirangee*, the indigenous people. Or at least she tries to hire them both; Thorem is down on his luck and agrees to help her, but Hanlin wants nothing to do with her. He's forty, has enough battle scars, and feels bad that his old chum is going along with her plan. Inevitably, things turn messy, and they all find themselves in the middle of something that the rich woman should never have started.

About the Author

David C. Smith (born August 10, 1952, in Youngstown, Ohio) served for sixteen years as the managing editor (research), of the *Journal of the American Academy of Orthopaedic Surgeons*, and managing editor, *JAAOS Global Research and Reviews*. He is the author of nearly two dozen novels and of many short stories and articles, as well as of a post-secondary English grammar textbook. He lives in Palatine, Illinois, with his wife, Janine, and their daughter, Lily; their cats, Rosebud and Corabelle; and their anole, Spikes. He is on the web at http://blog.davidcsmith.net and on Wikipedia at https://en.wikipedia.org/wiki/David_C._Smith_(author).

Made in the USA
Las Vegas, NV
09 January 2021